CONVERSATIONS WITH
LAARKMAA
A PLEIADIAN VIEW OF THE NEW REALITY

REBECCA SMITH ORLEANE, PHD
CULLEN BAIRD SMITH

One Water press IN
ASSOCIATION
WITH authorHOUSE®

AuthorHouse™
1663 Liberty Drive
Bloomington, IN 47403
www.authorhouse.com
1-800-839-8640

The information contained in this book is intended to educate, delight, and expand your understanding. It is not intended to diagnose or treat any medical condition, nor is it intended as medical advice. If you have concerns about your health, please consult with a healthcare professional.

Hard cover and soft cover first published by Authorhouse in association with One Water Press™, 3/21/2010.

ISBN: 978-1-4490-9324-2 (hc)
ISBN: 978-1-4490-9323-5 (sc)
ISBN: 978-1-4490-9325-9 (e)

Library of Congress Control Number: 2010903537

Bloomington, Indiana, United States of America
This book is printed on acid free paper

Original cover art © Ann DiSalvo
Author Photo © Ron Russell
Cover design by JP Graphics
Special thanks to Rowan Design

IN MEMORIAM

In memory of Hamish Miller,
who knew, and who took the first steps.

DEDICATION

We dedicate this book to Gabriealla and Skaalora, our High Self
angels, to Laarkmaaa, our Pleiadian family, and to all other beings
who have come to assist in the birth of the new humanity.

CONVERSATIONS WITH LAARKMAA: A PLEIADIAN VIEW OF THE NEW REALITY

TABLE OF CONTENTS

PREFACE

We should have known. I (Rebecca) had experienced unusual "knowings" all of my life. I "saw" little people and fairies. I had regular conversations with loved ones who had "died." When I related what they said to other family members, they simply did not know what to do with my experience. I saw colors and lights around people's bodies that helped me understand about them. (Not until I was an adult did I understand that I was seeing the energy body called an aura.) I often heard beautiful music when there was no obvious source for the music. I saw spheres of light dancing around me, leading me to where they wished me to go. I had inexplicable feelings of elation, love, and connection around each of these experiences. In short, I lived in a world filled with magic. As I discovered the "normal" world did not understand the magic that was part of my everyday existence, I became disenchanted with normal life but refused to give up on what I knew was real. I continued to allow the magic to fill my life with awe and wonder.

I (Cullen) reached into the body of a childhood playmate when I was four years old and removed some kind of toxic material (possibly a tumor). It was a spontaneous action that I just knew was right. Unfortunately the reaction from adults was not favorable. I could not understand how I could have possibly done anything wrong. It simply seemed necessary. For a long time after that experience my healing abilities went underground, yet I continued under the cloak of disguise to continue to help others when I could. One of the ways I maintained contact with those who were guiding me was to listen to my intuition to start a garden. Having no idea how to plant or care for a garden, I managed to grown my own version of a "Findhorn Garden" when I was seven years old all by myself (predating the actual Findhorn Garden by almost ten years.) My parents took huge vegetables that I had grown with the help of the devic kingdom into the local market. People were astounded by how tender and succulent the vegetables were in spite of their enormous size. It was years before I understood what had happened to me as a child and knew that it is possible for humans to contact the devic kingdom of plants. At age ten, I had a first hand experience of regeneration in my own body. One of my eyes had been so severely damaged that the current medical knowledge held no hope or technique for repairing it. Without medical intervention or explanation, my eye inexplicably and magically regenerated itself. I regained full and complete sight.

As children we experienced unusual contacts with dolphins. (Even as adults, we continue to share special connections and communications with dolphins and whales.) Beginning as children and continuing into adulthood, each of us noticed activity in the sky and the presence of something other than the stars and planets we learned about in school. These occurrences were, until now, completely mysterious. We had no idea we were actually being approached. These are just a few of the events that were part of our daily lives. There were many, many other extrinsic experiences that were inexplicable until we began to grow into the wisdom that helped us understand things differently as adults.

So collectively, we should have known when things started to get more and more unusual. We should have known when we started to hear footsteps in our house. Or when we saw waves of "something" or "somebody" moving in front of our eyes. Or when we heard what we now call "bleed through" voices or sounds from other realms. Or when we put things in one place, and they turned up in another. Or when the front doors of two separate houses we lived in were locked without our locking them. Or when the water was turned on while we were out of the room (a message to get us to "flow" a little more in our understanding, rather than being fixed on our own ideas.) Or when the heat suddenly switched to air-conditioning in the midst of a "heated" discussion. (A little help from our friends to cool down the interchange?) Or when my (Cullen's) shoes were placed facing another direction as a clear message to look at how I was walking in my life. We might have known that more was going to be revealed to us.

INTRODUCTION
THE ARRIVAL AND THE BIRTHDAY GIFT

Our lives were changed forever on my (Cullen's) sixtieth birthday. Something happened that was nothing less than extraordinary. We were celebrating with a simple meal. We kept a short wave radio that was turned off in another room. Outside snow was falling, and we commented on the deepening beauty and quiet. Suddenly from the other room, we heard the radio switch itself on. We looked at each other and realized this had never happened before. One of us glanced at the clock and noticed it was exactly the time of my (Cullen's) birth: 4:31 pm. We got up from our meal and moved into the other room, wondering how it was possible for a radio to turn itself on. After checking all the plugs and switches, we decided to add it to our list of inexplicable mysterious events.

The next night, and the next, and the next, our radio continued to turn itself on at exactly 4:31 pm. By the fourth night, we had begun to anticipate this phenomenon, and so we took seats in front of the radio and waited. When, right on schedule, the radio once again turned itself on, we turned it off and asked, "Who is here?" At first there was no audible or understandable response, yet we both felt a presence. (Later we would joke that we got, not a short wave, but a long wave communication.) With practice on subsequent nights, as the radio continued to self-activate, we found we were receiving simultaneous thought messages. When we compared notes, we quickly realized that we were receiving identical messages, word for word. With further practice and an expressed intent to better communicate, we discovered that the thoughts that formed in our minds could be voiced out loud. In short, we began speaking the messages that were being given to us. We realized that it was possible for this information to come through either of us, but only when we were together. And so we alternated who was audibly speaking the material.

We were informed quite quickly and definitely that what we were experiencing was a new form of communication, not the old style channeling process. The difference was that the information was not given in a one-way delivery, but required active participation on our parts. They wanted to hear what we had to say! They wished to learn from us as much as they wanted to disseminate information. This was accomplished through a synchronization of vibration that they call "merging." They communicate through tones and heart wisdom rather than speech and intellectual thought formation, matching their tones to our words as they access our library of words used for human communication.

As we continued to refine our communication skills, we began to notice certain themes emerging in our conversations.

This group feels these themes will help humanity evolve. In order to move beyond humanity's current illusionary reality into the understanding and Truth of a greater reality, the ideas presented in this book may be used as tools for change. The book is organized by the themes these beings have brought to us. We want to make the readers of this information clearly aware that these are not the words of Cullen or Rebecca; these words are directly taken from years of recorded dialogues and conversations with our Pleiadian friends. They have taught us that there are eight primary principles that create reality. We have consistently capitalized these eight elements throughout the book. They are Love, Healing, Trust, Grace, Truth, Transformation, Illumination, and Connection. Unity encompasses all of these elements. Because we humans learn through patterns, Laarkmaa repeats their information from varying angles throughout the book in order for every human to have the opportunity to hear it from a different perspective, hoping that different presentations of the same Truth may help each human break old patterns in order to move into the new reality.

We have done our best to keep Laarkmaa's original words as spoken to us with little editing. There are places where the flow in conversation reflects Laarkmaa's inimitable style, taking unexpected and surprising changes of direction. They are not linear beings, and therefore, what they present does not always follow logical human sequencing. Through time, as our conversations deepened, the language style became more synchronistic with the way we humans speak. Please bear with the unusual style of the original presentation. What Laarkmaa has to say is still profound!

Laarkmaa has explained to us that our vibrational level as a couple enables us to closely match their vibration to allow the synchronization they call merging. It is only together that we can reach their vibratory level to accomplish this communication. It takes both of us as a couple, through Love and Unity, to access this wise and wonderful source. Who are they? We invite you to discover the Truth of who they are in the pages of this book.

WHO IS LAARKMAA?

When we actually began having conversations, we asked a lot of questions. We wanted to know, "Who are you? How many of you are here? What is your name? Where are you from? And why did you start coming to us at 4:31 pm on Cullen's birthday?" We can tell you that this is a loving group of beings, with a sense of humor, great wisdom, and the desire to share their wisdom and learn from us as humans. Here is what they shared:

We are Pleiadians. You perceive us as six, but we perceive us as one. Our names are not easily translatable in your language. You may address us as Laarkmaa. We are here because this is an opening for humanity that has never happened before. There are possibilities in place, potentialities that may occur through choices that individuals make, and we wish to support your making the choices for the highest good for all. For when choices are made for the highest good for all, you feel more Love and more happiness in your own hearts. We know you understand this. We are, as we are here, resonating with you. You may not see us as you see something in your three-dimensional material world, yet your other eyes, your other ability of hearing, seeing, and sensing will become more and more open, both through communicating with us and through the work each of you does individually through your own growth and your own interest. If you were able to see us today you would see us as one of six and six of one, so we have some individuality within our group, and yet we are a unified essence of Love. Sometimes a specific topic is more resonant with one of our six than with another of our six, and a different energy may help transmit the message of what we speak. This is how we describe ourselves. We move in wavelike motion, and we teach humans that they too may move out of stuck positions and unwanted patterns that no longer serve humanity through your learning to be more like waves.

We resonate most with the color blue because blue is the color of Trust, and we wish when we are communicating with humans that they know that they are *safe*, that they are Loved, and that they may Trust in our presence. We have nothing but Love and peace and goodwill in our desires to communicate with you, and we bring the blue vibration of who we are into your vibratory field so that you may sense you are *safe* and that you may Trust, and so that we may all be welcome in gathering together.

We will explain how we communicate with you. Human words are formed from mental constructs. We have needed to learn to access languages in order to understand words that humans use for communication. We do not communicate through words between ourselves; we use tones, sounds, colors, and an energetic vibration that you may perceive as electrical impulses. We use these forms for communication. They come forth from our heart, for we are not based in duality where heart and mind are separated, and thought is necessary to link heart and mind together for expression, or in some cases, to hide what is in the heart by manipulating words through mind. We are much more simple than this. If we experience a vibration of joy; it comes from Connection in some form, either Connection to each other, or in our case Connection with you, or Connection with seeing lights emanating from Source, hearing tones of universal music, yet it is more than music. These things bring us to the vibrational level of joy that your laughter does for you. We also know that you reach these joy vibrations through some of your own experiences outside of laughter. It is when you are in the joy vibration that it is easiest for us to communicate with you, for then our vibrations match. You already receive communication through your heart in our presence. When we communicate with you, your heart receives the energy that you have translated for us as a smile upon your face.

At this point, we felt a strange sensation around our bodies and asked, "What is the energy we feel on our fingers and on our ankles?"

What you feel is related to Healing. We are showing you about Healing. We are behind you, on both sides, in front of you. You perceive the ankle, but you are unable to feel it in all places. Some places are blocked. We meld with you, much like a story you know of someone sewing his shadow back on (in the story of Peter Pan.) We wish to match our energies to yours. Partnership; we wish to offer the two of you partnership. That is why we have chosen the two of you to work with us to bring new understandings to humanity. We wish to focus

3

on partnership between interdimensional beings and humans with the mutual goal of raising planetary consciousness and human consciousness.

We want to meet you physically. We want to look at you, touch you, if that is permissible, and have a conversation like we are having now but be able to communicate with you more directly.

We wish that also. We very much desire face-to-face communication. We do not hold back on our part; it is an energetic place of meeting and non-meeting. It is not our choice to remain out of the reach of your hands or view. The etheric body and physical body in humans are not as well integrated as they are for us, for humans are generally unaware of the etheric body. Yet the physical is created from the etheric. We will discuss this more with you later. We have been actively opening receptors within your brains to increase your levels of understanding. We ask you, if you choose, to move away from things you hold as solid beliefs and expand your imagination towards other possibilities. If you chose to do this, you will be in full partnership with us for your expansion. We help. You help.

Why now? We have waited for sixty years, and humanity has been waiting even longer. Why are you here with us now?

We came to you at 4:31 because those numbers add up to 8, and 8 is the number of infinity. The energetic value of 8 is infinity abundance, and Connection. We wish humans to understand that Love and Unity are infinite. Eight also signifies the team we are asking you to join, for there are two of you and six of us. We will move from being 1 of 6 and 6 of 1 (six individuals within

4

one unit) to 1 of 8 and 8 of 1 (eight individuals within one unit) if you agree. We started communicating through the radio on December 31st because we have been watching you, and that day is a special time for you. Additionally, that date carries the energy of 7, the vibration that assists in moving between the veils. (December is the 12th month; 1 and 2 add to 3. The 31st is created from 3 and 1 which add to 4. Together 3 and 4 add to 7.) We honor your growth and development by coming to you on Cullen's sixtieth birthday. You have both waited for a long time. Now is the appropriate time for us to Connect and begin our work together.

The time for spiritual progress is *now*. There has been no other opportunity to make this big a difference until now. The light, the opportunity, the thinness of the veils was never available for you in this or any of your other lifetimes until *now*. This is the first time the energies, the stars have lined up this way in your lifetime, in fact in many lifetimes, to give you the challenges you now undergo. Do well with them, for they are your opportunity to go home. Do not be afraid. You are being lovingly guided and cared for. Use the challenges. They are created for you to enable you to surpass your final limitations. Rise above what you think is challenging you. Rise above: *break through* what you think you cannot do. Change the unchangeable by opening your eyes to other possibilities. The erroneous belief systems and judgments humans place upon themselves when facing adversity need to be counterbalanced with corrective measures as soon as possible. You have a limited time yet to use this opportunity, and the choice to use it is yours. You have been waiting many lifetimes for this opportunity. Especially this lifetime. The time is at hand. It may not unfold as you expect or predict, but you are losing your expectations, so what difference does it make? You become more open, fluid, flexible, and able to see Truth.

Why now? We are talking to you because you asked and because you have done the work to be able to hear what we say. We are here to make a partnership with you to support humanity's evolution. Humans all over the world are always watching the clock. We want you to know the eleventh hour, to use your linear understanding, has arrived. It is time to know what is possible. Time to change what you think. It is the hour of Illumination.

Humans all over are increasing their levels of fear and denial because most are not doing the shadow work necessary within this opportunity. We will explain more about shadow work later. Additionally, the devic kingdom is opening up to enter communication with humans again in a way it has not for hundreds of years. Also angelic and other presences are here helping with the changes at hand. Elementals of the earth, like humans, are sending up frightening astral waves for they undergo changes they do not understand. All of these things together create waves of fear throughout the astral planes. You feel these because you are becoming more and more sensitive. The two of you have been commenting on and noticing increased abilities of smell, taste, sight, hearing; all of your senses are increasing. Your abilities to sense the astral waves also increase, so you are more vulnerable for experiencing things because the two of you are aware of changes that are occurring where most of the general population is not. When they sense some of these energies, they move into their familiar emotional patterns of fear and blame and do not look further.

We come to speak to you today about your part in how to make a change in this. Those who are drawn to our conversations in person or in print are opening to greater and greater awareness of the opportunity at hand. You probably will not be surprised to hear that what we suggest comes from focused intent, and what we ask you to focus on with your intent and to send out into the astral world, into the astral realms, can you guess? It is Love. We are trying to raise the human vibration because it is easier for us and other interdimensional beings to reach you and communicate more harmoniously when the vibrations are more in alignment with each other. Love is the perfect tool for raising your vibration. In fact, Love *is* a higher vibration. Your willingness through your own choices to achieve this is your contribution to our overall goal.

Many humans at this time are finding what they thought would bring satisfaction or abundance will not satisfy or support their lifestyle or their beliefs. You will, if you take a survey, find the same emotional and financial frustrations and challenges in many. It is part of the breaking down of the belief system, and collectively humans must learn to search for satisfaction and abundance through Unity, through doing what helps all. Part of what you both experience is sensing the level of frustration humanity feels from realizing that their dreams are based upon false beliefs. Trying to work within the fabric of a structure that is crumbling cannot bring positive results; yet the new structure is not in place. This is an interim period where the new is not yet present and the old falls away. All you can do is persevere in what you know best and continue deep listening for guidance on how to make positive changes. You make changes every day. Honoring time to be quiet rather than constantly being busy is a positive change. A cheerful attitude, laughing and joking, which you may maintain in the face of difficulty or disappointment is a major change, not a minor one, a big step. The more you practice it, the better you will feel, not only for yourself, but you offer extended benefit radiating joy and Love immediately to your Loved ones and radiating outwardly to affect many others. In fact it actually affects others even when you are not in close proximity; the waves of energy do travel. It is an uplifting thing that reaches far greater distance than you imagine. We are Laarkmaa, and we are here to help you change into the future humans for the new reality.

2

FIRST SENSE

We Pleiadians and other interdimensional beings do not communicate with language. We communicate through wisdom of the heart, through intention, through Connection. Because we are able to be many places instantly, we are also able to receive and transmit what needs to be shared instantly. It is part of Unity. Humans, when they come into the human body as infants, carry some of this with them. It is called the First Sense. It is the intuitive ability that exists throughout the universe. The First Sense is very prevalent in ones such as you two, and many women also remember the First Sense. Yet your culture squashes the First Sense, diminishes its importance, preferring to focus instead on the five biological senses of seeing, hearing, smelling, tasting, and touching. These senses are involved in describing your physical world through what you *feel*. The First Sense is a universal sense, not merely a human sense. It is a way to know Truth, and it Connects you to your divinity. When humans arrive in the earthly plane, infants must make an adjustment from the watery realm of their mother's bodies to the air realm in which they arrive. They are guided by their First Sense and begin to develop the other biological senses, one at a time. The biological senses do not spontaneously arrive at once. The First Sense leads infants to develop smell and taste in order to orient themselves towards food and nurturance. After smell and taste human infants develop the sense of touch as they adjust from the watery place they just came from to the air environment where they are. The next sense humans receive is external hearing, which develops more slowly than the other senses, for infants are still very much internalized from hearing the internal heartbeat and sounds in the mother's womb. The last of the biological senses to develop is sight. The world looks fuzzy to infants until they learn to adjust their vision for incoming perceptions. These are the biological senses of the physical body, which humans use for receiving input and understanding. Humans perceive their world through these five senses, often forgetting the First Sense. As they develop the biological senses, humans develop an emotional response to express what they are sensing. Babies cry and laugh; this is the way humans integrate the perceptions that they receive from the five biological senses, through their emotions.

The next developmental step is the formation of mental constructs or thought forms that give meaning to what humans feel and what they emote. This is where language becomes involved. Humans, who have forgotten their First Sense as a form of knowing and communication, need to Connect and communicate, and so they develop language. That language is derived from thought forms. The wisdom of the body also carries a language, a non-thinking, non-verbal language based on the perceptions it receives, but this language is often ignored in favor of the language of the mind. The First Sense can Connect the two when it is used. Have you noticed the synchronicity in how we sometimes answer questions that you are thinking about discussing or have not yet asked?

Yes.

We would like to use this example to demonstrate that we are using telepathic communication to communicate with you through your First Sense. At appointed times when you ask us to join you or when we sense you would appreciate our exchange, we are beginning more and more to use telepathic communication as a form of communicating. We wish to help develop that in you. It has long been dormant in humans, and frequently referred to as a sixth sense. In the past humans were punished for using this ability. It is actually not the sixth sense; it is the first. It is the sense that arises out of oneness. Other senses are more aligned with survival in physical human form on this planet. Yet the First Sense, intuition, is the sense you brought here and will take with you when you leave. We wish to reawaken it and help you use it now in human form. It will guide you and help you in creating the reality you desire and in making better choices to attain that reality.

We ask you to pay attention to all synchronistic events. Every time you notice a synchronicity, you are moving out of time. Intuition occurs out of time. Time constructs prevent free flowing intuition because humans are watching the clock, so to speak, putting limits and parameters around what is happening. They watch the clock to see what time to satisfy the sense of hunger. They watch the clock to see what time they will see the light of day or what time the dark will arrive. Taste, sight, many senses are constrained in time. If you begin to enhance your intuitive abilities, you will simultaneously enhance your ability to move out of time and also move out of the patterns that keep you blocked. Follow every intuitive idea. Some, of course, will not manifest instantly because you are practicing. But the more you follow the energy with an intent to understand intuitive guidance and wisdom, the more you will enlarge universal Connection in communications. You in effect are building Trust, which is so desperately needed in the human world. You build Trust through reliance on intuition, and you build Trust through understanding the intuition comes through you from a greater source, the higher aspect of yourself that is reaching from the other side of the veil to reconnect with your human form. So telepathic or intuitive communication broadens and deepens you as humans. You two and many others already have openings and intuitive understandings that lead you. Try to learn to follow those hunches more than what you would call your logical, rational ones. They will not lead you wrong.

We appreciate your insight. It is good for you to tell us things that we wish to learn and need to learn. Thank you. We recognize that we are using our intuitive, telepathic abilities, what we humans call ESP (Extra Sensory Perception.). We are now reading each other's thoughts more easily and thoroughly than we have before. We are recognizing that it is possible and that we are achieving a higher level of this at this time.

That's very good. Perhaps you would like to lose the term *extra* sensory perception. It is aligned with the old paradigm in which humans considered it the sixth sense. It is the First Sense: intuitive communication. You can help others understand the necessity of changing their terminology to honor and promote a better understanding of what the First Sense truly is. We mention it to put in your file of things to teach. If those who wish to awaken telepathic communication want to make the first step, they need to start by honoring the process with a more appropriate name than a name that relegates it to something that is extra or not needed. Those who choose to ascend will very much need it where the world is going. It will be the source of both communication and creation. Perhaps you might wish to start a notebook together of items that you can teach when you speak or write. In this way you begin, one human at a time, one small group at a time, to larger and larger audiences to teach what you know is Truth.

Understand that we do not ever leave each other; we are always in contact through the First Sense. You may communicate with us through your First Sense without our verbal conversation, if you choose. We see it as a higher form of exchange to meld our energies and communicate in the way humans used to communicate before the advent of verbal communication. When we meld our energy with you, there is telepathic communication, where we put ideas into your mind and body (the water of your being) when you are in that state, you may put your thoughts and ideas into our minds. The speaking vehicle is a temporary, intermediary process. We are helping to awaken what's in your consciousness from before you came to this earth. We are helping you remember things that you only have the edges of now. We touch upon things that you have read, or things that you have thought, or things that you have discussed. Everything does not have to be a new revelation. New revelations are woven between existing understandings, building on a stronger and stronger foundation for a new Truth, a new paradigm of understanding. Please do not be afraid of inserting your own ideas into our communication. We correct those things that you may wish to insert and tell you if they are not accurate. We do that through your questioning mode. When you have questions, we respond. We also steer our conversations always towards the light of Truth.

Since your First Sense comes from heart awareness and actually governs the other five biological senses, your other senses operate more fully for interaction in your third dimensional world when you increase listening to your First Sense. You watch, listen, and perceive your environment more closely. You may also tune out the environment and perceive in an altered state and therefore, hear on occasion some of the musical tones of communication that we use to communicate with the earthly plane. Humans are capable of this when they use their First Sense. The more you honor your First Sense and allow rigidly held patterns that have kept you, the Great Being, locked inside of the small being, to dissolve, the more open and expansive you become, and the more easily you may discern all manner of communication from us and others. You two already know how to do this with each other by assessing and watching through your heart Connection. You may do it with us as well.

I have a question about how you communicate within your own group. When we become closer to ascension, will we be able to communicate with you directly through tones, sounds, colors, and electrical responses?

Well, yes, but you do not need to reach ascension to begin communicating as we do. You two are already experiencing electrical responses, hearing tones, and seeing colors that guide you to communicate through the use of your First Sense. You are developing your ability to *know* rather than to merely feel or think. We will speak more about *knowing* later. We are working with your brains presently for you to perceive the vibrations of colors. We thought this way would be the easiest for you. You already receive communication through your heart in our presence. When we communicate with you, your heart receives the energy that you have translated for us as a smile upon your face. So you are already way ahead of others who may eventually wish to share in communication with Pleiadians. Search for the color blue. We need to have a discussion about the importance of colors at some point. It is on our list of things to discuss. Blue, the color of Trust, is essential to understanding Truth. It is difficult for humans to find Truth if there is no Trust. Therefore you will note what you call an aura or emanation of the color blue around Pleiadians, for we dwell in Trust. With Trust, we will teach you how to re-remember and use your First Sense.

3

THE MAGIC OF WATER

There is a link between your First Sense and Water. We do not believe this has been explained to humans before, and so we wish to discuss it now and have you share this understanding with other humans. Humans tend to forget the importance of water in your being. You tend to think of yourselves as static, unchanging, solid. You are *not*. You wish to put your hand through walls, yet you cannot do that while you retain the concept that you are solid, unchangeable. When you focus on experiencing the fluid within your own body, your own water makeup, you will see and begin to learn that you can change your form. Ancient people in ancient times knew this as shape shifting, and they knew how to do this. Hardcore beliefs about possibilities and human structure have denigrated those beliefs about possibility. People tend to view those thoughts as impossible or witchcraft today. Yet the Truth is, when you focus on the water makeup of your being, you will begin to do the things you wish that are not understood in this dimension. It is also Connected to what we have yet to speak of, of having your physical and etheric form meet in vibration, and yet what we tell you today comes from a totally different perspective and understanding, as if we were turning it inside out to show you from the inside what is possible.

Water is magic. The energy of water is a teacher because you are water. When you turn to water to learn, you are honoring the body that carries your light body. The *water* you are cannot be controlled or polarized. Pay attention. Water cannot be polarized; it can only be affected by emotions, but it will not stay in a polarity for long. It is through fluid that you allow movement past things you need to Transcend. It is important that you understand that water is a special element, and you being made of water, your body is a special, special element. When you learn that water cannot be polarized, you will find your emotions flow more easily without hanging you up, so to speak, at one point or another. You learn to move beyond the limitation of discomforting emotions, and your world becomes less emotional.

Focusing on the water within you from a cellular perspective for change is one way to learn about who you are and how you may communicate differently. Understand the water within your own being cannot be polarized; it can merely be influenced temporarily. It holds more power than you can imagine. This power within your water is the part of the secret of unlocking your DNA. Your DNA is a pool of material like water; it is not layered linearly as humans currently perceive it. The other part of the secret comes from removing the rigid structures of your belief systems. When you remove your beliefs and allow possibilities you have not yet imagined, you open the channels for your DNA to manifest in the way that it was intended. We will speak more about this later. For now, focus on discovering all you can about your own water. When you go to the sea, experiment with the water in a way differently than you ever have. When you enter the water, enter it as one, enter it as if you are *it* and *it* is *you*. It will have much to teach you.

Do we get intuitions in our lives more when we are involved with or near water, such as doing the dishes and having our hands in water, taking showers, or having other association with water? I don't mean swimming in the ocean; I mean simple, everyday water experiences.

Oh, boy! We are so pleased with you. We gave you suggestions for paying attention to the water within your body, and before you even get to the ocean, you've already figured it out! Very, very good. Now take that and apply it when you become water in the ocean. Water, we said is magic. It is also a medium of communication. Telepathy, and we have not said this before, but this is *most* important, telepathy travels on waves of water, magnetic resonance from one human being to another. You are water beings. Have you ever heard this? We don't believe it's been said.

This is very interesting. We wondered earlier today if this could be the case, and we looked at each other and said, "Why didn't we know this before?"

You didn't know it before because humans don't know how to think outside of their structured patterns. It's like you're in a maze and you can't get out. This is why we work with your third eye, expanding the parameters of the water within your being to accept other magnetic communications. This is part of what you will experience with crop circles, too. Telepathic reception. The more you tune into the water of your body, the more you resonant with what is being communicated. Working with water is most important for humans. You will teach this and take it into the world. Humans do not understand the concept that telepathy is relayed through water. It is a new unthought-of of concept.

A new unthought-of concept.

Yes. Meaning, humans have not thought of this. To them it will be a new idea. It is actually a Truth, an ancient Truth. Humans will be amazed and surprised. They think telepathy is about some form in the air, traveling from one person to another, and it is *not* airborne, *it is water borne*; it is magnetic resonance between human-to-human water that makes understanding and communication easier and more direct.

Carl Jung and others asserted that the collective unconscious is out in the air or in the atmosphere, but what you are saying is, I'm getting Goosebumps, that the collective consciousness is in our bodies and in the waters of the planet. So we actually are able to communicate directly to each other and to the planet through the resonance of water.

Yes! All life communicates through the magnetic resonance of water. The more humans separate themselves from Nature and the water of this planetary being and the crystalline and liquid grid underneath, the more separation occurs through lack of communication. Humans experience communication blockage and separation through ignoring the importance of water. It is impossible to communicate thoroughly when you are separated and do not understand the very nature of your being, both the magnetics and the water carrier manifestation of *how* communication occurs. Listening to the earth, listening to each other is listening to water.

Did you give me this thought today?

Yes! Although we have to say your communication with your High Self (every human has a higher self, some call them guides, some call them angels, who guide them towards their divinity) gave you this thought as well. It is not only us; it is the open communication pathways and channels that you have engaged in and opened through *your* willingness and devotion to having a receiving mind and heart as well as a heart and mind that think and speak. You have decided to listen, and you both listen well. So, you can thank your High Self and, we are so excited, you don't need to thank us. It is a resonant communication that you provide yourself as divine co-creator simply opening up and listening. Do you now fully understand the importance of water for Connection and communication? It is electrical magnetic resonance that is carried by all of Life. We are most excited about this! Now, you need to remember it is *you* who listened and came up with the concept and the understanding, the knowingness, the Truth, the goosebumps, the whole package, of *knowing* that telepathy and communication and ideas travel *on waves of water,* not through the air waves. Have you heard any other human say this?

Never.

No, of course not. This is new understanding being brought to human awareness, and it came through you. We put messages from our water telepathically into your water, and they naturally Connected. In order to translate incoming water messages, you must surrender to listening. You deepen your listening skills by listening to your own water. We are very happy with discussion of this concept of telepathy and water. This has been a joint team effort of all of us working together.

We will continue our conversation about the Connection between the magic of water and First Sense. You have understood this and have begun to transfer thoughts, feelings, and messages back and forth rapidly between yourselves through this understanding. You have the understanding in your body now, not merely in your thoughts. You are noticing instant communication with each other, instant feelings of what you see, what you touch, what you feel with each other in a larger way. It is the water that carries this, and through your interaction with the water on this life journey, the lesson has been discovering the power present within your own water. Notice how water shifts. At the ocean you may watch what you call crosscurrents and swiftly changing ocean patterns moving from agitation to calm and calm to agitation. You are assessing and verbalizing deep understanding much more quickly, in the same way you observe how quickly water can change. Notice the difference in yourself. You received the very big lesson about movement: that *everything* always moves. Like your understanding about gaining wisdom from household water and other access to water for telepathic communication, now you understand the wave-like nature of water and its ability to inform. In understanding that everything is always in movement, you gain the ability to see *yourselves* always in movement rather than in static form, and you grow closer to being able to see us. Shape shifting is nothing but constant movement. It is inherently possible for all humans to move the form that contains your water. It becomes possible through breaking up existing patterns of structure that the human

22

mind believes erroneously is the way the body moves and functions. Placing your hands through the walls is moving beyond time and space from what appears to be rigid and solid into recognition that the wall in fact is moving, the hand in fact is moving. It is in the meeting of the two movements that you place your hands through the wall. It is in the understanding of movement that you grow closer to being able to travel and communicate instantly. The secret for both is held within your water. The biggest lessons you have learned so far are in understanding that everything is movement and understanding the power that you carry in your own water; water makes up the majority of your physical body, carries your thoughts and intentions, and provides the ability for instant communication. These are your greatest lessons, and they are some of the biggest lessons for humanity.

If all humans could learn the possibility and the power inherent in their own water for shape shifting beyond current constructs, whether it is a headache, a backache, a stomachache, or a bad mood, they would be infinitely more at peace. It is a pathway humans would greatly benefit from if they chose to pursue it. Humans need to understand that they carry power within the fluid of their being. This power is in their water. Within it lies the power for communicating, for Healing, and for Connecting. You both have been experiencing synchronistic and linked thoughts recently. This is evidence of your Connecting through your water.

You just read my mind; I was just thinking of that.

Yes, we know. Another synchronistic linking, is it not? This is what it means to be one of eight (the two of you and the six of us) and eight of one. We link together through wave motion speaking from our water to your water. The more you focus on recognizing this as it occurs, the more it *will* occur. It will cease to be something that you remark, "Isn't that something!" Instead it will become a norm, and as you move towards it's being a norm, you will miss it when it is not present, which is also a good thing, for missing it when it is not present shows how greatly you value it when it is. It also helps focus your intent to make it occur more frequently. And as you begin to understand how your water affects the water of others, you can see that your attitude, feelings, and thoughts affect the water of all those around you and of the collective consciousness of humanity. As you can put one drop of chemically harmed water into a glass and the whole glass is contaminated, so one drop of negative human thought form water affects the whole of Earth's water, polluting it as well. We will speak more about thought forms later.

Most humans do not yet understand that they have the power to purify water through their own thoughts. They may simply purify the water within them as well as their own drinking water. Yet most human consciousness is not developed enough to pursue this, although there are some who understand and practice this concept. Placing the human energy field around a glass of water and putting Love into the water can simply purify whatever is there, yet most are not aware of how to do this. The power you have been discovering of your own water goes beyond the power of telepathic communication and thought and is also about the relationship of *movement* and communication of your water to the water of the planet.

We would like to note with some excitement your linking understanding between what we have been teaching the two of you about feeling the energy of the land with your hands and the science called dowsing. Both are connected to feeling Water to Water: your human water to the water of the planet, your human water carrying messages between us and others, and the water of the planet containing messages acting as a receiving and transmitting device for communication. It is quite exciting that you have made these Connections and are interested in pursuing them. As you continue to explore your understandings about water, you may wish to spend some time in loosening the container that holds *your* water (*the body)*, moving it in unaccustomed ways and awakening the cells to possibilities of redirection with your intent. This will be an exciting exploration. We will be with you. We watch your molecular shape and structure change as you gather more and more wisdom in your water and focus your intent. We are also interested that you two begin to Connect with others who understand and think as you do, even if they are not on this continent or in this world. You two have much to look forward to in sharing what you are discovering with other humans. Remember: Water is magic.

4

BELIEF, REALITY, AND TRUTH

We want humans to understand that there is no such thing as belief. Beliefs are made up conglomerations of ideas incorrectly built upon assumptions and experiences. In reality, only knowing, Trust, and Truth exist. The word belief is used in communication to support individual positions about what one thinks is real. We wish to help humans learn to understand reality through Truth rather than through their belief systems. Beliefs are individual; they are not a shared Truth. Truth is universal for all. As you learn to communicate through your water rather than relying on your belief systems, there will be less of a boundary between "you" and "us". Humans are accustomed to polarization and duality, always separating into a "you" and "other." Truth is universal, and reunion with Truth cannot be simultaneous with a separation of "you" versus "other." We are the same and we share the same Truth.

I often have the idea that someone is contacting me or that a Truth has been given to me from outside

of myself when I experience what we humans call goosebumps. Can you speak about that please?

Yes. It is an experience of accelerated vibration. You spoke of it occurring when you hear the Truth. You might call it the Truth vibration. It is something that will occur more and more as humans are more inclined to use their intuition and recognize the difference between Truth and their belief systems or their made up reality. Usually, when Truth is given about something, it comes from an outside source or from one awakened human being to the awakened portion of another human being, speaking something that is Connected with Truth. When Truth is spoken, goosebumps occur. You are not the only ones to whom this occurs, as I am sure you are aware. It is a human reaction to the elevated, *pure* vibration of Truth, for Truth is a pure, high vibration, not simply an alignment to right or wrong, which most humans *believe* is Truth. Most humans try to access Truth by assigning meaning of "right like me" or "wrong, not like me." That has nothing to do with Truth; that is simply a made-up belief system about reality. Goosebumps occur when you are in animated states of conversation with someone, speaking about something that is important to you. When you have been aware of and responded to our touch with goosebumps, you are in an awakened state of consciousness. Goosebumps are associated with Truth. They are the sparks that occur from human to human in the divine space that comes when humans are hearing Truth. Both of you are beginning to see Truth more and more in ways you can feel it through your physical body. You've always been able to do this, but it will increase for you as your intuition and telepathy also increase.

We understand what you are saying, but we would also like to know, is it an understanding of vibration of Truth only, or are we also actually being touched physically by something other than our own bodies?

Sometimes, when you are with another person, and something is said that you resonate with as Truth, it is simply the spark of the vibration of Truth Itself. Other times you are indeed touched by us, angels, your High Self, or other energetic beings who are in effect giving you a physical awareness that you have achieved understanding of something important. So yes, sometimes you are being touched by us or others. Sometimes it is merely the spark of the Truth that humans can receive between each other when they for that brief moment are touching all their divine remembrance and living in Truth. It is both.

Thank you. I suspected I was sometimes being touched by you.

Yes. Do you approve?

Oh, yes.

It is important for humans to understand how their reactions and their belief systems create their reality and how deeply those belief systems and patterns of reactions are etched into who they *think* they are. It is your choice, humans, to move beyond your beliefs about who you are. You are so much more than that. When you hold on to the belief that you are powerless to change things, you continue to make circumstances that create that reality. Your *power* is in your *knowing*. Change what you believe is possible into what you *know* is possible, and other possibilities begin to exist. You are capable of so much more than your human reactions to external and internal stimuli. You are so much more than what you believe.

There is a big difference between what you *believe* to be true and Truth. Truth has nothing to do with whether you believe it or not. Some are fond of saying, "That's not my truth" because something doesn't fit within their experience or their belief systems about the way things work. Truth cannot be successfully resisted or denied. It just *is*, whether you believe it or not. Beliefs are such human things. Trust and Truth are all that matter for Trust and Truth lead to Love. You are learning that beliefs have no validity. They are traps. We will be glad when beliefs no longer exist and humans dwell in Truth with Trust. This is one reason we ask you to continually drop beliefs. It is not only about change. It is about understanding that beliefs entrap you and do not allow you to move towards flow and Unity. From the human perspective, Truth evolves as new facts are discovered. Humans have always believed that facts are Truth, but facts are only what is known at the moment, certainly *not* the Truth. Those humans who are beginning to broaden their understanding and drop away from some of their facts or some of the things they believed were true, are beginning to understand that universal Truth does not change, even through new scientific discoveries. We maintain that Truth is Truth. It is only from the human perspective that it evolves and changes as new understanding, alignment, and recognition of other realities become clear in the mental constructs. As you bring this work into the world, you will have moments where you are challenged and where you may doubt, for things can contrast causing challenging ideas to arise. Put your doubts aside, feel inside your heart, join hands, and remember that we are a team, a family of Loved ones, and doubt will quickly subside. Certainly do not be wounded by accusation and questions, doubting questions of others. You may know what feels right in your heart, and *move* more in the direction of accepting possibilities outside of your former awareness every day. As you develop communications among all aspects of yourselves *(conscious and subconscious)* you create deeper telepathic awareness, and you may use that awareness to link with each other and the Silver threads Connecting the collective consciousness. You may draw needed things towards you by sending out telepathic waves through your water. This is real communication. You may begin it now, and it will increase; it will be enhanced. Those humans who understand how to co-create reality in your world demonstrate Truth and the greater understanding of reality. What do you say to this?

Yes. I believe what you are telling us is the absolute Truth, and I believe we are growing into this understanding. I can speak for both of us in knowing that you are real, we are real, and that we have nothing to doubt.

Yes. And we agree. There is more about creating reality. It is not only your belief systems that create reality; the beliefs of humanity's collective conscious also create your shared reality. Collective consciousness has a general understanding and belief system that defines collective reality. It is confined by time. Collective consciousness has determined for humans what is possible and what is not in three-dimensional reality. Collective consciousness implies shared fears, shared thoughts, shared visions, everything humankind puts into the energetic pot for humanity. You know, as we said, you see us as six but

31

we see us as one; collective consciousness is similar. We see you *(Cullen and Rebecca)* as two, but humanity as one; it is much the same concept. So collective consciousness is the organism that desires to evolve into higher form. Your two parts act as heart and brain for the entire organism, sending your light, your positive thought forms, your dismantling of beliefs, your moving outside of time, space, and form, all of these things are affecting collective consciousness, just as if someone had brain surgery or heart surgery to make the human being function better; you serve to change the collective consciousness. You are not alone in doing this; all humans participate in this change.

There is also subconscious collective consciousness: we mean that forgotten longing that all humans have within them to return to Source, to act with Love, to have true Connection, the yearning for beauty, the longing to know as humans define it to know God. All of this lies within the subconscious collective consciousness. In our work together, the two of you will act as *way changers*, addressing what needs to be brought from the subconscious to the consciousness of humankind. Teaching what we have shared and living by example will serve to prod at humanity's subconscious and bring it to the light in order for humanity to evolve to a collective consciousness that knows its own shadow and remembers from where it came and that it is made of light. Rebecca interprets what we say as an opening of the heart. The subconscious is opening the heart of the collective consciousness. Revealing the divinity within the subconscious opens the heart of collective consciousness in order to move into Love. But most humans cannot settle themselves into quietness at this time in order to do this because most of humanity is simply afraid to contact their shadow. Humans make themselves so busy that there is no time for reflection or the quiet time needed to delve into their own shadow work. They distract themselves with many "duties" and the many "things" that make their lives noisy, such as television, radio, and computers. This avoidance of quiet examination can be summed up into one word: fear. We will speak more about this subject later.

So the collective subconscious carries information that scares people. The longing that you talk about must be a battleground between wanting to remember, and when fear becomes the stronger element, it cancels out the longing to truly remember.

Not quite. The subconscious is where the light and the remembering live that need to be brought forward. Fear lives in a middle ground. The shadow work is not subconscious; it is a middle ground where humans are afraid to go to any depth whatsoever. In three-dimensional understanding, you might see it in layers. The first layer is the collective consciousness where humans speak about the mundane things of the world. Beyond that is a layer of fear that humans either try to work through, or they refuse to examine at all. If they were to actually go through the fear and make friends with their own shadows and understand what the shadow tries to teach them and tell them, *then* they would penetrate into another layer where the light dwells. Understandings about the true nature of reality will unfold as humans gain courage to examine their shadows and go beyond clinging to their belief systems about what is "real" and what is "True." Doubts from questions of "What is reality?" will occur in all humans as the veil lifts or drops, depending on your perspective. As what humans counted on as sturdy, solid reality shifts and changes, humans will attempt to prove their point, grab on, make sure that what they believe is real all the more, as it crashes and slips beneath their feet. You two are experiencing a topsy-turvy (we like that phrase) maneuvering between existing realities: the reality the two of you know is real, and the one the majority of other humans *believe* to be real. When you bump into the true reality unaware, it can be disorienting for most. When you bump into that reality from a place of more awareness, you understand and see it for what it is. As you understand what this is, you will experience calmer resonance within yourselves. Reality *is* changing, and reality *never was* what humans believe it to be. Both are True.

Would you say that humans throughout history have called things that appeared outside their normal reality miracles?

Yes. Because humans believe anything outside their belief system is impossible and cannot exist, they define those occurrences as miracles. They are *not* miracles; they are simply divinity at work through the power of intent applied to one's own personal water, or even stronger, collective water, when similar intents are applied in group form. There are no miracles. Miracles are simple divinity awakening within human occurrences. Or you could say it the other way around: It's *all* miracles. We prefer that version; it's all miracles. Humans simply close the doorway to divine interaction through fear and through clutching and clinging to the structures of belief that prevent them from seeing Truth.

And it appears to me that all of humankind can live in a miraculous way by stepping out of our way and allowing the divinity that is part of all of us simply to work as it was designed.

We believe that is the divine plan for this planet. And you two are forerunners in knowing how to manifest this through moving intention into action.

Is that the same meaning as bringing Spirit into matter? People have used that phrase for a very long time in attempting to explain that if we bring the spirit or the original sense of Source into our human material world, life will simply run more easily and we will be in the flow. Is that the same as bringing Spirit into Matter?

We believe the understanding of bringing spirit into matter is limited from the human perspective because most humans believe matter is the most important. Physical form is what they count on and rely on as reality; therefore they wish to infuse it with spirit. From our perspective, we see instead of bringing spirit into matter, awakening the divine that already exists and reconnecting, re-remembering *(to use your phrase)* the Connection that is already there. Spirit or divinity exists already in physical form; it has simply been disconnected through fear, suffering, and all of those negative emotions humankind has endured and clung to for thousands of years. As humans move beyond the emotional clearings and integrate more fully all the realities of past/parallel lives and present understandings, they reconnect the fragments that allow the flow of divinity to move back and forth from Source to person and person to Source. So we see it rather as clearing a channel, opening the way to what already exists within matter, rather than bringing something into matter for the first time. Do not use linear, hierarchical thinking to make one more valuable than the other. Both are important. Spirit or Source is within and without you. Let us help you let go of your beliefs, learn to know Truth, and journey into the new reality. You are being waved into Truth.

5

THE POWER OF THOUGHT AND INTENT

We want to thank you for your willingness to converse with us. We wish to understand how to help humans with their difficulties. We wish to understand what is difficult or challenging for you. We do not understand why most of you are so frequently challenged with things that seem quite easy to us. As we have these conversations, we learn how your thoughts and emotions contribute to your difficulties, so we can give you more tools and assistance. We thank you for the opportunity to learn about human thinking. What thoughts can you share today?

Last night Rebecca was awakened all through the night with random thoughts and visual pictures in her brain. Would you please address the patterns she was seeing and tell us if there is anything we should know about that?

We showed her fractal patterns of energy waves and angular components of thought forms and how they appear in energetic form, rather than the way you understand thoughts.

Thoughts have structure, although humans cannot usually see the structure. We showed her the structure of mental thought forms. She was puzzled by the geometric, angular shapes, which were perhaps unusual to her. It was somewhat of a stretch for her brain to perceive these patterns. There are many visual patterns that are different from what humans are accustomed to. We expanded her brain, enhancing her ability to use more of her brain in the way that you use more of your brain. Had you seen these things, they would perhaps not have been as unusual for you, for your brain encompasses more of things you remember from before you arrived in this life than does Rebecca's brain. So we gave her a visual, a form of seeing the template energy of thoughts. What else?

She awakened with two phrases in her mind. The first phrase was "a cellular memory of living without restriction." The second phrase was "the roots of the world tree keep us from spiraling out in illusion." Can you tell us what these thoughts mean?

Ah, yes. Well, you have the interpretation of the first one already. It refers to your knowing that it is possible to be omni-present. It refers to the way we move and the way humans were able to move before they entered the physical body. The memory of this way of being lives in your cells. We help to awaken that memory by giving you the thought. The phrase is a reminder and a confirmation of what you already know. The second phrase is a symbolic thought reference to keep yourselves grounded as you are learning other ways of being. The world tree must have roots in the ground as it reaches up to the universe, and if one is not grounded while living in duality, one may have difficulty. The tree is a symbolic suggestion to slow down and connect with Nature. Don't be concerned with accelerating too quickly. This suggestion is for all humans, who are part of Earth reaching up to the universe. We give humans symbols and thoughts to help them understand and grow. Last night we gave Rebecca some visual representations of how the mental body and the mental pathways work. This was a communication. Here's how to interpret it: if you are looking at a foreign language and you see the shape and the flow of the letters moving from left to right (or right to left, as in Asian languages), you see certain patterns that you understand as a form of communication. What Rebecca saw last night were patterns, and we are telling her today that it is a form of communication, yet one that she is not familiar with because there is no flow from left to right or right to left as is standard in human languaging. Yet it *is* communication. Mental constructs travel on geometric shapes, bouncing against each other as they either resonate or bounce away from one point to another. It is a form of chaos and order all at once, for the energy moves the thoughts.

Yes. I believe the Butterfly Effect refers to the fact that even something as small as the flap of a butterfly's wings can cause tiny changes that can alter everything. The hundredth monkey effect refers to the fact that a learned behavior spreads spontaneously from one group of monkeys to all monkeys once enough have been exposed to it. Thought travels in the same way.

All right. Mental constructs move in this fashion. Thought energy moves from one place to another, splinters into fractals, create other colors, bounces back, and then moves off again, effecting every place it touches, some quite unexpectedly. Thoughts have tremendous power.

This is very important.

Yes! It is very important. What thoughts do you wish to add?

It seems you are giving us a primer to understanding who you are, how you are, how you live, and how you experience energy, light, color, and movement. You are giving us a condensed form of who you are and what life or what existence is on the other side of the veil that separates humans on planet Earth from the True reality of what the universe really is made of, what it does, and how it works.

Yes, but we wish to take this one step further. It is not simply a view of the other side of the veil; it is also an unveiling of the reality on *your* side of the veil.

Do you mean what can be?

No. What *is* that you are not aware of, what humans are unaware of that exists on both sides of the veil.

What can be if we can see, understand, and feel it.

It is here whether you see, understand, and feel it or not.

We humans have to unblock our habits and all of our "bad training" to understand and live in the way you are showing us.

Yes. Very true, and that is why we tell you to *drop your belief systems! Manage your thought forms!* If you get into an energetic negative place, watch what you think, because those thought forms create a reality you do *not* wish. They in effect build a prison around you, holding you in a structure that prevents you from getting the very things your hearts desire. It cannot be any plainer or more clear than this. Do you understand the importance?

Yes, I believe I do, although it is difficult for humans to conceive of how to constantly watch their thoughts, particularly when their emotions get involved.

We say thought patterns create more reality than you are aware, and we have given Rebecca a visual representation that you may share with other humans of how that happens. We are trying to break down your prison walls. The phrase that we gave Rebecca in her sleep *("a cellular memory of living without restrictions")* is about breaking out of the confines and the structures that humans impose upon themselves through their mental thought forms. The key to thought forms is *form*. If you understand that human beings believe dense physical material is form, then "thought form" makes perfect sense: you *think* something, and that something becomes structural form. We mean by this that if you think good thoughts, you manifest that which you are seeking. Conversely, if you constantly think negative, fearful, emotionally charged thoughts, you create an uncomfortable and unpleasant reality for yourselves and everyone else.

I believe I understand on several levels what you are explaining; however, this is the way humans have been trained. What you are saying is all new to most humans.

We know that, but we also know that you have many enlightened ones who have taught the principle that "thoughts are things." The *form* is the key thing. *You are creating form through your thoughts every moment of the day.* The more you focus on what you have discovered about resonance with water and communicating without the patterned structure of thoughts, the more you communicate as we do from the resonance of the heart. As long as you communicate through thoughts and words, they have the power to manifest into reality. Form is not what you think. Communication occurs through water. Form can be held within a construct of Love and fluid movement, flowing, as it needs to, joining where it needs to. We use ourselves as an illustration: You perceive six of us, but we perceive we are one unified being. We can separate and move around at will to surround you with our Love, or touch you from different angles, and we form one energetic mass together with no boundaries because we are able to move as water, with no specific boundaries. We communicate through our water without thought forms. We believe those humans who are reaching for growth and evolution are ready to hear and understand everything we are saying. Some will listen and figure it out. Some will just listen and accept it. Truth is Truth.

This will be a revolutionary understanding for human beings. How can we help make a change for humanity with these new understandings?

We are sometimes amused watching human thought processes; how interesting and curious you can be! We are all Connected, and we are learning so much from you about how associative thought processes move through human awareness. The more we understand this, the more we can offer assistance. Many humans at this time do not display evidential curiosity, the expanding of their brains to wonder, and we are delighted and amused when one of you creatively weave your thought patterns in a positive direction. It delights and amuses us because it is so very different from the way that we do things. Yet we would like to share our way of communicating, for humans are capable of communicating like we do. Our way is to start from heart; we feel emanations of vibration that communicate what we feel. We encourage you to please become aware of what you feel in your body, because this is a way of opening your understanding to communicate as we do. Almost all of humanity has been damaged by incorrect ideas that the body is less than the mind. The separations of dualistic Cartesian principles that mind and body are separate damage communication. Communication occurs *best* when the one communicating is (whether it is you or whether it is us) in a state of complete openness and receptivity. Better communication between humans and interplanetary beings such as us will benefit not only your world, but also the entire universe.

Let us return our conversation to the power of thoughts. It is important for humans to understand the Connection between intentions, thoughts, and feelings. Intentions can be heart-based, stemming from feelings, or intentions can be mentally based, stemming from thoughts. Intentions create reality, especially when they are coupled with emotion. (We will speak in great depth on emotion at a later time.) When someone says, "I never intended that to happen," there is always a misunderstood intention that precipitated the creation of that circumstance. Often there is known intention to express what one is feeling, while there is simultaneously a subconscious, unknown (and misunderstood) intention to stir things up in order to promote change. If the underlying intention for change is not well

43

governed and if it is not matched with conscious thought, if it is released through unbridled emotion in the moment, the energy for change becomes like a river raging out of its banks, creating an overflow, a surplus of what is really needed for positive change. How you apply your intent and your thought with emotional feelings directs the creation of your reality. What you think must be thought and intended consciously, for humans do not yet understand the full power they possess for creating their own reality. When you find yourself "out of your own emotional banks," immediately practice compassion with yourself and everyone else to re-establish balance. Search for the link between the conscious thought, the conscious and sub-conscious intents, and the emotion being felt. Humans are not very good at this. We are trying to teach you to monitor your thoughts, control your emotions, and focus your intentions to create a better reality.

You can accomplish much for humanity as you learn to consciously control your thoughts, your feelings, and your intent. More can be accomplished with group intent than the intent of one or two, for you are battling consensual human consciousness, which does not understand these concepts. Group intention makes a bigger impact. This is why it is important at this time to seek Connection and communication with like-minded beings where you can band your intent together and send it like a laser beam into the collective consciousness of humanity to shatter and break apart those rigid belief systems and structures that hold humanity captive. It is a time of calling together those of you who have waited all this time to do your work. This is part of our teamwork. Now is the time.

Thank you. That was a very large answer to a very small question. That's great. We notice that on some days we seem to be able to calmly monitor our thoughts, intents, and emotions, and on some days it is markedly more challenging. What happens to cause such an internal difference? Are we responsible? Is the universe responsible? Are we partially responsible? For example, today we both feel extremely light and joyful. We would like to know who, what, or what combination is responsible for this extreme lightness of being?

Ah, your question teaches. It teaches what we are most interested in: teamwork, Unity, moving towards Source. We have been telling you that the intent of a group, or even two, does more to shift the collective reality than the intent of a single individual. To answer your question piece by piece, we are neither allowed nor capable of making changes for you, for you control your own attitude. That is your power, the power of your water, and we cannot change that. Our portion is to open the pathways, rewire the brain, help educate, and show you other possibilities, yet nothing can be done without your permission, your choices, and the control of your own water, your own power through your own thought forms. Humanity's thought forms have been holding humanity back for some time. The two of you provide through Love, pure unconditional, genuine Love, the kind that is rare in humanity, a safe place to be able to receive what we offer. In this safe, Loving space, humans may do the shadow work necessary to clean out old, erroneous beliefs and fears, creating a space for a new attitude to exist. These elements are part of total teamwork, yet each human must take the largest amount of credit, for it is accomplished individually *first* through one's own power. Humans have *always* had the power to live in the light energy the two of you are experiencing today; they simply refuse to do so because of their attachment to familiar patterns and belief systems. Humans get stuck in ruts where the discomfort is more familiar than a new path of joy and ease, so if anything occurs to tip them out of balance, they literally fall into their own rut, the rut they continue to make through their own thoughts. We expect once humans understand *how* to do it differently, they will practice and make better track marks for their attitudes through their thoughts. So, to answer your question, each individual human is the only one who can change his own attitude; no one else is able to do this for him. It is not only the conscious self of each person; it is also the subconscious that makes a difference. When the subconscious and the conscious communicate together, functioning as an integrated whole, it makes a difference. It is then that humans may experience the holiness and the divinity of who you are supposed to be. As you move towards this understanding, you will discover that you are living in a joyous time *if* you will allow it.

The last thing we wish to say for now is that your thoughts do not belong to you. Isn't that an amazing idea for a species that focuses on individuality?! It is a strange concept for humans, is it not? Think of how we have shared with you about how we, Laarkmaa, and other Pleiadians communicate. We communicate through First Sense and through heart. That allows us to be able to read one another, for we want the highest good for all concerned. There is no need to hide our thoughts as private. Think also of how we have discussed how humans have the power of their water to carry thoughts back and forth. For example, you read Rebecca's wish for lunch today. If her thoughts were entirely her own guarded secret, you would not have been able to read her water and provide the meal that was beneficial for you both. Think further of how we are eight of one and one of eight. Human beings on the long road of development have marched further and further down steps of separation. It is now time to turn towards Unity. Claiming your thoughts as your own private territory is a step in the wrong direction. It is a very novel thing for a human being to think that *one's thoughts are not private.* Humans have been taught to hold their thoughts because it is the only thing that they can keep for their very own: their thoughts and their attitude. But this is incorrect teaching and training. In order to be able to approach Unity and oneness, you must be able to communicate freely for the highest good of all without separation, and understand that your attitudes as well as your thoughts affect everyone. Thoughts need to be open. You do not benefit yourselves individually or together by holding your thoughts quietly to yourself. Remember, when humans place intention and thoughts into the world, they begin creating a reality for all. When humans use their individual thoughts, with or without conscious intention, they are creating for their community as well as for themselves. On a grander scale, human thought put out into the universe goes into the collective thought pools for all of humanity into collective consciousness, which is the reality humans share in the third dimension. So you see, the idea that your thoughts are private and that you have the right to think what you please is actually incorrect, and that belief has harmed humans for some time. You need to be *so* aware of your thoughts that at any given time you know that your thoughts are co-creating the reality that your future self and others will be living. It is wise to remember that you are creating not only for yourself but also for your loved ones and the world at large. There is no more time or space for indulging in private moments of feeling sorry for oneself or thoughts of a negative nature that carry emotional upsets. Recognize thoughts as they arise, change them when necessary, and use your intention to create a greater reality.

Do not simply allow thoughts to run their course; that is an old way of being. The time for that has passed, and when thoughts come up, it is appropriate and important to examine what you feel and what you think and ask yourself, "How do I wish to arrange my thoughts around this issue to create a better environment and a reality that I choose, which always affects everyone else?" You must always ask, "What part do I play in this?" The two of you must teach other humans that thoughts are not private material for their own inner consumption. There has been a strong push in your culture for individuation, which is built on separation. While developmental psychologists teach that individuation is an appropriate stage for children, actually teaching concepts that support separation is not correct. It is time for humans to move away from individualism and towards Unity instead.

This process will be difficult for most, if not all humans, to correct their erroneous beliefs that their thoughts belong to them individually.

No more difficult than any other belief system. It is the letting go of belief systems that proves to be difficult for humans, and it matters not what the belief system is. Each person's *attachment* to specific beliefs makes it difficult to let go; it is holding on to entrenched beliefs that are familiar that makes it difficult to monitor one's thoughts and to change. Once humans begin to let go of beliefs, once that process begins, there is a certain form of surrender, and new possibilities open. Many humans will kick and scream, clinging to their beliefs until Truth overrides their beliefs and they can no longer hide from the changes that the universe presents. At that point they will have a choice to surrender with a positive curiosity of "What comes next?" You two are already doing that in some of your discussions where you stop mid sentence and acknowledge, "Uh-oh; here is a belief system; let's try this a different way." This process allows humans to change *how* they think about reality.

Yes. We have considered inventions or inventors in our human history, people like Albert Einstein. We never thought that he came up with the new ideas on his own. We always believed that he was connected into a greater or larger understanding. He simply slipped in and out of that understanding, bringing new ideas into the collective consciousness.

Yes, that is very well said and understood, much like when you think you originate new ideas. Sometimes it is Laarkmaa nudging you, and sometimes it is your High Self being Connected to Source that gives you access to the idea.

So when that happens through our High Self angels, do we experience that thought alone or are many having that thought at the same time?

It would be like seeing Starworks, you call them Starworks when the sky lights up?

Fireworks.

Fireworks. It would be like fireworks. Your High Self sparks you with an idea, and all across the planet many others may spark simultaneously, for you are Connected.

That is what we have called "simultaneous invention."

Yes, indeed. And simultaneous invention has existed for some long time. But this goes beyond simultaneous invention. We are encouraging humans to approach group Unity more and more rather than holding onto individual separation. It is a profoundly simple practice. You may have great fun with this. Pleaidians have group unity consciousness, so we understand that when one learns a lesson, all learn a lesson. If one is in distress, all are in distress. Since we do not have individual ideas about separate thoughts and we communicate with our hearts and our First Sense, what one learns, we all experience simultaneously. Practice what we have shared with you. Humanity will benefit from this greater understanding of Unity. Make your thoughts intentional. Use intentional thoughts and make them for the highest good of all. The power of your thoughts is profound.

6

ABOUT THE EARTH

So you wish to understand more about the earth and Earth's non-human beings?

Yes. Can you explain dolphin intelligence to us? Who are they, or who were they in another form?

Dolphins carry energy from Mu, a continent that existed long ago, where humans who lived there shared the knowledge of how to breathe underwater and communicate their intelligence through vibratory communication. They were able to move around in the omnipresent fashion that you call zip, zip, zip. Dolphins today know this method. They know joy raises vibration, and they have offered to teach humans about the vibration of joy through their play and interaction with humans. You may watch them play. You may interact with them. Notice the resonance of joy. It is this vibration the dolphins teach humans, trying to get them to remember this within themselves. When you are in the vicinity of dolphins, they will respond to your own joy vibration and join you where you are, if they are not busy on assignment in another place. Sometimes they avoid particular waters because of both human hazards and technical hazards where it would not be advantageous for them to come to you even if they wish to spend time with you. Do not be disappointed if they do not come to particular waters where you are, for they know best when to be near humans. However, if they are nearby and you wish to engage with them, it will be helpful to know that they respond to musical tones, for sounds are how humans and dolphins can communicate vibrationally at this time. They recognize particular tones as vibrations that are pleasant and communicative to be around. You will find similar profound communications with whales. Whales spent more time in Mu than did dolphins. Whales are older. Spend time with whales when you can. Do not focus only on dolphins. Sea turtles also have much to teach; on Earth they are older than whales or dolphins.

Thank you. Rebecca has been suggesting that we go swim with whales for some time.

We are aware. We put dreams in her to remember her own time in the ocean with whales. She remembers this within her. Rebecca has been asking for and entering into dream states with us for a very long time. We do not put dreams into people spontaneously. Some people ask through their High Selves, and their conscious selves are not as aware of the request, yet the request is still necessary. Remember we said humans are co-creators. You must have intent. Those humans who have been asking for guidance, for wisdom, to understand, are in effect opening the portals, opening the doorways, in waking time and in dream time for communication. Sometimes it is easier for us (Pleiadians) to enter your dream state than your waking state, for humans leave time when in the dream state; humans are constrained by time in their waking state. Therefore, we enter during dreamtime. Rebecca's Connection with whales was a remembrance of who she is and the water she carries. The eye of the whale looking at her through her dream was the eye of one of her kindred spirits awakening her, calling her to remember. We simply facilitated placing these images together, moving time from her human past, human present, and human future into one space within her dream. So in effect she dreamed of being in the water with a whale in the past and she dreamed of the whale's energy in the future, yet the dream occurred within her present to tie it all together. We also are responsible for many of her dreams where she is going to a school. Some of these schools have Lemurian teachers that are familiar to her, and she always feels at home when she visits these schools. There are other ways we have communicated with her and that we strive to awaken her remembrance of who she is. We are striving to awaken all humans' remembrance of who they are! Time at the ocean will benefit you both. In the water. Be in the water. You may awaken memories deep within you from times when you lived in the water, and it may help you in being more flexible and fluid as you walk on Earth. This is true for all humans. Water can do many things. The whales know this. The dolphins, for the most part, know this. Those who are drawn to the sea have a remembrance within their body of the importance of water. It is why humans yearn to go to the sea.

There are other earth animals with whom you may communicate. We have watched your energetic engagement with deer and their response to your voice. They respond to your verbal communication as if understanding your words, yet it is because you use energy that is more closely aligned to their own that they respond. The ability to do this demonstrates changes within yourselves. More humans should practice matching their energy to that of non-human beings in Nature. It promotes communication from an energetic perspective and increases resonance so that humans may improve their communication skills. Interspecies communication is not just about the Pleaiadian-Human exchange. It is about animal-human exchange, rock-human exchange, and water-human exchange. You are learning within your being, rather than as merely a concept in your mind, the Truth that all things are one, and you are being shown ways to teach this to other humans. All non-verbal communications with rocks, water, deer, and us open the pathway for you to listen well and receive the guidance that is yours. Remember the joy vibration. It is a wonderful tool to help you evolve.

Rocks and water provide much information about any human's particular resonance with any place. If you wish to understand the energy of any place on Earth, look for the energy from the rocks. Feel the land. Put your bare feet on the ground. Pay attention to rocks, for rocks hold energy and information. Humans notice their color and their form; we ask, if you choose, to feel their vibration and take in what they can teach. Many humans are drawn to rocks and understand that they carry energy, yet they do not understand the possibilities for communicating with rocks. The energy of the stones talks to the human crystalline body. Humans must slow down in order to hear what rocks have to communicate. Rocks are teachers on Earth. Stores that sell rocks are Healing places; they are places where humans can get a large does of crystalline energy. Rocks can also teach humans how to break down patterns they hold within their structure.

You have spoken about what rocks teach, and you have spoken of water teaching us about changing form. Could you elaborate on the difference in what these two elements have to teach us?

Ahh. A very excellent question. Energy may be understood at a small molecular level. Tiny changes lead to huge waves of change. Rocks hold patterns of wisdom and energy; humans may learn this wisdom from rocks by placing their hands on the surface of the rock. There is much to learn from rocks about slowness; rocks move with infinitesimal slowness. It is in slowness that humans may change the electrical particles of their being. It is in the slowness that humans may attain what is considered miraculous movements. If humans slow their consciousness down to that of the ancient rocks, they learn communication through resonance. We do not wish to confuse you. Slowing down consciousness allows *raising* of vibration. This is why meditation is helpful for humans. Let us explain. The electrons of the human body move very fast within your being, within your DNA when you are vibrating at higher vibrational levels, such as the levels you seek for melding with us or for ascension. Yet within that speed there is a slowness that is out of time, perhaps most akin to your meditative states. That may be the way we can explain it best. It is a slowing down beyond time, while speeding up the energy. It is allowing molecular change by slowing down your human speed and accelerating your divine vibration. From this then, you can understand that rocks move in slowness. Rocks *do* move, but most humans think of rocks as static: rocks chip away with the wind, or from contact with moving water, but humans do not see rocks as moving on their own. This view is actually quite wrong. Rocks do move on their own. Crystals grow. Rocks shift positions. It just occurs in a different time reference point than human time. This is one thing you can learn from rocks. It is *important, very important* for humans to understand how to break all of their patterns. Patterns keep humans stuck. Slooooww down. Slooooww down enough to understand potentiality held with slowness while simultaneously speeding up the electrons of your vibration into a higher and higher spin. This creates light. This type of spinning movement can be experienced at the human heart center. It is a slowing down and a speeding up simultaneously, and it relates to both change and higher levels of communication. We wish humans to experience such openings of awareness.

Place your hands on rocks, listen to what they have to say, feel the heat and the cool. Listen to their stories, which you may not hear in words, but you may have a feeling of understanding. Rocks are a form of stardust. They are part of this planet, the crystalline grid coming up form the heart, the core of the liquid crystalline being you call Earth, and part stardust coming down from other realms. Not all rocks, but many, have been, shall we say, kissed by the stars. Most humans do not know how to respect, listen, walk lightly on rocks, and listen, listen, listen. Rocks sometimes withhold some of what they have to teach for they are disrespected. Yet their wisdom is freely given to those who are willing to slow themselves, be quiet, and listen. The same is true for crystals. Crystals primarily are focusers of energy. Rocks teach you to slow down and listen. Water teaches you to flow and to surrender. Water teaches through resonance.

Water's resonance has to do with understanding that you *are* water. It teaches that if you surrender with what is and flow with what is, you merge together with oneness. The duality of polar opposites ceases to exist when you become water. There is no more conflict or polar opposite arguments about who is right and who is wrong. As you resonate with each other through your one water, you communicate with each other in a different way that involves less separation. Rocks teach slowness and listening. Water is a Unity teacher. Both are great, great teachers of humanity.

Humans still do not understand the concept of Unity, oneness. You view your hands as separate parts of your whole physical body, and you view yourselves as separate from the earth. You and the earth are not separate. You are part of the earth. Earth is a water place. Humans are made of water; you come from the sea and from the stars. You use your power as humans to project your water *(thoughts)* telepathically outwards, and it affects the earth. Earth is on Her own spiritual development path, as is each human; yet you affect each other. The earth causes storms, not to only to purify, as some believe, but also to offer humans a chance to better understand cooperation, Connection, and Unity. Meteorologists study storm patterns but do not make the Connection that human thought forms contribute to the formation of storms. Humans do not yet understand the concept that their thought forms and mental agitation contribute to Earth's storms. Humans offer Earth a chance to enhance or diminish Her own spiritual development according to what humans project from their water into the earth's water telepathically through their thoughts.

Humans may see the earth as a dense, physical being or they may see Her as a place of sparkling, crystalline energy. Both realities exist. Reality is created through the power of water put out in thought forms. Those humans who are able to understand the physical, etheric, and universal Connection and reality of everything will see the earth in that form. Those humans who focus on their negative thoughts and physical separation will see the earth as a dense, separate physical being. These different levels of thought compete to create the reality that is shared by the collective consciousness of humanity.

Can you tell us about crop circles? Are crop circles intended to enhance our understanding or help us?

Humans believe that understanding comes through the mind from learning and from questioning. Crop circles are another form of education. When humans experience crop circles, they visually take into their bodies different patterns as if they were reading by Braille. In the presence of crop circles, humans take in patterns of learning and understanding that help to open their DNA. The crop circles help humans to address patterns that already exist within them. When humans visit crop circles in a meditative and open, respectful state, they may experience the true purpose of crop circles: aligning human patterns with the patterns given in the crop circles. It is one way we have been able to communicate with humans.

Several years ago when Rebecca and I were visiting the Yellowstone super volcano, I predicted from a vision that I experienced while there, that there would be huge eruption bringing major changes. It has not happened. Can you address that?

You were completely accurate in perceiving that possibility. While you were there you began to experience with your hands and with your body energetic change within the earth. Your vision was activated and you were given a sight of what is going to occur. There are either volcanic or earthquake fault lines in places that have been dismissed and overlooked by geophysicists who think the major focus is only in California. Only recently are they beginning to see the potentialities in these other places. Much will change. Flexibility and movement are necessary for survival, as you move towards being creatures of the universe and creatures who honor the of wave motion of the water you are rather than the particle stability you *think* you are. One of the most important things humans need now as the earth changes is to expand community and heart. Work together, for there may be challenging times as the earth moves towards Her own ascension. Those who are able to act in Love rather than fear may be able to manifest, to create a reality that is different, a place that is safe through unified thought forms. This is the reason humans need to gravitate towards places that are building community.

Please say more about how we affect the movement of the planet and how it affects us. What we can do for the benefit of all?

Movement is a necessary step in changes that are now happening and will continue to happen in order for human understanding to change. It is partially related to the magnetic grid shift and partially related to solar flares, the change of energy received from the Sun. The effect of the earth's magnetic shift is hard on the human system. You are being called into alignment with new magnetics. It causes many to feel a sense of destabilization. The earth is beginning changes internally that feel much like disruptions and energetic disharmony; sensitive humans such as the two of you experience this disharmony as you move towards higher levels of understanding Unity. Earth does the same thing. As everything is one and Unity is the goal, much of what you experience as humans parallels what the earth experiences. You and the earth are one on some level, and reflect the feelings of growth within each other. When humans are emotionally and mentally careless with their thought forms, emotional debris, and actions, the energy unsettles the earth. When the earth is distressed, moving towards change, it distresses humans. More than you realize, you and Earth are one. Humans magnetically, energetically align with place; you influence Earth, and Earth influences you. You may focus intent together to change the energy of the earth. Use the power of your water to soothe, calm, and Heal energetic disturbances within the earth. Earth has long provided sustenance and protection for all her creatures. It is appropriate that humans begin to understand how to energetically and vibrationally protect and sustain the planet and how to sustain life through proper thoughts. As goes one, so goes the other. When you are in pure etheric form and the earth is in pure etheric form, you may join together and re-integrate into the physical, for the physical comes from the etheric. We will expand more on the etheric-physical connection at another time. From the human perspective, we are teaching you about magic. From our perspective, it is simple reality. The most important thing for you to know and remember now is that Earth is part of you and you are part of Earth.

7

HUMAN MAKEUP

Can you speak to us about how we are being affected during these times of change? Some humans are experiencing sleep disruptions at this time. We have read that low levels of stress hormones in the blood are related to external hypersensitivity, which may cause internal sensitivity and disruption of sleep patterns. Could you please address that for us?

Most humans see the hormonal system only as a physical system and ignore the energetic components. The pituitary, the thalamus, and the thyroid are all linked, and their hormonal flows are regulated by energy. The energy of emotion affects the output of the hormones and chemicals that are needed for human physical function by each of these parts of the system. They are interconnected. Each of them needs to produce a specific output of particular things, yet stressful emotions and demanding work loads cause imbalances to occur. There are five elements within the human brain structure that are extremely sensitive to emotional energy. We refer to this system in humans as the Five Pack. The thyroid, which is regulated by the pituitary, would be the sixth; it is lower in the body. The heart, the lungs, and all organs and glands are also quite sensitive to the response of emotional energy. Everything in the body communicates with everything else.

We will define what we call the human Five Pack. The Five Pack is formed of the hypothalamus, the thalamus, the pons, the pituitary, and the pineal. The pons is in the center of the brain, the pituitary resides behind the third eye, and the pineal gland is between the two, more or less. The thalamus and the hypothalamus form the remaining part of the Five Pack. The thyroid interplays as a sixth part of in the system. Each is responsible for its own job in balancing and regulating the endocrine or hormonal substances, and they communicate with a flow back and forth to each other. Humans do not yet understand how energetic input from emotions affects flow or blockage of the communication pathway between these five in the brain. When these five are not communicating properly, it creates a stress response within the individual that is then picked up by the thyroid. The thyroid regulates the hormones within the body. So if these five within the brain are picking up cues of negative energy, lack of safety, or emotional instability, they create a hypervigilent response, setting up a constant internal stress. This constant stress overrides and overworks the Five Pack of the brain. In trying to avoid external stress or over stimulation, the individual actually creates hypersensitivity of the internal organs. The human system is designed to enable stress hormones to move through the blood and return to the normal communicative state when the stress is removed. In the current human situation of continual stress (both collective and individual) humans have developed an inner alarm system that is always on. Such a continual state of alarm stresses the human system to a point where the Five Pack becomes extremely unbalanced. Loss of sleep or disrupted sleep is one of the effects of an imbalanced Five Pack. Additionally, right now, humans have the opportunity to receive and integrate a tremendous amount of new and unusual energy and information that is out of the scope of your three-dimensional understanding. This influx of energy, designed to help you return to the remembrance of your divinity, is also partially responsible for disrupting your sleep. When you receive and integrate this information, your brains shift, and your bodies need to rest from the shock impact of what you receive; you need to rest. This is not illness; it is adjustment. We will speak more about this later.

So our sluggishness, our sleepiness, and our sense of not being completely "with it," is because of what is happening to us, our acceleration?

Correct. You will continue to have cycles of integration time where you are fuzzy and lethargic as your mental concepts are stretched and as your body adjusts to etheric changes. It is quite normal for humans who are developing. Yet the overload of toxicity that is carried in the human system from taking in harmful thoughts and foods and from stresses can also contribute to Five Pack imbalances if humans do not make conscious choices for improvement. Those humans who face their shadows, take in healthy foods and thoughts, purify toxicity, can support their physical bodies during these beneficial shifts.

Could you tell us how touch affects the brain?

Many humans were not appropriately nurtured as children and did not learn to soothe themselves as infants through being rocked (the rocking motion affects the pituitary and pineal) or through being touched (which stimulates self-regulation of the hormonal system.) When humans do not learn this as infants, Trust drops away more easily and hypervigilence takes over. Continued stress through life contributes to an imbalanced Five Pack. Humans at this time would do well to attempt to balance their Five Packs through meditation, through controlling their thoughts with intent, through seeking Love, and learning to Trust. Trust involves relying on human intuition. These things help to repair the Five Pack mechanism. The Five Pack of the brain is an interlocking system including all Connective portions of the brain that emanate outwardly in the physical body. Touch receptors lying along human skin act as electrical signals, sparking the portion of the brain to receive information or to offer information flow in both directions. The peripheral, energetic realm where we touch you, where you feel tingles, and where those you call energy workers affect you, affect the brain also. Most humans are not aware of this level of touch yet; they respond more to direct physical touch. You two and others who are sensitive about energy understand that touch is possible on or outside of the skin. Touch, both physical and energetic, is more important than humans recognize.

Thank you. Can you address the use of psychoactive plants and hallucinogens for spiritual development?

Many humans wish to gain understanding and do not know how to elevate their own vibration or remove the belief systems that block understanding on their own, so they seek outside help through ingesting substances instead. It is not appropriate to take drugs in order to be on the fast track without examining one's own shadow; many humans wish to attain the "high" of an altered state and experience the Illuminated state without equally embracing their own shadows. In fact, most do not wish to look at their shadows at all. Those who courageously delve deeply into their shadows over and over again while asking for help and Illumination can attain the same Illuminated state of altered consciousness without the use of drugs or plants. We note that many aboriginal and native peoples have used plants in a sacred way to access the spiritual realms. Yet those who do that have been more balanced in accepting the plants as their brothers, accepting and understanding oneness, rather than trying to *use* the plants to selfishly gain something for themselves. Most humans have tried to gain things without understanding the Connection of oneness. They want it for themselves because they want to stop the pain. They want to feel better, and they want instant answers.

Do you mean that if we do our own work by looking at our shadow and by utilizing energy and intent, we don't need to go that route?

It is rare for humans to be able to take a shortcut and truly receive the wisdom they receive from experiences of oneness while they are in this state. Most who take substances for insight go back to the substance again and again to repeat what they have experienced, rather than keeping the experience within them. If they do not do their shadow work, they cannot maintain the wisdom they access. If humans use energy, intent, and willingness to Love all of who they are and all of who everyone else is, if they use these things, they attain that heightened state of awareness, seeing the colors, seeing the vibration, and feeling Unity on their own. It is not necessary to use drugs. Yet most do not know how to do this. Understand that what we have shared with you about working with water and slowing down like rocks can help you achieve the same elevated vibration as taking the plants into yourself. You do it through your own intent and energy without expectation. Humans have lost understanding of their own power, so they go to doctors for Healing, priests for Connection to God, and use drugs to see Truth. This is mere human fallacy. Confronting your shadow and dropping belief systems that no longer apply brings you to the Illumined state of Unity. Taking drugs to find Unity is not necessary. Additionally, the effect of substances has a different effect on the human body now because your magnetics have changed, as the magnetics in your physical bodies, your etheric bodies, and the earth have shifted in the last twenty years. You now have a closer alignment to help you open more. Because of this, we suggest humans choose wisely what they put into their bodies now more than ever. For those who wish to take advantage of the opportunity at hand, they must choose carefully. Take in only nourishing substances, both in thought and in food. Take in substances that support the natural openings that are occurring as you do your own work. What you take in and what you put out are related and Connected. The inner and the outer are the same. There *are* no shortcuts.

What can you tell us about dancing? Is it about Connection?

First it is about movement, moving circularly, around and around. It moves humans out of linearity because the body leads the mind. The Sufis know about this in their divine

66

spinning. Moving in circles with flow and harmony is another step towards oneness. This *then* leads to Connection. This is why dancing has become important with humans in the mating ritual. It is the first approach to oneness together. It is a way of moving beyond the conceptions each gender has about the other and moving directly into flow. Try it sometime from this perspective. Even those who are afraid to participate in dance often enjoy watching the movement of Connection. Watching the movement brings them to the edges of Unity. They see something happen as the dancers move away from linearity and into the spirals of Connection with universal flow. It is appealing to their desire for Connection, no matter how remotely remembered. Those who are afraid of the body have more difficulty dancing, for the body with all its cycles, brings one closer to Unity and away from the linearity where the mind rules. The mind tries to maintain control by keeping everything in linear order- sequential steps of cause and effect. The body knows differently. The body is designed to keep you aware of cycles and circles. Look at all the body does. *Nothing* is linear. Everything is cyclical.

How do you perceive the human smile?

We see it as waves of energy patterns and colors emanating from your face. We perceive exactly the energy that you are experiencing. We believe humans respond at a molecular level to things that make them smile, things that give them promise, pleasure, and understanding. Smiling carries the vibration of joy.

Would you say that a smile on our face is a silent form of laughter, with the same energetic component? Does smiling raise our vibration?

Excellent understanding. Humans may change their dynamics through the energetic components of laughter. Laughter raises your vibrational being, as does smiling. Laughter can help correct physical and emotional imbalances; it can help correct all of the things that keep you in a fragile, complicated state. There is a reason that many spiritual teachers laugh. Laughter raises the vibration, and smiling raises your vibration.

So when we smile in joy, we are in joy.

Yes, and when we are having our conversations together, the joy you feel from communicating with us raises all of our vibrations. Laughter is *truly* for those on the spiritual path. Laughter comes from the heart; it is spontaneous. If you watch human children, you will see them laugh at a butterfly landing on a flower, or something funny the dog does. Children know how to spontaneously emit and share the joy vibration emanating from their hearts.

And that stops when children become socialized between the ages of five and six.

Your age estimation is too high. We will speak more about that later.

Laarkmaa, thank you for helping us smile, and thank you for helping us laugh. We appreciate the many gifts that you bring!

It is a great pleasure for us to share in the vibration that emanates from laughter, and we appreciate the ability to be in that vibration with you and share it. It is one thing to watch humans moving in and out of that vibration; it is quite another to share it with you. We broaden in *our* understanding through sharing with you, so we all benefit. We find the complexity of humans most interesting, for your brains and hearts both have so many thoughts. It is also why others in the universe (not Pleiadians) wish to study you. They are most interested in the energy of the emotional aspect, but also curious about the ways your thought patterns move through your world, for it is known in the universe that thoughts with emotion create reality for humans. So those who study humans are interested in how this works.

Humans are very limited in their understanding, and it sometimes seems that we are constricted in our abilities to move forward by a larger hierarchical system. Are Pleiadians also involved in a larger hierarchical system where you must follow rules?

Very good question. We wish to address first your understanding of human limitations. Yes, humans are, as you so rightly ascertained, limited in understanding and abilities. Yet the limitations come from fragmentation within the totality of who you are. The more you integrate all aspects of your being, both conscious and subconscious, the less limitations apply. You suffer from fragmentation of not only body and mind, but also past or parallel life remembrances; this separation has caused deep fragmentation of your total system. To move beyond human limitations, you must integrate body consciousness with both the conscious and the subconscious mind. It is fragmentation that causes feelings of limitation. As you more coherently integrate the fragments of the stories that you have carried through all of your many lives, cleaning up your shadow as you go, the *limits* of your understanding *decrease.* You have experienced lives both as male and female selves. Humans must work to integrate all of the feelings and belief systems held by each of those aspects of who you are. You have a High Self that guides you. As you clear out the shadows of incorrect belief systems that cause you pain, you open your own pathways towards divine understanding. Much of your human perception of limitations is guided by your inability to communicate with and integrate the varying aspects of yourself. It is the fragmentation that keeps you separated both within yourselves as individuals, from each other, and from us. Humanity is now ready to step back into wholeness, holiness, and oneness with the divinity that moves within you and beyond you and is Connected to Source so that you may complete the contract you made to be here at this time in service to Earth and the evolution of humanity. We are here to help. The limitations you perceive are in effect because you suffer from living in three-dimensional consciousness. As humans break away from belief systems that have kept them prisoners within what they *thought* was reality and move towards the concepts of cooperation and Connection, limitations of all sorts disappear. We are here to help you to awaken to re-remember what you have always known. The power is within your water. The abilities to move from place to place and to communicate without words are all held within your water. As you meld your physical and etheric bodies more and more, you move towards experiencing possibilities of limitlessness in your own world. It can be disorienting, yet profound. Humans experience more disorientation and forgetfulness because they begin to let go of their attachment to time.

Yes, we do have a higher source that we use as guidance. Yet we do not see it as controlling or limiting or preventing us from doing what we choose in the way that humans do.

We perceive it as alignment with flow and being Connected to Source, understanding the appropriateness of "'everything is as it should be." When we explained to you that you see us as six, but we see ourselves as one, we were telling you about Unity. When there is only one, no one is controlling. The Mayan understanding, which we gave them, of "I am another yourself" is a way of understanding that there are no limits, for everything is one. If you look at everything and everyone as yourself, how could you possibly be controlled? You simply are manifesting a different expression in the moment for whatever story is helping you to re-awaken and remember who you truly are. You are part of Source; you are divine. When you act on that divinity using your own power, recognizing that emotions are merely tools for cleaning out old belief systems and patterns that keep you constrained, then you see that everything is as it should be; all is one, and you are *not* being controlled. Everything has a purpose and a place, and you have choices. This is a very challenging concept for humans because they have a sense of how it should be, and yet they cannot quite do it, so it becomes frustrating. We are here to help you break through these concepts. Humans have not yet mastered the ability to use their own water and their own power to discard their belief systems and move outside of time. You allow time to control you. Time interferes with your ability to be who you are as your future selves; it is an imprisoning limitation. And now, time begins to fall away as you approach 2012. The future humans will exist in the world very differently without the effects of time.

So humans feel controlled, but actually we are only controlled by our own beliefs and the constraints

of third dimensional time. We are only controlled by not being in the flow and not realizing who we are as we develop going towards Unity and Source.

Yes! Yes! You have it exactly. The only portion you omitted is the emotional packaging around all of your experiences from parallel/past lives and present lives. Those emotions carry energy charges that keep you attached to patterns that no longer serve you.

This is a question I've wanted to ask you for a long time. Are humans the most fragile creatures in the universe?

Ah, interesting question. Humans are the most *complex* energies in the universe. Most other energies are more simple and straightforward. As you know from participating in the materiality of your world, the more complex something is, the more likely it is to break and the more difficult to maintain and stay in balance. Because humans are fragmented by having moved away from light and divinity over the course of time, allowing their power to be taken by others, forgetting their own divinity, and separating themselves through the division of subconscious and conscious memories, and mental-physical separation, it is more difficult to maintain balance and agreement for all your parts to work in harmony. This separation actually makes humans more fragile than they need to be. Additionally, consensual beliefs about death and the linear progression of aging contribute to human fragility, for humans *expect* to begin to deteriorate once they are, "over the hill," to use one of your phrases. Humans look around and observe everyone they know aging and passing through the process of death. Because their subconscious selves know that they have experienced death many times, humans attach to the belief that this is the only reality. What they are doing through this process is setting their own intent for physical decline, leading to ultimate death of the physical body. We wish for humans to understand the power of intent and to begin practicing it, using it as we expose you to other possibilities, other realities. As long as humans focus their mental thoughts and enhance those thoughts through emotions, those thought patterns will build and build to manifest what it is on which they focus. It is a practice of intent. For example, if a person sees all of the females in her genetic line die from breast cancer and she focuses on this, she instills fear within herself and a dread that this is her future, thereby magnifying the genetic potentiality. Or if a person sees all of the men in his genetic line have had heart attacks, he expects one to end his life as well, therefore intending manifestation of his own death. Human fragility is a very complex concept because humans are complex in themselves. Yet the principles which we are teaching you, which align with your own divinity, serve to integrate varying aspects of yourselves so that you may re-remember the simplicity of who you are. Once integration and divine Connection are attained on a regular basis, many of the complications drop away, and humans become not only less fragile, but more simple and truly powerful.

So in other words, in very simplistic words, whatever we focus on we bring to ourselves.

The only portion that needs to be added is that you are affected by consensual reality, and there is a battle when you are trying to disengage from that reality. Consensual reality has its force. The more you strengthen your own intent and focus on correct thoughts with positive emotions, the easier it is not to be pulled into consensual reality; in fact, you begin to *change* consensual reality by the power of your own thoughts and intent. The more humans practice this, the more the consensual reality will change.

Would you please speak more about waves and particles in human makeup?

Humans perceive themselves as static or fixed in their third dimensional reality. This viewpoint relates to being a particle, a solid form that moves in solid patterns. Yet as humans engage in movement and emotional changes, including positive thoughts, they are more like waves. It is through being like waves, through wave motion, that you are able to better perceive and participate with other realities from the other side of the veil. Wave motion also relates to what humans consider impossible or fantasy, such things as reaching through walls (for in wave motion you and the wall become the same) or shape shifting. We wish to keep this topic uppermost in your consciousness and in your awareness to help humans better understand the water nature of their being. Humans have the concept of "thought waves" (notice the word *waves),* but they do not make the connection that those waves are experienced through shared water. Humans also do not understand that their emotions are the fuel that power their thought waves and direct the creation of their reality. We are encouraging humans to move more and more away from particle rigidity (both in thought and physical form) and move more towards being waves as a form or way of being. Particles are unchanging, although they can move about. The third dimensional physicality is the basest of forms, the most dense. Waveform is closer to the etheric world where we live, where humans came from and are once again going, and by moving your understanding about who you are from particle to wave, you help move your physical body closer to becoming a wave body. You may use elements of Nature to help you understand your own bodies as waves. Watch the movement of water or stare into a fire. You will see waves there. Such exercises promote your ability to see us, to see another version of yourselves, and to have a greater understanding of the true reality. The more you can see waves of movement and light, the more likely you are to perceive us and get glimpses of your future selves. It is the wave motion that will help in the ascension process of taking your physical body with you, which is the desired way of transition at this time. We will discuss more about ascension later.

Humans may better understand and move towards wave motion by noticing all movement: breath, physical movement, and movement patterns with which you are not accustomed. Anything that is out of your patterned normal response helps humans move away from being particles and move more towards being waves. Approach the ocean and other forms of water as being part of water, rather than entering into it. This understanding helps humans prepare for the shape shifting which allows them to move between kingdoms, to move between veils, to move beyond time and space and dimensionality. You two are already beginning to manifest those abilities in small ways. Anything that you can do in your consciousness to promote movement as flow and difference, whether it is in your thought patterns or in creative movement assists in this process. Humans may practice thinking in different ways, walking in different ways, putting their bodies in different postures and positions, anything that breaks down habitual, structured patterns that their understanding of the body has carried from lifetime to lifetime. We *wish* you to focus on wave motion, rather than having your eyes scan for things remaining in a fixed place. Look for waves everywhere. Don't focus on looking for solid objects. Solid is only a condensed form of many waves. Humans have been taught from childhood, "Oh, look at the dog. Oh look at the cat." No one ever taught you, "Look at the running. Look at the sitting. Look at the eating." Human teachers and parents have taught a reality based on nouns, not verbs. In order to facilitate seeing us, raising your physical and etheric to meet for the ascension process, we wish you to think more in terms of verbs. Flow. Movement. Change. Instead of thinking "there is the table or there is the dog," think, "We are sitting. The deer are walking." Movement is of utmost importance in changing humans from particle status to wave status.

Emotions also cause structure, and the more you are engaging in elevated joy, Love, and Trust vibrations, the more you are aligning with the flow of movement. The flow takes you from separation towards oneness, which is where your physical and etheric will join, and where you may join with us on the other side of the veil for true communication. We will continue to bring this up again and again from different angles until it becomes a natural part of who you are.

Last night Rebecca was given two amazing understandings. The first came as a direct experience of being able to see everything completely and **clearly with her eyes closed in the dark.** *The message that came with that experience was: "Look Beyond." The second understanding came as a vision where she* *was shown to penetrate more deeply than what her biological senses normally allow: to listen more deeply and reach past normal touch to find other awareness. The message of the vision was: "Penetrate your 3-D reality. Go Beyond." Both messages seemed to let us know that we as humans must let go of what we feel and what we think by using more than our normal senses to determine what is real. We must go beyond our human thoughts and our human feelings in order to arrive at the place where* Love *is all that exists. We must refuse to be stuck any longer. We need to* move, and the time is now. *How wonderful it would be to stop seeing altogether in the limited way humans have been taught to see! It's very interesting to think about looking beyond, looking with heart rather than with the eyes, and simply being aware of waves of energy.*

You are becoming more aware of what is possible. Humans move towards wave rather than particle, but you still exist in particle in your three dimensional reality of time constructs. It is up to each individual to determine how much she moves towards waves or how much he may experience the sensation of waves. The two of you are well on your way to seeing differently and being able to experience what we describe. Other humans may practice as you do and do the same. But please do not forget that humans are functioning in the duality of the third dimension at this time, and as long as duality exists it is more challenging for most humans not to attach to polar beliefs about what is real. As humans approach understandings of Unity rather than the duality to which they are accustomed, it makes them a bit unstable, and they must adjust. It is still necessary to honor what exists in your human form in the third dimension while working towards the future humans you are becoming. We would not wish for any human to become completely destabilized by moving too quickly towards the energies and understandings that we address. Focusing on seeing energy, movement, and color rather than static form is an exercise to help you. But by way of analogy, we dip your toes in the water; we do not wish you to fall in headfirst. You will at some point have moments or longer periods of time of being completely immersed in the waveform of being, for it is what you are moving towards in joining your physical and your etheric bodies. All of this is coming. In surrendering your beliefs about reality, humans are capable of moving more quickly than they ever thought towards a different reality. Remember please that you are here in human form on purpose. To completely move towards wave motion at once would simply move you from your side of the veil to ours on a permanent basis. That is going to happen, yet it is not time. You would not be able to sustain that level of vibration on a permanent basis yet. We are merely expressing our complete joy and excitement that you are resonating with and understanding these concepts and moving towards them.

We humans have been told for a long, long time, "you're not ready yet." Many of us have been very anxious to speed up this process because we know that there is a better way. Knowing that you are here to help us to make this switch is very reassuring. We can be more willing to slow down in the process and be more patient.

We are pleased to speak about the development of humanity. In addition to the understanding of moving from particle to wave, you must be aware of the elements that support the evolution of humanity at this time in concurrence with Earth's evolution. The light from the sun infuses you with wisdom and helps you to obtain higher and higher states of vibration. Humans need sunshine. Rocks teach you the value of slowness. Water helps you understand yourselves as waves, teaching you to accept your own fluidity and to manage your own water. All of these elements support your approach to becoming wave forms. From a physical standpoint, as the earth goes through changes, human needs for physical food and water may be challenged in coming times. Being near water will assist in growing food to nourish your physical body. Using the water of your being to form community will support you because like-minded humans will be able to weave intent together to elevate and direct the creation of a better reality. There is more water power in joint intent. Sunshine, water, community: these three are the most important for you, yet rocks and trees help ground you into being where you are; they support you, Love you, teach you, and nurture you as you do what you do. All five elements are important, and all five elements support your moving into the flow of Unity. Do not focus only on the thoughts and intentions in the mind; remember the wisdom that is held in the heart. The heart naturally leads you towards Unity.

We have often said that native intelligence is much greater than book-learned intelligence, and that seems connected to your statement about heart wisdom. We don't know where the term "native

***intelligence" comes from, but we think it means the
same thing that you have just explained.***

The term came from those very old elders who recognized
listening to Nature, their own inner nature and external Nature
(which are connected,) was the wisest way to live. Native
intelligence is listening directly to the nature of this world *and*
listening to the rhythms that exist in the universe, looking for
natural flow and Unity, rather than building artificial separation
through thought. Recognizing the wisdom of cycles can help
you to better understand the importance of Nature and Her
rhythms. Listening to Nature's rhythms is indeed a step towards
remembering that you are divine beings. Follow them with the
wisdom of your heart. The most important thing to remember
is that you are waves. Waves are the rhythms of life.

8

EMOTIONS

You have counseled us to focus on energy rather than **time,** *and to watch our thoughts. You have also told us that emotion powers thought to create reality. Can you tell us more about the cycles of emotion that we experience as humans? How can we best handle the surges of emotion that arise unexpectedly for us?*

Ahh. You are asking us to answer what we are interested in about you. It is how you deal with emotions that other beings are most interested in studying. We know and understand the different levels of vibration affiliated with varying emotions. We know how to teach you to guide your thoughts away from negative emotions when you are in a downward vibratory spiral; you must focus your thoughts on more positive things until you re-stabilize and balance yourselves. We are most interested in what makes the negative emotions arise when things seem to be floating along, as you would say, most smoothly. To the best of our understanding, this surprise of emotion occurs from parallel/past life triggers where shadows need to be cleaned out. In the shadows of your subconscious lurk old belief systems and incorrect thoughts that must be corrected now in the present life. Because they are in the subconscious, you are often surprised when you suddenly find yourself being overly emotional "for no reason," when your emotions seem far larger than the issue at hand. The emotions serve as a sign pointing the way to the belief system that needs to be cleaned out and corrected, usually something you have been attached to not only in this life, but also many others. The emotions occur and take you off guard because in this life you are unaware of existing patterns, or because an old pattern from another lifetime is rising to the surface now to be addressed. Those things that are minor in your outward understanding are points of entry to address the larger emotional issue from your parallel or past realities. You do not expect them because you do not perceive all of your parallel/past lifetimes simultaneously. When humans focus their thoughts more positively as they are experiencing a negative vibration, they empower and energize themselves so that they may move into higher vibratory states.

Why do emotional upsets keep happening when we think we have learned and moved beyond them?

It will happen again and again because this is humanity's *opportunity* to clean out lifetimes of old wounds and the old beliefs that keep you in a state of separation. All life is spontaneous when you are in flow. When you experience disruptive emotions, you have moved out of flow. The emotions serve as a pointer to change directions to move back into flow. Every time you move through an intense emotion and understand that the *belief* attached is *not* true, you move closer to your future self. Emotional purging will continue until you reach full understanding of your divinity. It helps if humans can stop being angry about what they don't have and be thankful for what they *do* have. Gratitude supports movement towards flowing with Unity.

Shadow work exists within each human and within the collective consciousness of humanity. On occasion humans must release an energetic block as they remove and work through an emotion that has been stuck. The release may be explosive, volatile, and uncomfortable. The blocked energy escapes with the release of the block. This is appropriate. What is not appropriate is to release this energy *towards* another human being or animal. Releases of this type need to be accomplished privately or with the support of another human who is trained to accommodate and redirect the energetic release of emotion.

We have our own understanding of shadow. Please define for us how you view the shadow.

We define shadow as dark or unresolved issues within you. We mean the dark aspects of yourself that you are either afraid to look at or that you choose to work with when you are not distracted or frightened by them. We use "shadow" to refer to those aspects of yourselves that you have forgotten about that affect your behavior. Your shadow represents aspects of yourselves that reflect poor choices from habitual patterns or cause emotional reactions or "triggers." They are the places that need cleaning out from all of the present and past/parallel lives that you may not remember within your consciousness but that bring up emotional triggers and make you react in certain ways that upsets you and others. Most humans are either unaware of these shadow affects on their behaviors or they are too frightened of them to want to address them. Your fears and reactions come from unresolved situations that have occurred in this lifetime or from the many lives that you have lived besides this lifetime. You may not remember the patterns that cause you to be fearful and to react, but the emotions you experience point you towards what needs to be addressed within your shadow. There are fragments within you that must be addressed and resolved for Unity. Without dealing with your shadow you will remain fragmented and unable to integrate all of the parts of yourself that need to be aligned in order to be whole. You must begin to make friends with your shadow and look at all the triggers and fears that live in your subconscious. *This* is shadow work. Shadow is an important part of who you are. You should get to know it, dance with it, and hold it very, very closely until you learn to work with it as part of you. Shine your light of Love into all the dark corners, and the shadow eventually evaporates because you merge with it and integrate it into the wholeness of who you are. As you do this all of your essence becomes more filled with light, and you Connect more to your own divinity. Advanced humans know that if they want to evolve, they must investigate all of the parts within themselves, conscious and subconscious, to better understand and integrate everything that exists within them.

Most humans are too afraid to look at their shadows; if anything makes them uncomfortable they run from it. They keep the recognition of their shadows at bay by keeping themselves too busy to address what needs attention or through addictive behaviors that occupy and numb them, thereby preventing themselves from delving into or recognizing that there exists within them aspects that need to be consciously approached and dealt with. Humans keep themselves so busy with duties, constant thoughts, errands, and continual social activities that they avoid recognizing the need to examine themselves. All addictive behaviors are utilized to obscure or cover up the things that need to be brought to light. We will list some examples of things we see that addictively distract humans from the true work of evolution, although the list of these behaviors is extremely lengthy, for humans will go to any extreme to avoid the uncomfortable parts of their humanity rather than making the necessary changes. Examples are:

- Leaving your radios and televisions on all the time to prevent the quiet because in the quiet your thoughts make you too uncomfortable or lonely;
- The social need for *constant* interaction with others, including continued cell phone calls, one immediately following another, without the balance of quiet introspection;
- Taking addictive substances that "calm you down" (alcohol) or "speed you up" (caffeine);
- Turning towards "comfort foods" rather than listening to what your emotions are trying to tell you;
- Over eating; sex addiction; Internet addiction; use of nicotine, stimulants, and recreational drugs;
- Basically *any* disquieting activity that distracts you when done with regularity can be considered an addiction that prevents you from doing your *real* work.

If you want to evolve into the new reality, you must make a different choice. You must *choose* to pay attention to the uncomfortable issues that live in your shadow. The first step in doing that is to become quiet, allowing time for contemplation. Allow quiet time to notice what is occurring within you. Without the use of quiet where you may listen more deeply into yourselves, it is difficult to reach the places where you need to work, and it is difficult to recognize the patterns that keep you in destructive cycles. So first step away from your normal activities, become quiet, and begin to notice what needs attention. Notice when you begin to feel the very edges of an emotional field that are not calm, joyful, and peaceful, for peace, joy, and Love, are not emotions. Emotions are a human construct. Peace, joy, and Love are universal; they are states of being, not emotions. Emotions are your signposts that something that needs to change. So notice when you begin to become emotional, and then notice the thoughts you are thinking. Are you *blaming* yourself for making a mistake or *blaming* someone else for hurting you or doing something "wrong?" Stop your judgments. Clear your emotions by breathing through them and start thinking more Loving thoughts. When you turn your thoughts from blaming to Loving, you are correcting a pattern that exists within your shadow. The next time an emotion related to that pattern arises, it will probably come from a completely different direction and you will receive a different understanding. The continual arising of emotions trigger awareness that your shadow needs Loving work in those places. The bigger the reaction, the more the opportunity to work through it. As you begin these practices of noticing your emotions, looking at them, noticing what you are thinking, and then beginning to think differently, you will determine for yourself what the patterns are that you need to clear. This is how we suggest you work with your shadow.

Each individual has his own shadow work to do because each individual has an accumulation of trauma carried forth in the emotional body and in the body consciousness that was specific for the lifetimes lived by the individual. When humans share shadow work by agreement, as they move through a shadow episode, each person benefits. Each must take responsibility for understanding what the shadow reveals to her without understanding what the shadow episode may mean to the other. Each shadow experience gives each person an opportunity. Sometimes when humans are sharing shadow work, one person has a release, and during the release the other may simply learn the lesson of, "Do not be affected by what is not yours." Deflect the energy and sit with Love and compassion for each of you. The lesson here is learning how *not* to react, for *reactions invite even more reactions*, which continue to separate and divide you from the understanding of Unity. When emotions are in charge, humans may not like the change that is created. To keep from reacting, humans must monitor what they think and say. Do not attach a negative thought to the emotional energy that is arising, for if you do, each individual adds new and repeated triggers that further aggravate an already negative communication between you, keeping the cycle of separation going. Through a joint commitment to do shadow work, humans may rid themselves of their own habitual thought patterns and emotions revolving around shared experiences as well as doing your personal work around individual shadow.

Just as your house gathers dust and dirt and needs to be cleaned on a regular basis, so you must continually do the work of cleaning your own shadow in order to create a better environment. Humans must learn to live through their emotions without attaching negative thought forms to them in order to keep from getting struck in the entrenched patterns and old beliefs that need to fade away. As you move closer and closer to this oneness, and as you understand the dynamics of form and emotional packaging, you are able to sit with each other in Love and compassion, allowing emotions to surface and to serve their purpose without becoming entangled with them, thus clearing out all of the things you carry from parallel/past lives. It is the dustpan version of sweeping up what still remains. When you have things arise that feel like, "Oh, no, here we go again," just recognize that the emotion serves the purpose of clearing out, cleaning out something unresolved, and it may not necessarily come from this lifetime.

Humans do not need to expend so much effort in trying to make sense out of so much garbage. They simply need to allow it to arise, Love each other, support each other, and if you can, laugh through the hardship saying," Here it is again. Just like we have to clean house, we have to clean this. Getting dirty is part of living." It is what humans have come to do in this lifetime: collect the aggregate of all your experiences, link them together, and disband the beliefs, the thought forms, the traumas, the incorrect patterns that you have carried forth from one life to another unresolved.

Thoughts, energy, and emotions create form. When you combine these three in a particular way, you send a signal of what you wish to create. If your thoughts and emotions are positive, you begin the creation of a positive reality. If they are negative, they are usually connected to something you remember about being afraid or unhappy at another time. The remembrance is a sort of bleed through that occurs from something that existed in your past. In a way you are stepping from one time into another, outside the present moment. Your deepened emotions allow you to step more deeply into a former reality that was quite real for you at another time, and so it *feels* like it is real now. The emotion and the thoughts make it real, and you carry the pattern of an unhappy reality into the present. So why not remember how you felt at a more positive time and focus your creations on *that* energy? Humans would benefit from learning how to do this.

We notice that the majority of humans tend to move in two directions of negative thought while experiencing emotion. The first direction is an outward projection of the emotion in the form of *judgment and blame of others*. It manifests in thoughts such as, "It's not my fault; he (or she) hurt me; or the other person is wrong." This typical reaction is prevalent in all those who refuse to look at their own shadows or do their own work. They blame other people and other circumstances, refusing to see the opportunity before them to change their *own* patterns of reaction. They judge and blame anyone rather than taking responsibility themselves for their own opportunity to create something better through new thoughts. While this choice of behavior is unfortunate, and it does nothing to further one's spiritual growth, it is far, far worse to take the second approach.

The second approach is absorbing the emotion in the form of *self-judgment and self blame*. Self-judgment is not the same as taking responsibility. Self-judgment comes from living *too* closely to one's own shadow, to the point where the human begins to feel that all they are is shadow. The reason this is worse for humanity is because while blame comes from fear, (specifically the fear of looking at one's shadow,) self-judgment comes from a lack of Love, and the inability to feel self Love creates more fear and so perpetuates cycles of separation. Humans must Love themselves *first* before they can Love others, so when one does not Love himself, it stops the flow of light into the world. Love and light are very closely related. A complete immersion into shadow obliterates an individual's light. If a human cannot Love himself, he cannot generate Love into the environment, and everyone suffers.

When humans move into positions of self-blame, self-judgment, and lack of self Love, they cross the wiring within their networks; they forget how to think of anything reasonable. When this happens, their discernments become harsh judgments, and the emotions they attach to their distorted judgments blind them from seeing that *they* are responsible for exaggerating the size of the incident. At that point, their emotional projections actually create more harm than the original situation to which they are then reacting.

What about taking full responsibility for bad behavior by retreating? It seems a natural reaction for a conscious person to wish to change the energy of what they have created by retreating.

The potential problem is that often in the retreat, the person continues to focus on self-judgmental thoughts, energizing them with the emotion of grief. Thoughts such as, "I'll never do that again," which are too harsh and do not allow room for gradual improvement, create a cycle of not being able to move forward, for the person adds to their sense of failure when he makes the same or a similar mistake another time until he learns to change the old pattern. Humans need help. You are not yet in a position of being able to do everything with self-responsibility only until you break all the patterns that do not work and drop all of the belief systems that constrain and confuse you. You are not separate entities. You are linked with all, and help is always available.

I believe many people who are striving to become more aware, try to right imbalanced situations by themselves. They know they made a mistake. We do understand that we cannot do everything alone; yes we need help; yes we need Grace. But there is also the pull from inside that tells us to retreat until we have calmed down, until we have the where-with-all, the strength, and the wisdom to repair what we have done.

Thank you for your explanation. Retreating to calm down and gather wisdom is beneficial. We note, however, the pattern of many humans who withdraw to indulge in continued remorse and self-judgment for entire situations rather than only taking responsibility for making changes within themselves. They falsely *believe* that if they do *all* the work, everything will be fine. We notice a prevalent pattern of self-responsibility that is tilted too far out of balance in those who have taken care of everyone else all their lives. You call them "caretakers" or "caregivers." Many of those who focus on caring for others often do not properly care for themselves. Those humans who have been overly responsible for everyone else while ignoring their own needs are already out of balance on the responsibility scale, for most of those have never learned how to Love and care for themselves. They often tend to judge themselves harshly when they feel they have done something incorrectly, moving out of balance into self-blame with habitual thoughts of insistence on fixing the situation all by themselves. Humans must learn to balance between taking responsibility to change their thoughts and actions and releasing responsibility that is not theirs. Withdrawing until you calm your emotions and assess proper responsibility is positive. However, humans must learn in the withdrawal to change the directions of their thoughts, and asking for help supports that change. Many human spiritual masters have taught throughout the ages the concept of balance. The New Age movement has done great harm to the idea of balance, for New Agers often focus only on moving towards the light. They focus on just seeing the light without seeing the shadow. They repeat positive affirmations without claiming what exists in the shadow that needs to be changed. We find this approach to be as highly imbalanced as taking too *much* responsibility. Ask for help in determining self-responsibility and properly directing your thoughts for change.

We must learn the difference between care-taking others and not taking care of ourselves, taking on too much responsibility and enabling others through enmeshment.

That is a major leap in understanding. The test for humans is to stop the downward emotional spiral when it occurs and to instead turn towards self-Love, rather than self-blame. Humans are meant to generate their own Love in order to Connect the divinity from their own water and send it outward to aid each other, in a webbing network of light. Most, at this time, are unable to do this because they are so far removed from any sense of balance. Most suffer from misguided emotional attachment to erroneous beliefs. Yet for those of you who are what you term "light workers," this is your job, to spread the light, and when you find someone's light has been snuffed out from lack of self-love, you may send your own Love into their shadow with compassion.

The two of you, as human ambassadors of our work, must experience these changes yourselves in order to learn how to overcome patterned reactions so that you may teach others. *Emotions can be used as tools for change or they can be deadly.* You are beginning to understand that, yet it is human choice to grasp the grenade of emotion in your arms and hold it as it blows you to bits or to fling it from you and turn your face towards the light. When you fling the emotions away after having examined their message and turn towards lighter thoughts, you will notice moments of waves where you feel a lightness bringing peace. In those moments, we are holding our hands out to you as you reach back to us on levels of which you are not always consciously aware. We are watching humans break patterns that must be broken one way or another for you to step more fully into what is real.

We were reading an author who says that he is surprised and cannot quite understand why he has been chosen to have the teachers and the helpers that give him so much insight. I often wonder about that myself, as you are helping us. Humans seem so dull and so habitually contracted that sometimes it's hard for us to understand why we have energies and Love like you in our lives. Not that we don't deserve it, but that we don't seem evolved or mature enough for you to bother with.

We have a laugh. Humans are often dull and habitually contracted?! What's new? Yet within all humans there is a brilliant light, a great knowing, and a huge Connection with divinity. You might say we are helping you mine for the gems within yourselves. With your work and our help, you are scraping off all the incorrect beliefs and assumptions as you would scrape off a rock to find a polished gem inside. It is the same process. In advanced humans such as the two of you and many others, there is less to scrape off to get to the gem. It is simplistic and not *quite* accurate to use the example of mining for gems, for you are always in charge of your own choices; yet we thought the analogy might be a good teaching one. Is it acceptable?

It is. However, do you ever think, "Oh my. We thought this was the right mine to delve into, but maybe these gems are too encrusted or they are too deep?"

We stretch our hand out vibrationally and stroke the very gem within you. We know what is there. We make no mistakes. Humans always have choice. While we know what is there and what is possible, you may continue to choose otherwise. The only thing that can get in the way of the certainty is *you*. The two of you are not built for failure. Understand that.

Thank you for knowing and Trusting what you see in us.

We ask you to remember that we Love and enjoy and benefit from our time with you, no matter what you place in front of us. We watch your moods, your emotions, your thoughts with Love, as we experience your energetic vibration. While we encourage humans to acknowledge and experience their emotions and to learn what they have to tell you about the direction of change, we do *not* encourage you to attach to your emotions, particularly the negative ones as humans are so accustomed to doing. Humans attach to what is familiar rather than letting go of old patterns in favor of more workable, new patterns that may seem unfamiliar or even strange. When you are in the process of creating your own reality, as humans are every second of every day with every thought and emotion you put into the world, you are more able to create the reality you wish to exist if you do not attach to negative emotions and you flow through and accept what is occurring in the moment. It is simple in reality, yet complex to try to explain. Basically, humans must let go of the familiar sense of fear of what they do not know or understand and learn to Trust that everything is perfect exactly as it is. Direct your emotional state from fear towards Trust. Direct your mental state through such thoughts as "what do I wish to create? How am I creating in this moment through my thoughts and emotions? What reality do I wish to create for the highest good for all?" Use the power of your water, your focused intent. Know that your emotions feed the direction of your intent. It is for this reason that we teach, "Do not be afraid; accept with Trust and Love that what is happening is correct and that something beneficial will come out of the discomfort you feel *if* you do your part." Remember that you are co-creators, and you are constantly making changes through your thoughts and emotions. Humans must always do their own part for other possibilities to become available. If you take your own personal responsibility by doing your part with your thoughts and emotions, you will be helped. It's teamwork, returning towards the Unity of Source. The universe presents a situation, and you help to change it.

Emotions have a real impact. Humans must learn that they are employing emotional fuel to where they place their intent with their thoughts, creating reality. You are co-creating through the collective consciousness with other humans and with the universe. It is best to acknowledge your emotions, recognizing that their purpose is to point the way and provide fuel for change, then clear the emotion, turning your thoughts in a positive direction, and moving into pure Love, which is not an emotion. Pure Love is light and is not part of the emotional spectrum. As humans move closer to Unity with greater understanding of the purpose of emotions, you become more able to sit with each other in Love and compassion, allowing the emotions to surface and to serve their purpose of propelling you towards positive change. Remember, how you experience and use emotions is each human's personal responsibility. It is your choice. The choice is yours.

Are there techniques you can teach us to help us not spiral down emotionally?

When humans are engaged in full-blown emotional experience, they are usually asking for three things:

1- To receive unconditional Love;

2- Acknowledgment that they matter; and

3- Reassurance that they are "OK"

Change those requests a bit. Ask for these three things:

1- To *be* unconditional Love;

2- To make a difference in the world; and

3- To Connect through Unity.

We will give further suggestions that each human may adapt to their own needs.

- Do an inner survey when you start to feel your mood deteriorate, as soon as you notice you are moving vibrationally away from the peace of your True self.
- Remember that emotions serve the purpose of clearing out, cleaning out something unresolved.
- Call on spiritual assistance, asking for help.
- Infuse yourself with the Golden light of Grace to help you move beyond the patterns of your karma.
- Experience the emotion, knowing that it will soon pass, and do not attach to any mental thought forms that arise or give too much meaning to what you are feeling;
- Remember that thought and emotion feed each other.
- Say to yourself, "This energy no longer belongs to me."
- Refuse to place yourself in old patterns of "victim-hood" by thinking you have been wronged or are misunderstood.
- Be thankful for everything that works in your life.

We trust this will be helpful. Just remember, emotions are pointers to redirect you towards flowing in the right direction.

9

TIME'S ILLUSION

Could you please explain what happened the night Rebecca awakened at 4:25, then 5:00, then 3:11, and then 4:25 again, and 5:00 again? How was it possible to experience several times over and over again in the same night, or did she simply misread the clock?

Rebecca experienced the disintegration of time. She has had many occasions of, shall we say, dancing with time. She has been aware of suspending time when she writes or when she travels alone, superseding human limits of time and arriving more quickly than "time" would allow. There is a reason she is interested in time, and a reason she dislikes references to the past. The past makes her feel restricted and detracts from the now that she knows is all that is real. Through her memories of past/parallel lives, she understands more clearly than most humans that past and present exist side by side, and when others continually refer to the past, she feels infringed upon, as if something or someone from the dimension of the past are taking her away from what is present in the *now*. Rebecca is pained by the past. Not because she doesn't want to hear the stories, but because she feels those energies take away from the energy of what she can experience in the *now*. Not many humans understand the dynamics of past infringing upon present. Rebecca knows that reality is not built upon the past but is created in *every present moment*. We continue to work with her, taking her out of time as often as she wants to go. This movement back and forth between dimensions is what occurred last night. She did not misread the clock.

To understand the limits humans experience because of the illusion of time, you must work on your linear perceptions. You must understand that cause and effect are not bound by human understanding; universal laws have more bearing on the true reality. Reality is created by energy, not time. Time is an illusion that exists only in three-dimensional human reality, and as such, it holds humans captive under the false belief that future and past exist. Only the present moment truly exists. Consensual human made-up reality has created the idea that occurrences have a life before they occur and after they occur. You call this the past and the future. Actually, everything happens simultaneously. Since humans are trained to think linearly, they believe that everything progresses from one direction to another (from the past to the present to the future). This is not Truth. You experience many things simultaneously, and yet you compartmentalize them within your awareness in order to make sense of them. What humans refer to as past lives are really parallel lives. You may actually go back "in time" to recreate what happened in an "earlier" or parallel time and change the event for a more positive and productive outcome. You can do this for any uncomfortable "past" life experience to clean up your karma and forever change the dynamics of what has happened to you in past/parallel lives, thereby changing your present. When you begin to understand that the past and future do not exist, you can begin to create your present more fully without relying on what you call "history." History is just a story. It is not real. You may enter the story at any time and change the outcome. Do you understand?

Yes, we are beginning to have more clarity about this concept. How can we expand our understanding of stepping away from linear thinking?

We would like humans to be comfortable with bending time a little bit. That's what meditation is. It is a dispensing of time in order for humans to connect to their future selves (which already exist.) The reason you feel refreshed and calm after meditation is because you are in contact with your future self, and you bring some of the peace and Trust back into the present time-space with you. Cullen, you once stated that you don't know where you go when you meditate, but you "go somewhere," in the process of leaving your self behind. You do in fact leave your personality behind and you meet your divine future self, which is total and complete. You may do this with anything or any situation because everything exists simultaneously. You may Heal yourselves through understanding that you may revisit an occurrence from the past and correct it in the present, for they exist simultaneously. We will say more about this later, but for now understand that moments where humans step outside of time reflect a cellular memory of living without restriction. *Time* is the restriction. There is cellular memory within humanity of what it is to live without time, and that memory is being awakened now.

How does time affect the accumulation of what we call shadows that we must work through?

Humans experience many things through your parallel lives in male and female bodies. Your current bodies also have a consciousness of what exists in parallel lives. Many humans today believe that the personality is only what is conscious and that the body arrives at birth and dies at death. Dust to dust, and there is no more body. Yet you have stories contained within your subconscious from the past/parallel lives that you lead, and there is a body consciousness that goes with you through all of your lifetimes. The body consciousness accumulates experiences just as the male and female selves of past/parallel lives accumulate experiences. Humans are very ignorant about their bodies and the consciousness that lives within their cells. They only see the physical biology and not the eternal energy that is present. When humans awaken to the consciousness held within each cell and recognize that each cell carries a universal consciousness that exists beyond death and beyond time, they will awaken great memories within their DNA. The body consciousness and the male and female personalities that exist in parallel/past lives are just as vibrant, alive, and conscious, as what you are aware of in the present. They all exist simultaneously. The illusion of time has confused humans about the Truth of reality.

The male and female personalities who live in parallel realities carry remembrances of specific stored emotions. This is the story line, so to speak. You carry emotional packages of all the stories that the male and female selves experience in all of the parallel life times you live. The body consciousness carries the pain held from those stored emotions. The shadow is the accumulation of the emotional patterns created through living all those stories. The reason shadow work is so important now is because this is your opportunity to merge all of your lives and clear out all of your incorrect beliefs and the patterns that keep you from understanding your own divinity and power. As humans work to release the emotions stored in their shadows, the incorrect belief systems that are carried from thought form in parallel lives rise to the surface in the present for emotional cleansing and re-integration. You have the opportunity to bring what you believe is *past* into the *present* for integration. Sometimes you are not even aware of what causes the emotion that is being released in shadow work, yet as you consciously clear it and redirect your thoughts, you Heal things in all lifetimes simultaneously. Old injuries, physical and emotional, do not have to last. Communication with the human body is the first step. We will speak more about this when we discuss Healing.

We are here to help humans to expand their consciousness beyond current understandings of time. We have told you time is a human construct. Now we tell you, humans actually create time through their thoughts and beliefs, which are co-created and supported through consensual reality. Humans must learn to honor what they feel through their First Sense and to stay focused on the present moment. Time's limitations form a type of compressive energy, blocking your flow. We understand that in consensual reality you must schedule appointments; it is impossible to avert that completely right now, yet as humans collectively develop your First Sense and move towards Unity, your need for operating within an artificial construct called time will diminish, and you will rely on your First Sense for what needs to occur, always staying in the present moment.

Time is a disconnect that occurs when humans move away from their physical sensations and the rhythms of nature and begin to make meaning of life through the thoughts they think and emotions they express. It is at this juncture that humans participate in the creation of time. Human infants arrive with only their biological rhythms and no understanding of the time constraints they are entering. Small children live in the present moment; their emotions are closely bonded to their physical sensations, with very little thought. As conscious awareness becomes attached to mental thoughts, they begin to move away from living in the present moment. As they accumulate meanings from what they sense and what they learn through acculturation, they break away from living in the present moment. A disconnect occurs at this point. Meanings begin to accumulate, and separation occurs that pushes them towards living in the consensual reality of duality, which is full of polar opposites that carry meaning. As the children are guided by their caretakers to attach to the meanings of polar extremes, time is born for them, for past and future are simply polar opposites of duality. When small ones begin to accumulate meanings, they form a historical framework of their experiences, such as, "If I cry, I'll get hugged," and rather than acting from sensations in the present moment, they begin to *think* about what they *are going to* do. Have you ever watched a child fall down and look around for someone to see them *before* they cry from the pain of falling down? They move away from responding to their environment in the present towards creating the future through their thoughts and emotional responses. This is how humans begin to create their reality. Parental and other caregiver responses shape and mold this process even more as caregivers impose their own meanings accumulated from *their* experiences, and the young ones accept those meanings as "Truth." So children begin the process of separation from Unity by moving into the consensual illusion of time and creating their futures through their emotions and thoughts.

If children were not socialized or acculturated at approximately the ages of four, five, or six, would they never enter separation and duality?

It is an interesting question. Your age estimate is too old. The process begins as soon as human infants and children begin to attach meaning to their physical and emotional sensations. They begin to express the conflict between what they feel and what they are told when they begin to say, "No." It is at this point that they learn that what they are told is Truth does not necessarily resonate with their experience of Truth. At around the two-year mark, they experience a separation. They are entering duality. Because parents operate in linear time of past, present, future and they wish to bring their children into a shared conceptual reality, they build upon past behaviors in training their children. As children grow into their environment, they begin to form their own loops by disregarding what they know from their First Sense and attaching to the meanings they are being taught. They move into the loop of time, thinking about past learning and future actions, separating themselves from their understanding of only the present moment and Unity. This moving into separation is the beginning of their experience of time and duality. Humans begin to move away from knowing they are part of Source when they create the illusion of time.

What happens to humans when official time changes occur (the twice a year Day Light Savings time)? Even when we are not watching the clock and don't realize a "time change" has occurred, we both feel disoriented.

Humans experience biological shifts when they are forced to sleep and awaken in a different rhythm. These artificial time shifts cause disorientation as your alignment with the planet becomes even more unbalanced than normal, further separating you from Nature, so that you become even more out of touch with your own inner rhythms and wisdom. When humans are out of alignment with the planet and their own biological systems, (their electrical-magnetic relationship to life), they are more easily controlled, for humans become needy when they feel off balance. Governmental powers understand this and seek to control you through continually manipulating your consensual time so that you remain off balance. We dislike your government's artificial manipulation of your accustomed consensual time and agree that it does disorient humans. What the two of you feel in disorientation without understanding why is directly related to your core self-awareness of being separated from Nature. As the consensual reality of other humans suddenly snaps into another formation with an "official time change," you feel the shift. Because you are within the energetic parameters of this shift and because the two of you are sensitive, you feel a greater disorientation.

The more humans align with Nature, surrendering to and flowing with natural rhythms (none of which are functions of time), the more you are aware of the disorientation that happens during official time changes. Move through the disorientation with understanding of what it is. That way, when you teach and help others you can share principles of what occurs to those who are open to hearing it, and you can help to reset their internal balance with your Healing abilities. It is another function of your work, and in order for you to learn to do it well so that you may assist others, it is necessary for you to feel what they feel subconsciously. Then you may help raise their awareness and empower them to correct the imbalances within themselves. You benefit yourselves and others by your diligence and willingness to honor and respect what *is*.

As the illusion of the consensual reality defined by time falls away, humans begin to feel pressured that there is not enough "time" to complete their many three dimensional tasks; they do not understand the ramifications of breaking free from those three dimensional constraints that will occur when time ceases to exist. Without time, humans will feel much freedom. But right now, as they feel the pressures of time's collapse, they feel insecure and frightened, for their frame of reference is falling away. As many humans have traded security for freedom, they look for more ways to feel secure rather than dealing with their rising fears. Many sink into false comforts. Many seek outside assistance from medicine or religion rather than dealing with their own imbalances. They comfort themselves by drinking more coffee, drinking more alcohol, taking more drugs, having more sex, eating more bad food, watching more TV, or distracting themselves with the computer. These "temporary comforts" become addictive behaviors that prevent them from doing the work of examining their own shadows and facing their own fears. It is only through facing human fear that one may understand, take responsibility for, and correct the imbalances that are present. Without addressing the subconscious imbalances, more fears and conflicts rise to the surface. As most of humanity seeks security and comfort, the powers that try to control humanity have the opportunity to make decisions or implement changes that a conscious, fearless human living in Love would never allow.

Did the invention of the clock by the monk in the thirteenth century enhance the human sense of time?

It put structure around it. The clock and the invention of the Gregorian calendar put structure around what was already in place by giving it a container and a way to watch the approach of the future. The structure of the clock provided a way for enforcing an artificial sense of rhythm, called time, taking humans further away from Nature's rhythms. Many years ago one of humanity's religious persons discovered that humans could be controlled by separating them from Nature. Focusing on artificial time separates humans from the natural environment, making them less comfortable, more fearful, and easier to control. The Gregorian calendar created an artificial rhythm, separating humans even more from their natural rhythms in harmony with the earth. Religious leaders encouraged humans to design their lives collectively around calendar time, and the imbalance that occurred by separating from Nature's rhythms instilled more fears. With rising fears, humans began to rely more upon sources outside of themselves to direct them, to control them, and to keep them safe. One of the most significant effects of this religious control through artificial time was the disempowerment of the females of your planet, who are natural rhythm keepers. Through the wisdom of their bodies, women had shown humans how to keep good rhythm in harmony with the earth. The rhythm was based on flow within the present moment. When this natural rhythm was replaced by the Church with an artificial calendar, humans moved further into separation of past, present, and future, stopping the natural flow of harmony and oneness on your planet; that artificial separation projected humans further into *believing* in a future and a past, while ignoring the present moment. Humans began to see movement from an artificial past to an artificial future as progress. There is no such thing as progress, for there is no past and there is no future. There is only greater understanding of Truth, and that can be obtained only in the present moment. Humans who mark off the days of the past and look towards the days of future on their calendars help to further enhance the illusion of time through their thoughts. It does not help, humans. When you focus on an illusionary time, you also experience more fear. You fear that you won't get things done; you fear that you will be late; you fear that someone will not Love you because you did not get things done or are late. All of these fears separate you from Love and Unity. Is it any wonder that humans are so challenged in obtaining peace?

Sai Babba often manifests wristwatches for his devotees. I believe he manifests wrist watches to show people that time is an illusion. Is this correct?

That is precisely correct. He also manifests precious gems for humans to clutch in the form of rings, teaching them the powers of manifestation. The true gem that he manifests is understanding of the power contained within the water of each human being; that power can manifest for the highest good for all when humans channel their water individually or collectively for community purpose. Humans have the choice of taking his teachings and beginning to manifest in their own lives or remaining stuck in their patterns of belief that only he can do this. Many humans clutch at a Messiah or a guru because they do not understand they have the same divine power within themselves. They do not understand the divinity they contain within their own human water, nor the powers possible within that water to create a different reality on their own. Sai Babba serves the planet and the universe through his teaching examples of manifestation and through the presence of his Love.

How do Nature's seasonal changes, and sun and moon changes relate to time?

They are *natural* rhythms. Time is an artificial movement away from natural rhythms through thoughts that create a "past" or a "future." When humans began to attach meaning to artificial rather than natural rhythms, they move away from Nature. Nature does not plan; Nature occurs in the present moment. Watch the deer around you or any other animal in Nature. Deer don't plan to get out of the rain when they see clouds form. They simply graze, and when the rain comes they either move or stay in the rain. When you focus on Nature's rhythms, you are moving towards Unity. It is important to do this now, for the illusion of time is ending.

10

DIVINITY

Humans have held a basic misconception about divinity for a very long time. We wish to correct this misconception, which is based on the false belief that divinity exists *outside* of you. Divinity exists *within* you, for all *humans are divine and all life is divine.* From our perspective divinity is quite simple. Divinity is your Connection to Source. Divinity is recognizing Truth and Trusting Love. Divinity is understanding your Connection and not judging yourselves or others, remembering the concept of "I am another yourself." All of this is divinity because all of this comes from an enlightened, Illuminated perspective. While we will answer your questions, we do not need to speak at length about divinity because the very simple Truth is that you are all divine.

Humans, it seems, for the past several thousand years, have needed to believe that there's a divine being or intelligence greater than themselves in the universe. Does the need for this belief have to do with

our partial forgetfulness that we came from Love and that we are a part of Source?

Yes, your forgetfulness, which is attached to your fear, causes you to believe in the illusion that you are separate from Source. Fear is the great divider. A human need for safety arises out of your fears and feelings of separation. Fearful humans feel powerless and out of control, so they look for someone or something outside of themselves that has the power to make them feel safe and Loved. Through this need, humans have created the illusion that you are separate from the divine omnipresent Love of universal Source. You have forgotten that you may create your own safety through the divine power of Love that lives within you, for there is a constant open channel between human divinity and the divinity of Source. Unfortunately, when humans believe in a divinity *outside* of them, they begin to believe that that intelligence has the power to help them or to hurt them. Your history is full of stories where humans have attempted to appease a wrathful god through human or animal sacrifice or the sacrifice of your own self-worth. So you have built an incorrect assumption on top of your incorrect beliefs about divinity. Your current understanding of sacrificing your own self worth and ability to Connect to Source is not divine. Love, or Source, does not require sacrifice of the divine understanding of who you are or the sacrifice of life to keep you safe. The only sacrifice requested by Source is the sacrifice of your cherished incorrect beliefs and the habitual behaviors that keep you from seeing who you are as part of the divine whole.

Human children come into the world knowing that they are divine and divinely connected to Source. They are coaxed and trained away from what they *know* into what they learn to *believe* as they join society and the consensual reality of the world you have created. We are asking humans to find their way back to what they knew as Truth before they were convinced otherwise. Wake up and know who you are, for you are standing in the doorway of understanding the Truth that humans are divine. Humans have lost the understanding that *divinity is right here, right now inside each of you.* We remind you again, each of you is Connected to and part of Source, for divinity runs both ways, from Source to you and from you to Source. Prevailing attitudes of fear have caused true understanding of Love and Unity to be misconstrued by many of your religions. Many good humans who long for divine Connection have been misguided and taught by their religions to ignore their own divinity while searching for or accepting divinity outside of themselves. Sadly, religions have confused humans about the Truth of divinity. While there are many good hearted people in organized religions who wish to help humans Connect with God or Source, they cannot make that Connection for others, for every human must remember the Connection to Source within himself. It is each individual's responsibility to Connect with the divine on her own in whatever manner is directed by your own heart. Humans who give over their divine power to a church, a mosque, a temple, a priest, or any person representing a hierarchical system that claims a higher Connection to Source, are giving up the right to their own direct Connection to divinity. Many of your religions instruct you that you cannot reach Source without intercession by one who is trained to directly Connect with God. While organized religions help many humans feel a sense of community, hierarchal structures actually prevent humans from understanding that they are each and every one divine. Humans need to know that they *always* have a direct Connection to divinity *because* they *are* divine.

Another misunderstanding about divinity occurs as religions encourage humans to have faith, for faith is not the same as Trust. Faith is based on belief rather than on knowing. Trust is based on knowing, and knowing comes from Connection to the divinity that lives in each human heart. Faith comes from hoping that something outside of you will take care of your lives. Trust comes from *knowing that you are divine* and together with Source, you can co-create your own safety. Most humans rely upon sources outside of themselves to keep them safe (including guns, fences, and their concepts of a separate God) rather than recognizing the divine power within them to connect to and co-create with Source. All humans need for a sense of safety is to Trust in your own divinity. Humans ultimately have the power to change any situation through Connecting to others and intending a different outcome. You are co-creators with Source. Focusing on cooperation rather than separation is divine. Yet human fear has turned cooperation into competition. Even religions compete for ownership of Truth, forcing their "beliefs" upon others as "the only truth," when Truth is constant and is always available for all. Often religions judge those who do not share their beliefs, even when their religious teachers have instructed them to "judge not or you will be judged." Judgment causes further separation and promotes more fear. Forcing one's beliefs on others is the cause of so many wars and the senseless loss of millions of human lives. Divinity is not something to fight over. We know humans think divinity is complex, but it is actually quite simple. Your divinity exists as a flow that comes both from within you and from Source; the light moves back and forth as you Connect. You see, you are part of Source; therefore you must understand that Source cannot be hierarchically more divine than your own physical form, for you are filled with the light of divinity.

Many humans are more connected to the Truth of their own divinity than the ones who make the rules that define who or what is divine. And many of those who make the rules of religion seek to control and disempower humans by separating them through the use of fear from their own divine power. They build into the collective consciousness that the world is a scary place and that humans can only be saved from pain and challenge through belief in a "higher" intelligence. Actually your pain and challenges are *gifts* to help you remember that you are divine so that you may reclaim your own divine power for the co-creation of your own reality. It is up to each human to re-remember and re-connect to his own inner divinity rather than looking *outside* for God.

Human stories from past/parallel and even current realities hold examples of divine beings such as Jesus, Buddha, and Sai Babba. We say that all humans, if they do the work to move beyond the fear of their own shadows, may act just as divinely as these examples. It is not good for humans to focus on hierarchal linear thinking where there is only God at the top and they are at the bottom. *Any* human who understands and lives what we are teaching about divinity can perform the same miracles that Christ did or what Sai Babba does, for they are not miracles at all. They are elevated understandings for advanced humans and eventually all humans. Christ was vibrationally advanced and divinely inspired. When humans remove their fears, they may use their own divine inspiration to achieve the same higher vibration achieved by those such as Christ, Buddha, and Sai Babba. All humans can attain this *because* you are divine. You must remember this and take back your divine power rather than giving it away to those you incorrectly *believe* are more divinely connected than you. You simply need to reunite with your shadow and remember your own divinity. Each of you is divine perfection waiting to be remembered.

What can you tell us about the true trinity Christ tried to teach that has been interpreted as the Christian understanding of father, son, and holy ghost?

The man called Christ used the trinity as a teaching tool to show the principle of individuality within Unity. He taught about three of one and one of three, as we teach that Laarkmaa is one of six and six of one. This teaching shows that there is individuality within Unity. Everything is Connected. For clarity of human understanding, we would define the trinity as the Present Moment, Trust, and Love. Another way to say it is the Absence of Time, Knowing, and Unity. The eternal now, or the present moment, is the absence of the illusion of time. Trust is knowing that you are divine and divinely connected to Source. Love is the absence of fear and separation, which is the same as Unity. *This* understanding of trinity supports human evolution much more than the current Christian idea of father, son, and holy ghost, which supports the belief that divinity is *outside* of humans. Modern Christians have become confused about what Christ taught. *Humans are divine* and have the potential to express the light of Christ *within* them. It is a large statement. We wish you to take it in and respond.

How are humans to understand the teaching tool of trinity so that they can correct their misunderstandings and false beliefs?

By moving out of hierarchal, linear consciousness of separation and fear towards understanding that everything is Connected to Unity through Trust and Love. One of three and three of one shows the Connection of each individual in Unity. Everything in the eternal now, no matter how individual and specific it may seem, is Connected. Trust in what you know is Truth, and stop judging each other's differences. It is now possible for the first time in human development for humans to move into a deeper understanding of these concepts, and we ask the two of you to help *teach that divinity exists within each human being.* All are part of Unity and Love *right now* in the Present moment. Humans may use discernment to help you to see individual differences, but remember that the differences are what give you a more complete picture of the whole of reality. Unity. Discern differences all you want, but do not judge. Help each other move into Trust in order to disband inappropriate beliefs that hold you captive. Judging others and insisting that you have the only version of Truth is Connected to the human need to be right, which comes from fear that you could be wrong. Humans should never accept another's insistence upon Truth, for each human must find divine Truth within herself. Nor is it correct to force your Truth on another. Each human must discover Truth on his own. Never Trust anyone or anything outside of yourself to tell you who you are. Trust the divinity within your own heart.

Because humans experience so much fear, they confuse judging with discernment. The true understanding Christ taught of, "Judge not or you will be judged" is that you judge yourselves when you judge another, for you are connected in Unity. It is time for humans to understand that Unity cannot exist at the same time as judgment and separation; Love, acceptance, and cooperation lead to Unity. Humans are Connected to each other and to the earth. When one of you is hurt or frightened, others feel it, and it spreads through the earth, water to water. You feel it through the collective consciousness. This is why it is so important for humans to maintain focus on your thoughts and emotions, for what each human creates through her thoughts affects all. When you raise your awareness of your own divinity, you raise the vibration peripherally of others, whether they consciously recognize it or not. Raised vibrations of Love and Trust, where each human feels accepted and Loved cause the fear-based need for competition and separation to drop away. All begin to feel safe through your divine Connection. When humans Connect to their own divinity, their own Source, and their knowledge that they are part of Source and co-creators with Source, you are united with the one; you are God. So understand that as one, you cannot judge each other. When one of you judges, others feel the separation of judgment. Judgment comes from fear, causing separation; separation is a disconnection from Source, from Unity, from Love. When humans engage in judging behavior, they forget their own divinity and the divinity of others. We taught the Maya to understand this by saying, "I am another yourself," which means, "I am divine, and I recognize the divinity within you." Fear and separation from divinity and from each other cause humans to judge one another, forgetting the concept of "I am another yourself." In their need to be right, humans often cannot see the divine light of another human standing right in front of them. Unfortunately many humans would rather be "right" than to be in harmony with others. The belief in a need to be right causes a continuation of separation and distrust between humans, which simply feeds the illusion that you are not the same. Humans desperately need to stop judging each other and recognize that Truth resides within each individual heart as a Connection to divinity. It is each individual's responsibility to Connect to her own divinity and know Truth.

So there is a difference between judging and discernment. Judging separates us. Simply noticing that there are differences without judging them is discernment. Discernment is a simple acknowledgment, and it is perfect that we see and do things differently. We are the same, but we are all also slightly different. Discernment need go no further than the thought of, "Oh, I see the difference." Discerning that there is a difference but going no further stops the thought form that could lead to judgment and teaches us that we may learn from the differences we discern.

Yes. That is well understood. It is the judgment that separates, for judgment is aligned with polarity and attached to emotion; it is aligned with a need to be right and a need to force others to see things as you do, which comes from fear. Discernment can help you to see Unity by showing you that each divine part makes the whole. Remember your divinity and create a flow of

Connection between you. Stay in the present moment and know each other as divine.

We must stay in the present. In the present. In the present.

Yes. For in the present, you are divine. Experience the divinity of Love and Trust in the present moment, for that reality is Truth. Wake up and know who you are, for Truth is the understanding that *all* humans are divine. This is the simple Truth of divinity.

GUIDES, ANGELS, AND OTHER HELPERS

Are you, Laarkmaa, what we have considered to be our guides?

We are always available with help, but we are not what you call your guides. Human guides come from many sources and a variety of energies. Each person's High Self is the most prominent and important guide, for your High Self is actually a part of you. The High Self brings in other guides from a myriad of energies. Sometimes Pleiadian energy offers guidance; sometimes Arcturian and other of our star brothers and sisters come as guides; some of your own human ancestors come to you through dreams with symbols to assist. For some humans, their High Selves brings in energy of animals to which you relate as animal helpers to guide you as well. Animal helpers are a collaboration between your High Selves and the energy of the particular species that volunteers to help. Often when humans have animal helpers in spirit form they will notice the same animals in physical reality. For instance, if you dream of bears, you may see living bears, which is indicative of the

Connection. Animals' spirits are solicited by your High Selves to help you. Many guides work with humans while they are asleep, suggesting ideas, questions, and insights to direct you on your path and help you to better see Truth.

Human bodies also have a consciousness that can be considered as guides. *Most* humans disregard, ignore, and abuse their bodies rather than listening to the guidance their bodies can offer. It is your job to listen to the consciousness of your own body and nurture it through listening to its needs and requests. Connecting to your body's guidance can be as important as listening to other guides. Stop your old patterns of dismissing the bodies as something lower than your minds. Humans have dismissed their bodies in inappropriate and incorrect ways. Raising the vibration of your bodies through true health supports raising your total vibration. Make or renew acquaintance with the consciousness of your own individual body, for it has intelligence and can help you. All guides are here to help you. Those humans who are becoming more and more open, such as the two of you, may experience an increase in guides as more beings in other realms become more interested in your progress. They will align themselves more closely with you as you raise your vibrations. Your High Selves, however, are constantly present and are your most important guides.

Can you define High Selves?

Human High Selves are angelic beings of universal consciousness who stay with humans through each of their parallel lives. They know all the stories. They are the ones who are able to combine the stories into an emotional package and instruct you, "It is time to deal with this now," and hold you lovingly while you do. They also are the ones to put the mental constructs in place to let you know what is connected from life to life. They present humans with the catalysts for change, and they guide your growth towards your divinity. We sometimes are involved in placing things in your head through your High Selves, but your High Selves are in charge of your spiritual destiny and well being. Your High Selves are the ones who bring the instructions for placing dreams, raising emotions, and whatever else acts as a catalyst for change and growth. We all work together. It is teamwork. Your High Selves are extremely gratified when humans ask who they are and notice that they are helping. Humans may fulfill their deep desire to meet their individual High Self angels through your intent to communicate with deep and lasting, profound Connection. All you need to do is ask every day and then listen. Your High Selves are also the ones who from time to time put bumps in your road, placing impediments in front of you to help you to remember prior experiences from past/parallel lives that are keeping you stuck. They help you effectively work to eliminate old habits and patterns, such as poor health, difficult relationships, or anything else that continues to get in your way, preventing you from evolving. Your High Selves orchestrate all of the activities that you need to move beyond unresolved issues; they organize the steps you need to free yourselves from your old beliefs and patterns.

Sometimes guides who have been assisting your High Selves move away as their services are no longer what you need, making room for other more appropriate guides at the request of your High Selves. You cannot simply say, "OK, I'm ready for a guide change," like changing the oil in your car. That is a bit simplistic. Changes in guides occur only when your High Self angels ask guides who have been working with you to step aside and allow more appropriate energies to work with you as your own vibration accelerates. Your High Selves design this. It is such human linear perception to think that if you request other guides you will get further along the path of enlightenment. Each human's primary guide is and remains your High Self. Does this answer your question?

Yes, that was a most wonderful explanation. And we want to tell you that we are not interested in exchanging you, nor giving you up, nor asking for someone else who might suit us more closely. We would never do that. We are so happy with you. We don't ever wish for you to go away.

Thank you. We are aware that the two of you hold us in your heart and with Love and respect. We feel it energetically. We have no intention of leaving your side.

Thank you.

We represent your family, your brothers and sisters from the Pleiades, and we have a certain perspective that we are able to communicate with you that resonates with your spiritual growth and our shared project of helping to elevate humanity's vibration. So we have purpose in our communications. We can assist you with all the things that really matter ultimately for humanity's journey to universal Truth and the new reality.

We know you influence our thoughts and perceptions when we feel guided at times; we are sometimes unable to determine whether our thoughts are coming from us or from you or if they are a joint effort between us.

That is the magic of water allowing our six to be one with you, sharing hearts and sharing thoughts. That is the magic of transferring messages through water. You have much Love around you from all those who wish you to succeed with what we teach: Pleiadians, Arcturians, Sirians, those from Orion, the Lemurians, a whole host of angelic beings that come and go, and of course, your own special High Self angels. All wish to assist the birth of the new humanity. It is as though humans have a cheering squad, helping you, wishing for you to succeed, watching you, guarding you, prompting you in certain directions, and respecting, of course, that you always have a choice. You have many, many around you who wish to see your success in learning to focus the power of your water through your intent in order to perform what most of humanity would consider to be magic and we understand to be divine possibility. As you become aware of, utilize, and enforce your own power, the power of your water, you develop the ability to prevent any harmful energy from touching you. We help keep you protected and safe, but you must always do your own part to keep yourselves safe. When other energies approach, humans may protect and empower themselves by stating from a place of knowing, "If you do not come from Love you are not welcome." Nothing that is not part of Love can exist in the presence of Love. So Love whatever comes your way.

Humans will need to work with that to lessen their sense of fright or discomfort with new or unusual energies.

The only thing humans need to remember is that you are powerful beings who contain the light of Love within you; if you focus your intent saying, "We shine our light outwards:

leave if you are not from Love," beings who do not come in Love cannot stay. Negative energies feed on fear. When humans are frightened, they draw closer. If you are fearless and sending out your power, there is nothing for them to gain and they leave. It is a simple battle between fear and Love. Negative energies cannot stand the vibration of Love; they will leave. Your choice is always to send Love.

So we can simply send out Love while saying that we surround ourselves with Love and light.

Yes, or you might try simply saying, "Oh, poor thing. You don't have any Love. You need Love. We'll Love you.'" They will run very fast from that! You saw a sign that says, "Love Heals." That sign tells you what to do when you feel negative energies coming towards you, whether they are human or not. Negative energy can come from disturbed humans as well as from interdimensional beings, you know. In either case, Love Heals.

We watch and help as humans begin to reclaim their own power. We are pleased when humans begin to understand what is possible and what you can do through joining your intent with the intent of others to circumvent or override circumstances present in consensual reality. Joining the power of your water with others who understand focused intent *does* change reality. It is very necessary now for those of you who are doing this find each other and join together in order to focus the light you are offering in order to create new realities and move beyond the old paradigms structured in your shared collective consciousness. The longing you feel for finding others like you is born out of the necessity that approaches. You *need* to find these others; the tasks at hand are large. The difficulties of surmounting consensual reality and the belief systems contained in that reality will be more easily mastered in the presence of several or many than in the presence of one or two, no matter how strong, positive, and joy filled the one or two may be. We are not saying that one does not make a difference; we are saying a greater difference is made by several or many. You noticed today the delay in our turning on your radio?

Yes.

We move away from the necessary signal of the radio, as you expand your awareness of our presence. We wished to test a little bit the abilities you are developing to notice our arrival without the traditional birthday gift announcement of the radio signal. You did well today; you are developing your telepathic abilities, your intuitive, telepathic, water communication. This will help you communicate with other like-minded beings in the future. Please share with us how you know that we are here.

We feel your presence by deep yawning. When we yawn deeply and we are not sleepy nor in need of extra oxygen, we know that there is another presence near us. Our signal that you are here is in the energy shift that causes us to yawn.

We take that to mean your life force Connects with our life force; very interesting. We would like both of you to understand on your own when we are present. You are moving in the direction of flow, attention, awareness, and communication without structure. We wish you to share these abilities with other humans. You may help others to listen for the presence of interdimensional friends as well. Awareness involves listening from the cells of your body for energetic movement changes. We know this sounds nebulous, but it is simply a matter of paying attention differently. Rather than focusing your attention on expectations of a radio signal, you focus your attention on listening for the presence of our energy. We, Laarkmaa, are sharing a joint purpose with the two of you for spontaneous conversation, which is a rather novel concept compared to other human-Pleiadian contacts. Each time humans make an aware Connection with the presence of energy they resonate more deeply, allowing more possibility for communication. Any time humans feel a Loving presence, they may express through thoughts or words, "Tell me what we need to know." That intention opens up communication from our side. You have both been aware of and experiencing increased activity of those who wish to enhance your development. There are other Pleiadians besides Laarkmaa. There are Arcturian and other light energies around you. You might say you are surrounded by Love from the many who promote and encourage your better choices and who fill you with Love.

Do know Monitor, Kryon, Abraham, Michael, and other channeled entities?

Yes, we know them and they know us. We are all colleagues. Many Pleiadians are part of the Spiritual Hierarchy and participate in giving guidance to humans through that system; there are many who wish to help humanity evolve. The Mary energy also comes through sometimes, bringing messages to humanity to wake up. The Mary energy is one of the strongest and most Loving energies present at this time. Use it to help you find what you have lost: your connection to the power of your own divinity.

How many humans do you work with at this time?

We work with most of humanity but not directly as we do with the two of you. Some have glimpses through dreams; most are completely unaware of anything we do; we work with the collective consciousness of humanity, trying to place light into that consciousness for guidance. We, Laarkmaa, work *directly* only with the two of you at this time. You are our team members who share the common goal of birthing the new humanity with Love. Additionally, you and Rebecca are part of a group that intends to bring about interdimensional communication. It is a small percentage of humans, and unfortunately, many humans who work with interdimensional beings allow their belief systems to interfere with pure communication of Truth. Attempts may start off quite well, but they often do not hold the integrity to keep the communication clean and clear. Humans begin to feel the importance of their role and importance of what they think they understand, and the communication deteriorates. Your alignment with Truth prevents that. The amount of Truth that comes through interdimensional communications depends upon how much each human has released attachment to his own beliefs. Because of the amount of shadow work you two have done together, releasing personal agendas and beliefs, we have reason to know ego will not interfere with our communications with you, nor will you choose to interject your own ideas and belief systems. The energies of the magnetic shift of the Earth and the influx of light from the universe at this special time allow greater communication for those who have done their work and set their intention for divine growth. It is the responsibility of all humans listening or reading such communications to listen with their First Sense and their hearts to see if what is communicated is Truth. As human sensitivity and awareness increases, your perceptions increase, and opportunities for intermingling with many, many interdimensional beings also increase.

Are all humans incapable of reaching higher understandings on their own?

Yes.

No human can do it without outside help?

Humans can reach higher understandings through *inside* help, by listening to the guidance of their High Selves. Helpers such as us may also nudge them, but higher understandings do not come on their own without Connection to guidance. There is a crucial point here: humans must consciously ask for this outside help. As humans begin to integrate the fractured parts of themselves that exist in their subconscious and Connect more to their own divinity, they will be able to better understand things correctly. You will begin to understand through resonating with energetic vibrations rather than seeking your understanding through your thinking only.

We are thankful for your help.

You are most indeed welcome. Humans may always ask their High Selves if there is more that can be disclosed either awake or in sleep to help with understanding, and we and others who are here to help you will join your High Selves in guiding you.

I'm amazed at how quickly help comes when asked for.

It has always been available. Most humans either prefer to figure things out by themselves or they forget, and so they simply don't ask.

I think some humans have a misunderstanding that if we ask too much, we feel that we may be bothering those who are capable of helping us.

Yes, it is a misunderstanding. Those who wish to help twiddle their thumbs waiting to be asked. Humans must figure out the edge between non-responsibility and over responsibility. Many humans prefer to seek answers on their own because they feel a responsibility to do it themselves. Yet the majority of the population refuses self-responsibility for anything. The more humans seek a balance between proper responsibility and asking for help, the quicker your growth will come about. Humans must do their own part, but without help, you have great difficulty in putting aside erroneous beliefs and false ideas in order to open to Trust, Love, and Truth. Ask for help to be able to see clearly, to Trust what you are shown, and to be able to understand so that you may act from Love rather than from fear. Each time you ask for help, your request is answered in ways that help in the evolution of your understanding.

Many of us have asked and pleaded for help. Sometimes we have felt that we were neither heard nor helped. I suppose we were not capable of proper listening or following the advice we were given.

Largely that is true. Also you need to realize that more help is available now because of the evolution of the planet and the evolution of humans. More help is available to provide assistance to those who ask. You have many guides, many protectors, many who are interested in your well being and in assisting you to develop the senses that will allow you to perceive them and recognize their help. While it is true that help often does not come in the form humans expect or appreciate and many humans do not listen well to what is said, it is also true there are more beings volunteering to help at this special time. The veil has changed dramatically since a group of humans elected to come together with intent to change the world for the better. You call that time the first Harmonic Convergence (1987.) This event allowed those who asked to gain greater access to information and helpers than any other time in the evolution of humanity. It also changed the collective consciousness, making help more readily available to all who now ask. So ask, humans, we are all waiting to assist you!

12

THE DEVIC KINGDOM

Does Pan exist? Is he like you, an interdimensional being? Will we meet him ever?

Pan is an interdimensional energy, a very large presence affiliated with this planet. Pan is a governing body of the devic kingdom and an energy of life for those dwellers in the plant and animal kingdoms. Yes, there is great likelihood that you will encounter Pan, although the structure you expect may not be what you perceive. In parallel/past realities, the energy of Pan represented itself in a certain form to those who could see or engage with Pan's energy, much in the same way the Christ consciousness was manifest in a single human being. The Christ consciousness is manifesting now in many people. Likewise, Pan's energy may be seen in many places other than one being you encounter. That does not rule out the possibility that you may meet someone from Pan's kingdom in the form of a single being. In fact, Rebecca sees fairies from Pan's kingdom quite often. The more humans understand the water and the rock similarities within themselves, the more they open up pathways for communicating with Pan, just as the two of you are opening pathways for communicating with plants, animals, with us, and with each other. We feel a sense of deep longing from you, Cullen, for this encounter. You have the longing because you remember encounters with Pan energy from another time. You carry that energy with you, missing that interaction and longing for that communication. You are re-awakening as the veil is shifting and lifting. Focus on Connecting in the present, seeing what is present now, feeling the energies that are here now. That brings the balance necessary for you to know how to communicate with both kingdoms.

Did my childhood garden grow in the manner it did because of Pan's influence?

Absolutely. Pan made his energy present as a reminder to you so you would not forget about going between the kingdoms and so that you would remember your pledge of service to that realm. Pan chose to do this when you were young and not yet imprinted by the collective consciousness through much schooling and socialization. You now approach a place of balance with Nature that enhances your abilities to merge with other kingdoms once again. You seek wholeness and Unity with what you remember from other times.

Thank you. When I listened to tapes about Rock and Pan's dialogue in The Findhorn Garden, Rock asked the same question I have asked: "Why haven't I been able to see you?" Pan's answer was, "You cannot see us; you cannot communicate with us from your side; only we allow you to see us when your vibratory sense becomes finer so that our energies mesh more easily, but that meshing only happens from the devic side, not the human side."

At the time the Findhorn Garden tape was made, the devic kingdom was greatly cautious of humans, who have caused such harm to the earth. The veil between the human and devic kingdoms was largely closed to humans at that time. The situation is not quite the same now as when Rock met Pan. Many humans have achieved a more elevated vibration and are now able to more easily match their energy to the energy of those in Pan's kingdom. Pan has opened the devic kingdom to those who wish to help with the joint project of raising the vibration of all. The fairies and the little people suffer from the effects of lower human vibration, as does the entire devic kingdom. Having humans consciously raise their vibration is a mutual benefit for humans, the fairies, the devas, the earth, and the universe. The fairies Rebecca sees more and more lately are delighted when humans continue to raise their vibration. When humans' vibrations are raised, they are less likely to cause harm, for they see and understand more deeply that they are Connected to the devic kingdom. Raising human vibration also promotes easier merging with the higher vibration of Pan's kingdom and prevents harm to the devas from Connecting with lower vibrational humans.

Thank you for explaining that. Please tell us where the music came from that Rebecca heard deep in the forest as we were sitting by a small brook of water on top of a large rock.

We were communicating with the devic beings in that forest, and we wove threads of communication between you, the devas, and ourselves through your Love for the devic kingdom. We feel so much joy when humans put together pieces of understanding and truly absorb the depth of a reality that is much larger than you have realized. We have a question for you. What can you tell us from the human perspective about snow? Snow has devic qualities. We understand the physical way it comes in your universe. As we are always interested in emotional expressions of humans, we notice that snow often seems to bring calm. What can you tell us from your perspective about the interaction between the devic beings of snow and the human emotions affected by snow?

Snow does indeed calm the atmosphere. I don't know if it's the crystalline structure of the frozen water, but it makes our environment seem quiet, calm, and often restful. At least for those of us who are willing to surrender to the effects of snow, it seems to slow time down. It makes our environment neutral, and that seems to make time elastic.

That is a very insightful. Thank you. We do notice the quiet that arrives with snow. We perceive that the quiet may cause human brains and bodies to slow down, so it makes sense that the humans would perceive that time slows down.

Some humans speed up around snow because of their nervousness; they seem to want to challenge it rather than being in synchronistic flow with Nature. Many humans wish to conquer Nature in an aggressive manner. So I perceive that there are actually two or more ways to perceive what humans feel when it snows. Rebecca and I slow down, become quieter, and sink into our true selves through experiencing snow. However, many other humans

speed up more aggressively in their relationships to snow.

To escape their fear of being trapped, to escape their fear of being confined with no one but themselves and the quiet. Perhaps your world needs a major two-week snowstorm, keeping everyone quiet and slow. It would be beneficial if humans could slow down enough to find harmony with Nature and return to the Connection with their own divinity, leaving their fear behind them. We believe the snow devas intentionally bring quiet with them, for the rain devas do not do that. Rain has its own song, its own tones, yet snow does not. We believe the quiet is a devic gift.

That's a very wonderful understanding. Humans often say that winter is the time to go within, the time to become quiet and ponder the questions of who we are. During snow, we have the opportunity to stop our activities, stop making decisions, and to be still and quiet until the snow melts, giving our thoughts and ideas a chance to germinate.

Have you noticed that snow comes more irregularly and less often or more often and intensely as humans refuse to heed the invitation into slowness?

Yes. As we watch the snow falling right now, we actually get a sense of wave motion, a slowness in the design of calm. The quiet movement seems to lull us into a sense of quiet peacefulness. It actually seems as though the material is there, and yet it is not there in the way it falls, in the way it moves in the wind. It is almost a wave motion.

Oh my, Cullen. You are certainly beginning to see the Truth of the world. How exciting for us! There is a linking between the components of the human physical body and the devic qualities of the earth. Earth responds to the vibration of humans. Humans who are so sped up with their Internet and cell phones and their addictions to coffee, nicotine, drugs, or anything that makes them speed up, are damaging their neurology. Much of human choice today involves things that promote speed, speed, speed, yet the neurological components of humans are not set up to handle speed. This constant speed causes burnout. Humans do not understand their Connection to the earth; humans are the neurological part of Earth. When humans are in harmony with Earth's rhythms, Earth blossoms and is able to follow Her correct path of divinity. Because most humans are sped up, Earth responds as if She has a neurological disorder. This is why you sense and see so much distress on Earth, for Earth takes the neurological impulses directly from the humans who crawl all over her. This Connection is little understood.

We believe that human technology has advanced rapidly in the past three hundred years, but our psyches have not been able to catch up with that growth.

Correct. The reason is because the human psyche has been separated from Nature.

And part of what is wrong today on Planet Earth is that those in control of money and inventions are governed by greed and power. With our newer, smaller, digital technology, we may be replicating the mistakes made in Atlantis. No matter how many wires we have coming into our houses, it doesn't

make us any smarter or wiser. Just like in Atlantis, we seem to be inventing things simply because we can. There is no Wisdom in that philosophy. That philosophy is based on incorrect beliefs, and the element of Wisdom connected to Nature is missing. Until we reorient ourselves with the rhythms and wisdom of Nature we will continue to devolve rather than to fulfill our agreement to evolve with Earth as She makes Her changes towards ascension.

That is why so many of us and others like us are present in these very important times, watching and preventing improper decisions and actions at higher levels. We, none of us, wish for human beings to repeat the mistake of Atlantis and other places over and over. As the two of you and others like you help to elevate human consciousness through grouping your intent together, you assist us in our work. It is very important.

Do individual devic beings or spirits work in teamwork? Or do they work at their own jobs independently?

It depends on the level of devic enlightenment. There are varying levels in the devic kingdom. Each deva does its own job. In the kingdom of Nature, your flowers and trees each have devic beings that govern their specific well being. Yet there is a more advanced deva who acts as an overseer. A higher organizing principle of devic energy links all the devas of the trees and flowers. It is all a webbing of life, much as each human being is an individual and a part of the collective consciousness of humanity. There is a collective consciousness of the devic kingdom as well. When advanced humans or devas weave their intentions for creativity together through offering their light, they interweave Silver threads of Connection, and light is shined into places where it is most needed. Humans and devas once worked together. It is appropriate and possible for them to begin teamwork for the highest good of all once again. Most of Nature operates under the greater plan for Unity, yet because Earth is influenced by the thoughts and activities of humans, there are levels of separation even in Nature. So devas who watch one thing are not aware of what other devas are doing. When the snowflakes fall and the devas of snow bring quiet, there is a group action, but each snowflake is individual and has its own characteristic and its own devic energy. There is individuality within Unity in the devic kingdom, just as in the human kingdom and within us. The devas move towards Unity, just as humans are moving towards Unity. The governing body directs the collective consciousness and the individual consciousness participates, just as in the human kingdom.

I have often called what you are describing "Overshadowing." But I see the better term would be "Overlighting."

Yes, yes. The underlying understanding is that all life moves towards Unity. All life moves in that direction. As we have said before, Pan and the devic kingdom are opening, or we should say re-opening, avenues of communication between the various kingdoms of the planet at this time in order to enhance cooperation amongst *all* the kingdoms. Humans often deplete the vitality of *all* the land, and Pan's creatures must vacate because there is not enough energy to nourish them. The devic overseers guide them to other places. Your thoughts of concern and your actions can honor, respect, and help those living beings. Your Loving thoughts will help to create a better reality for all kingdoms. This planet has long been under the spell of fear and separation. As humanity and the planet break away from that spell, nothing can be lost. You can only gain Love and Unity through this opening of communication. The human and devic kingdoms are equally responsible for keeping Nature in balance and helping the earth evolve. You may do it together through Love.

13

2012: THE END OF DUALITY

The easiest way for humans to successfully move through the transition of the things that are coming is to look at everything that no longer works and Love it. Move away from old concepts and be curious about what comes next rather than being frustrated about what no longer works and what you think you have lost. Relax a little, and try to float through the changes. Many things are challenging for humans now because you have no base, no framework for understanding. We are here to help humans understand. The basis for understanding is *Trust*, for it is from a foundation of Trust that all you desire will come. When you set aside your beliefs about yourselves and reality, when you Trust that everything is as it should be, knowing that you have the power within you to create the next moment, you are in contact with your future self, the divine one that you really are. The divine part of you knows and has the power, where your current self has neither. Openings for greater understanding come from Trust. We brought wisdom about the energies of the universe to the Mayan people many human years ago, in the form of what is now called the Mayan Calendar. The Mayan Calendar is truly about energy, not time. Understandings about the Mayan Calendar can help humanity flow with the energy of the universe and move past the illusion of time. Each day and each number on the Mayan Calendar carry a different type of energy, and the energies work together to help humans create a more successful and harmonious reality. Through the existence of duality, everything has opposites; it is the human purpose to find the way to move away from opposites towards Unity. The Mayan Calendar's "End of Time" is actually the "End of Duality." It is the place where humans may leave the separations that have divided them and move into the Unity of Love.

Humans have created through their thoughts, words, and actions a consensual reality that is based on an illusion: time. Through your clinging to the illusion of time, humans have created more separation, focusing more on the power of opposites and moving more towards separation. We are here now to assist humans move in the opposite direction, towards Unity, during the opening that has been provided by the universe. The end of the Mayan Calendar was set as a window of opportunity for humanity to drop away from the separation of opposites and move into Unity. The date of December 21, 2012 was chosen by its *energy*, not by time. That date carries the energy of eleven. Eleven carries the energy of Illumination. Within the eleven are two threes (the month of December is a twelve; one and two of twelve add up to three, and the day of 21 also adds up to three) and a five (2012 adds to five). Three is the catalyst number and the number of Creativity. Five is the number of Change. So the date was set by us to invite in the energy of creative change, not simply according to time. Even so, dates are not definite eventualities.

Humans think in definite or finite terms rather than *infinite* terms, for humans are accustomed to seeing reality as "fixed." It is not. Reality moves in waves and is changed in each moment by the thoughts and energy that are used to create it. Likewise, the "date" and "time" of the end of the Mayan Calendar, or the end of time as you know it, is not a fixed date. It is a *wave* that you approach as you move away from separation through dropping old beliefs and patterns and moving closer and closer to Unity as you begin to live in Love and Trust. Those who study the energies of the Mayan Calendar may see that the patterns have shifted and continue to shift. Some of your scholars (Carl Johan Calleman) have now set the "date" for the end of the Mayan Calendar at October 28, 2011. If you add the energetic components of this number, they add to six. Six carries the vibration of flow. Within the six are two ones (as the tenth month, October is a 1, and the two and eight of 28 also add to one) and a four (adding the numbers of 2011.) One is the vibration of new beginnings, and four carries the energy of stability or foundation. So your new date indicates you are flowing towards a new beginning with a stable foundation. An interesting development and an excellent understanding of how humans participate in changing reality. You are accelerating the end of duality through your thoughts. The more quickly you drop old beliefs and old patterns, the more quickly you change your own vibration, allowing an easier and more rapid transition from separation into Unity. *The "time" is not set, and the energy continues to change in waves, as you change in waves to match the energy of reality.*

Humans need to understand that the end of the Mayan Calendar is in fact the end of duality, not the end of life. Many humans have *no idea* what this means. Most humans will be quite shocked as the energy of duality comes to a close. They will experience what you may call "shock waves" as everything they believed was real falls away, bit by bit. It is already gradually happening. The waves, of course, are an accurate representation of the true reality, and as time's illusionary reality falls apart, the energy of that change can and will be felt by all. What will be left are waves. Those who choose to move from "fixed" positions in their beliefs about reality *now* through changing their patterns and learning to Trust rather than believe, will find an easier transition. They in effect become waves themselves, changing in each moment as the energy shifts. Those who choose to remain fixed will be broken apart by the shock. They will feel confused as everything they have ever "believed" was solid changes in front of their eyes and becomes waves, waves of energy. It is, of course, each individual's choice how and when you integrate understanding of these changes and how they will affect you.

There are signs along the way, symbols to help humans understand the energy of reality. The symbol of the cross, which many have long misunderstood, is a symbol that promotes deeper understanding of the end of duality that approaches. The cross shows two opposite energies coming from two different directions. The center, where those energies meet, represents Illumination. It is in the center, where opposites meet, that the divine spark begins, for divinity and Unity are the same. (It is the clash of opposites that creates the divine spark. We will speak more of this when we speak about the Divine Couple.)

The symbol of the cross illustrates how opposites meet in the center and spark illumination. The end of duality foretold by the Mayan Calendar is represented by the coming together of polar opposites at the center of the cross. Perhaps humans may begin to see movement away from duality and towards Unity through an understanding Rebecca has reached: by seeing opposites cross each other, come together, and spark the divinity of oneness, wholeness, or holiness. Very good, Rebecca. Many humans misunderstand the symbolism of the cross. They see it as a symbol of death and resurrection, but they don't understand that death (or ascension) and resurrection are the same. It is in the joining, the coming together of opposites, that resurrection occurs. It is in the center that the divine spark brings you back to oneness and the holiness of who you really are. It is in the center that you remember everything.

As we work with the two of you, we join hands, so to speak, in partnership, camaraderie, and Love, as true team members. We wish humans to join hands in Love as they move away from duality and towards oneness. There are many ways that you may bring opposites together towards Unity as you move out of stuck, fixed positions and into waves of being in the new reality. You may work to meld your physical and etheric bodies into oneness (we will say more about this later). You may meet each other on common ground in the way that we meet you in understanding. Couples may work together as a unit rather than as individuals. Communities may work with other communities. Goals for working together may include expressing Love through non-judgment, willingness to clean out shadow by releasing old beliefs and patterns, desire to make a difference through positive thoughts, words and actions, and focusing on seeing yourselves as we taught the Maya: "I am another yourself." These ideas all support movement away from your opposite polarities of pain and separation into the joy of Unity. You have the opportunity to step away from your illusionary reality that you have created together. You have the opportunity to move towards oneness. Use these opportunities being made available to you now, in this present moment. They are a present!

Can you say more about the effect of the Harmonic Convergence of 1987 on humanity's opportunity?

Ah! Yes. The Harmonic Convergence is directly related to energies of the Mayan Calendar. It represents group consciousness of humanity asking for help. Groups of humans joined their water, focusing their intent on creating a better world for humanity and the earth. Through their joint thoughts and shared emotional request, they participated in co-creating the opportunity that now exists. Through your requests, you opened a larger window for more light and energy to arrive to provide the help you need. That is the precise reason there are so many of us here at this time to offer help, guidance, and support. Take this understanding and help other humans to know why the intentions that you put out into group consciousness are so valuable. The more of you who band together in community with group intent, the greater the effect. Just as the Harmonic Convergence opened a huge window for more assistance and more light to flood in, you may now band together with others to take advantage of this opportunity for another form of elevated vibration is about to occur: it is the upcoming second Harmonic Convergence, which we will further discuss later. The incoming light helps you to move beyond the challenges of duality. Duality is the most difficult of circumstances in which to dwell. Remember time is a construct of duality, and as humans approach being able to step away from this structure, the experiences of duality are more poignant. You seek the balance that arrives through living without time. You will experience more balance as you flow more towards Unity. Let go of your beliefs based on dualistic ideas. Become more aware of what you create through attachment to patterns, beliefs, and what you *think* into reality.

Humans have trouble when they feel they are accelerating, learning, and moving with more flow, and then all of a sudden they run into an obstacle. When that happens to us we feel as though we're failing or not moving ahead as we thought we were. That often gets in the way of our progress towards Unity.

Progress is not linear. Part of the challenge is that your human culture believes that all positive movement progresses in a linear fashion. Therefore, if things have gotten better and then you meet a challenge, your consensual belief about progress gets in the way. It is your *belief* about progress that is the problem. You don't need linear progress in the true reality; you need understanding. Progress occurs in spirals or waves. The analogy of the children's game hopscotch makes more sense. You move in a non-linear fashion, bouncing from one understanding to another. There is no straight line for achieving progress. Understanding comes in waves, spirals, and circles. Humans need depth of understanding and the ability to explore their shadows, which hold so many misperceptions and incorrect beliefs. And so your High Self angels and the universe present challenges in many forms, and you cycle through them again and again from different perspectives to give each challenge the depth of understanding it needs in order to be completely resolved. The Maya used the energy of each day to move through these natural cycles. Often different aspects of your lessons and the gift of your challenges come from an opposite direction, moving towards the center for a greater understanding of Unity. When humans feel challenged, you can remember that forward progress is a *linear* concept, and that true progress is deeper immersion into the reality where opposites dissolve. Approach each challenge like the game of hopscotch, jumping from understanding to understanding. You do not fail; you experience cycling between duality that is unavoidable while living on planet Earth until you create the new reality.

Within the Mayan Calendar system, which affects humanity, there are portals of opportunity where the energy is more intense. These portals can be experienced as high intensity in either polarity: discomfort or insight, depending on what needs to be discovered. They are opportunities that offer humans either a recognition of "Aah-ha, this feels right" or "Oh no, this feels awful." They are guidelines for you to move away from separation and towards Unity. During intense portals of energetic opening, it may feel as if "the roof comes off," as a greater intensity of light is poured in. These portals of opportunity are designated as Core Days in the Mayan Calendar. They are opportunities to dig down into the core of who you are in order *to remember* your divinity and to change dysfunctional patterns. Most humans experience Core Days without much awareness of what is happening. We explain these concepts once again through the Mayan Calendar perspective of energy so that humans may use this opportunity to do their work in order to evolve. Now we have questions for you. If you understand that these are opportunities for breaking through dysfunctional patterns and erroneous beliefs, which color do you suppose is most utilized, which color light shines through this window of opportunity?

White?

Of course. We will say more about colors later, but for now we will speak of White. White is the color that humans perceive is the harshest, for White is the color of Truth. Truth always reveals what is incorrect in beliefs, and so humans become uncomfortable with that energy. And as humans are full of incorrect beliefs, Truth can be a very frightening energy to encounter. Now, why do you expect that these days of opportunity are so challenging for humans living through them? What is your understanding?

Because they are living in fear.

Very good. Not only are they living in fear, the minute things become challenging, they regress to old patterns that feel familiar. They believe that familiarity holds safety, when it does not. There is no security in familiarity.

And fear is the most familiar.

Yes, fear is the most familiar, and growing out of fear are thought forms that continue to support fear, so humans remain habitually stuck in their familiar patterns until they find the courage to change. In the last few years, the two of you decided to aggressively face everything, every emotion you were feeling and every thought you were thinking. You moved through them no matter how painful they were, and you lived through it. Many others on the spiritual path are doing this also. However, most humans are too afraid to do this; they don't have the courage or the skills that we are now teaching. They retreat into their addictions, or they gloss over their fears distracting themselves, or they flee the situation. We encourage humans during this opportunity to ask, "What dysfunctional belief or belief system is causing me this pain?" Pain is not necessary. Humans must ask, "*Why* am I feeling this pain? *What* belief system needs to die? *What* do I need to surrender that no longer serves me? *What* needs to fall away? *What* subconscious part of me is frightened?" These questions will draw you towards where you wish to be, experiencing duality without such intense pain. Use the pain as a pointer to make the changes that need to occur rather than allowing the pain to define your reality. Combine willingness to grow and understand with courage to change; you *must* work these opportunities in order to evolve.

So as you use the opportunities provided during Mayan Calendar Core Days, we ask all humanity to simply come towards each other looking for different ways to create a new reality. Ask, "What gift is hidden in this challenge? What are we supposed to discover?" We would like to point out that emotional volatility is a human element. And as humanity develops, it diminishes, for you move more and more towards the vibration of Love, which carries peace, calm, and harmony; yet on the path of development, humans experience intense extremes. Emotions are meant to guide you towards change, and the more intense the emotional reaction, the more intense the change that is called for. The task at hand for humanity is managing the emotional portion, neither denying it nor dwelling in it, but using it to guide the necessary changes. Many humans are blindly living their lives in a stuck mode with underlying tension, anger, and frustration. Those emotions need to come to the surface in order to cleanse them and make appropriate changes. That process allows the cleansing and clearing of suppressed parts that have held you captive in old patterns from lifetime to lifetime, and certainly within the present lifetime. As humans move through cycles of challenges, you may consider the process a spiraling up towards oneness. On some days you notice a sense of flow, and other days you may feel largely out of sync. Because you live in duality, cycles are part of life. Just as you and Rebecca have many days where everything flows smoothly between you, and then you have an uncomfortable surprise of misunderstanding each other or misreading each other's thoughts or energy, and then you move back into longer periods of deeper harmony. As humans move closer to Unity and away from separation, cycles of misunderstanding occur less often and the severity of the emotional cleansing can be less intense.

I suppose we are hoping for diminishment of duality, thinking that the more we progress, the further we will remove ourselves from the conflicts within duality.

Yes, but there's that word that throws humans off, "progress." Understanding is not linear; it cycles. It spirals; it swirls; it is wave motion, for it is part of Unity and oneness. The linear form of progression comes from the point of view of separation and fear, where competition exists. Humans use many thoughts and words that create competition, such as "the early bird gets the worm'" and "getting ahead." The use of those thoughts creates a reality of competition rather than cooperation. Cooperation is more based on Truth, for with cooperation there is always enough for everyone. The collective consciousness of humanity in this and many thousands of other lifetimes have built a reality based on dualistic-minded competition because of incorrect fear-based beliefs. Humanity's consensual belief is that there is never enough for everyone. The Truth is that there is always enough for all. Humans who are able to redirect their understanding towards more cooperation show true progress, rather than linear step-by-step progression where humans compete against each other to get ahead. Through cooperation and acceptance of differences, you absorb and integrate more into what you know, who you are, and obviously, how you observe and treat others.

Here's a key thing for humans to understand as duality comes to a close. There are only two forces in the universe: Love and fear. Everything else stems from those two. Everything in duality is based on separation, the separation of those two forces, Love and fear. When you unite the two, allowing Love to absorb and transform fear, you move towards Unity. Humans need to learn to assess every emotional reaction and every thought with the question, *"Does this come from Love or does this come from fear?"* If it contains judgment, you can be sure that it comes from fear and will cause further separation. Continually asking this question rules out human tendencies and old patterns of justification, blame, righteous, selfishness, all of the separating energies that arise from fear. Through this exercise, fear-based thoughts, emotions, words, and actions may be completely absorbed by Love. If humans could look at everything through questions about fear, they may learn a great deal about Love. Asking "Am I afraid? Is this person afraid of me? Am I doing what I need to do in Love? Is what I choose for the highest good of all?" promotes release of old beliefs that have kept humans locked into painful patterns. These are very high spiritual principles, universal spiritual principles, not only for Earth, but also for the rest of the universe. Approaching Life this way is approaching Unity through divine thought and action. With practice of this approach, humans participate in the end of duality as time comes to a close, and it may happen more quickly than you have previously imagined!

14

LIGHT AND COLORS

May we discuss colors?

Certainly.

Colors are specific vibratory patterns of energy that come from light. Each color carries a vibration of a specific energy that supports and upholds the true reality. The elements of reality are Love, Healing, Trust, Grace, Truth, Transformation, and Illumination, and certain colors resonate with and represent these aspects of reality. As colors are patterns of light, the vibration of a color represents a particular concentration or spread of light that enters into your world. Colors carry specific messages that humans may use for their growth. The energy and vibration of colors is the same throughout the universe; however, humans are able to *perceive* colors somewhat differently now. Most humans are only aware of the beauty of colors. Through becoming more aware of the energetic vibratory nature of colors, humans may gather information that leads you to larger understandings that clarify the true reality. You may learn what each color symbolizes and align your vibration with the vibration of a specific color to experience greater awareness of the effect of that color.

We will outline for you the seven specific colors that support and define reality and an eighth vibration, Silver, that Connects them all. We begin with the Pink color. While we introduce the colors in a certain order, hoping to instill the pattern within you, you may call upon and use of any of these colors at any time in any way you choose. Pink is the color of Love. Pink comes towards your heart and from your heart, for Love is the beginning. What else can exist in life without the beginning of Love? It exists in All That Is. All humans can greatly benefit from using the Pink vibration of Love, for humanity is full of misaligned thinking and emotions around perceptions that are causing pain. Following the Pink light of Love, we present the emerald Green light of Healing. We use the color Green to represent life; if you look all around you, you will see that one of the primary colors of life on this planet is Green, as is evidenced every spring. So to Heal physical, emotional, mental, or spiritual pain, or any painful situation, use the Green Healing light. Green light the color of emeralds is very beneficial for humans and helps them feel grounded with life.

Next we move towards Blue, which carries the light of Trust and clarity, for once the heart is opened with Love and a certain level of Healing has occurred, Trust is necessary to continue your awareness and your growth. Being able to Trust is stepping away from fear. If you live in Trust, you never have to doubt anything. Trust is implicitly necessary on the path of development away from pain and towards Unity. Fear causes pain; Trust erases the fear and so erases the pain. If you begin to Trust that everything has a purpose and that pain is a pointer to things that must change, painful places may be Healed as you make the necessary changes. So you move from opening your heart with the Pink vibration of Love, through Healing with the Green light, into the Blue vibration of Trust. Humans move into greater and greater harmony through using Trust to eliminate fear and a great deal of what is uncomfortable.

We will repeat our presentation of the progression of the colors. Pink Light helps the heart open; Green light brings Healing; Blue light helps you move towards Trust. Next we introduce the Golden light of Grace. The Golden light of Grace exists in particle form. You may envision the Golden light of Grace as tiny particles that rain down upon you. Golden light of Grace has a vibration that instills upon you a sense of "ahh." The Golden light is the color vibration that breaks apart patterns. Imagine Grace descending upon you. It is welcome and palpable. Because it is used to break apart patterns, there is a substance to this particular vibration. It is used to break away your karma and all the patterns that have been held lifetime to lifetime in your present and your parallel lives; it breaks patterns apart belief by belief, for humans have built one false belief upon another. Asking for the Golden light of Grace instills the ability for light to flow from Source towards your divine selves, breaking apart what is *not* Truth and opening you to receive what *is* Truth. This is why we present Grace before we present the color of Truth.

After you experience the Pink light of Love, the Green Healing light, the Blue vibration of Trust, and the Golden light of Grace, you may more easily experience White, the color of Truth. The White light is often called the Christ light, for the Christ energy is aligned with Truth. We have already told you that White is the color most difficult for humans to accept. It often is experienced as the harshest light because White represents Truth rather than illusion. It shatters false beliefs, yet when experienced from a place of Love, White is anything but harsh. It is freedom itself. Truth in full vibration shatters illusions and beliefs that humans hold dear. Your subconscious has experienced and met this vibration through your High Self angels, who surround you with the White light and vibration of Truth; you have a choice in how you wish to accept it. Truth is connected to beauty in understanding that everything is as it should be and in its own form, in all of our own forms, we are each of us beautiful. The energy of Truth shatters inappropriate illusions about self, about other, about the world, and about the universe. We ask humans to please accept the vibration, experience it without judgment, without assumptions or beliefs, just accept the feeling and know that each of you may open more fully to understanding Truth without the misguided thoughts and varying coatings of meaning that you so often layer over Truth. When human beliefs get in the way, the experience of the light of Truth may be quite uncomfortable. Truth causes emotional discomfort as it shatters illusions and beliefs. Working through emotions from a perspective of Trust allows you to see Truth without pain. With Love, Trust, and Grace, Truth is easier for humans to see and accept. Things take on a new light, if you will excuse our pun, and you may use that light to elevate your emotional state and realign the inappropriate thoughts you think. You may then more easily see and experience White Christ light with joy. The White light of Truth shows Unity. It shows that all is one. With this understanding you may also begin to see the shimmering Silver threads that Connect all of life here on this planet and throughout the universe to others such as us. These Silver threads attach through Love. Are you with us so far?

Yes.

The next color vibration we wish to present is Violet. Violet is the color of Transformation. It may be perceived much as you perceive the Golden light of Grace, in a sparkling form like stardust. It is not simply a color vibration; it contains poignancy within it, etheric material that may actually be drawn down to you or rained upon you to help you with Transformation. The Violet light may best be understood as the light that helps humans Transcend or Transform anything in the universe. The Violet light of Transformation may be used for Transforming specific situations that do not work or Transcending certain emotional states that are imprisoning you and keeping you from Connection to your own divinity. You may call the Violet light of Transformation around you when you wish to Transcend something, shape shift, or elevate yourselves. Access this beautiful light by tuning into a visual image of a cloud of stardust over your head or by opening to the channel between humanity and the universe, as if you are looking into the Milky Way and seeing a bright array of lights that are all Violet in color. It is one of the higher vibrations because it is Transformative. The Violet light of Transformation and the Golden light of Grace often work in Unity as a paired team for accessing change. They work well together because of their similarity and their formation. The Golden light of Grace eradicates old patterns and beliefs, and the Violet Light of Transformation helps Transcend and Transform them once the patterns are broken and released. This color combination is quite beneficial to humans. The Lemurians used and continue to use it.

Now we present Yellow, the color of Illumination. Yellow is different from the color Gold. Yellow is the color of the sun and the color of understanding. We present the Yellow light of Illumination next because Illumination naturally follows Truth. Once erroneous beliefs are dropped and the light of Truth shines fully on you, in you, and through you, you may Transcend old restrictions and move into an Illuminated place of peace and calm. Some spiritual masters call this enlightenment. We simply say you are moving into the light. Yellow helps you understand what the White light has shown you, that everything is one. Now you may have a true understanding of Unity and see the Silver threads of Connection. You cannot reach this place without opening your heart to Love, without Healing your wounds and managing your emotions, without stepping fully into Trust with clarity, without welcoming Truth, and without Transforming what needs to be Transformed. All of these things lead you to Illumination and the Silver threads of infinity where time does not exist. After you see this, what do you suppose you find? Can you guess?

Please tell us.

What did we start with?

Pink.

The Pink Light of Love. Where do you think you end up after you experience Truth, Illumination, and infinite Connection?

Love.

Exactly, completing a full circle. So Love is everything. Love is All. Do you understand? We repeat the colors that define reality: Pink, Green, Blue, Gold, White, Violet, and Yellow, representing

Love, Healing, Trust, Grace, Truth, Transformation, and Illumination. Yet the total of all colors come from and return to Love. All the color vibrations are woven together in Unity. You have a rainbow to work with, and we sometimes supply a visual rainbow in your sky to remind you. If you follow the pathway of the color vibrations that we have outlined and pay attention to how each step takes you away from fear, you will experience more deeply the vibration of Love. You may dwell there more and more and more as you practice managing your emotions through the use of color. The Pink light of Love helps you with acceptance and resonance with all the other vibrations and colors. The emerald Green light, often used for rebalancing and Healing, helps correct imbalances in your physical body. It can also soothe your emotions and your etheric body. Blue light, the vibration of Trust and clarity, carries energetic waves to break apart fears that have kept you away from Trust. It has an overall deep and calm vibratory effect. The Golden vibration breaks up your karma and old patterns, the White light shows you Truth, and the Violet light helps you to Transform. The Yellow vibration brings you Illumined understanding, showing you the Silver threads that Connect all.

Because humans learn through linearity, you may further understand the progression of color vibrations we have presented if you look at their numerical sequence. All numbers, all musical notes, and all colors carry a vibration. While we wish humans to understand that they may use colors in any order they choose, there is something to be understood in the numerical values as we presented them. The first vibration we presented (the number one) is the Pink light of Love. One is the vibration of Unity. The second vibration we gave you (the number two) is the Green Healing light. Two is the number of duality and separation. Healing is necessary because humans live in duality and often must heal misunderstandings from polar opposite beliefs they hold, and so we associate the Green light of Healing with the number Two, although it also carries other numerical vibrations as well. The third vibration we presented (the number three) is Blue, the color of Trust and clarity. Three is the number for creativity, a catalyst for understanding and clarity. Understanding helps you to feel a sense of calm and Trust. We presented Gold as the fourth vibration (the number four.) Four is the number of stability, and Gold both breaks down solid patterns that do not work and also helps you to feel stable as it embraces you for the changes you must incur. The fifth vibration we presented (the number five) is White, the color of Truth. At this point in the progression you have used five colors to support changes in your perceptions in order to arrive at Truth. White light of Truth could actually be five, the number of change, or one because Truth is Unity. We have presented it as five, the number of change, because every time you move towards Truth, a change must occur. The sixth vibration we gave you (the number six) is the Violet Light of Transformation. Six is the number of flow. What comes next?

It takes Transformation of ourselves to get to Illumination; the work that we have done through the first five colors opens us to the sixth vibration of Transformation of understanding, and we may then move to the Illuminative state.

Yes. And Yellow, the color of Illumination, is represented here by the number seven. Seven is the vibration for merging between the veils, the place where you move between worlds

164

to find Illumination. The vibration of Illumination is actually eleven, but it requires the vibration of seven to access it. The eighth vibration we gave you is Silver. Eight is the number of abundance and Connection. You may visualize it through the symbol of the Infinity Loop, for in infinity everything is connected. Through infinite Connection you always have abundance. Silver threads Connect you to all that is, and when you increase your inner vision you may begin to see them.

What can you tell us about the color and vibrations of metals?

Gold and Silver metals each have a different kind of vibration. There is a reason that people of the earth, going back to the Egyptians, the Maya, and beyond, particularly venerated the metal Gold. They used it not for its wealth but for the value of its vibration. Gold actually holds an elevated vibration of sacredness and safety. When you invoke the Golden light of Grace, you are calling in and asking for a showering of miniscule light particles the color of your physical Gold to help you shine and reflect your own light. Silver carries the vibration of Connection, and humans have used Silver in many forms in order to promote Connection. To compare the vibration of Gold with Silver, think of waves and particles. Gold showers down on you as tiny particles of that color of light. The vibration of Silver is more like waves. Tiny, tiny Silver waves emanate from you as threads Connecting outwards to other energies, other sources. One might say you are held together through tiny Silver threads. These Silver threads are Connection to the etheric; it is part of the make up of your etheric form. We will speak more about your etheric-physical makeup later. Your etheric form could be outlined in Silver lines that Connect to the physical form. Silver is quite malleable and moldable. It can be easily bent, as can Gold, yet Silver has tiny lines that can hold shape. When humans learn to work with the water in them, inviting your shapes to conform to your water's intelligence, you will learn how to erase and redraw the Silver lines of your etheric blueprints that govern your physical forms. So Silver and Gold each have great propensity for the new human being, the future selves you are moving towards. Enjoy the full flow of both; your High Selves dance and sing to be able to participate with showering you fully with the Golden light of Grace and the Silver threads of ultimate Connection. Colors and metals both carry vibratory information. It is of great spiritual benefit for humans to hear and understand the vibratory energy of the metals Gold and Silver, since humans have focused most of their awareness around either the beauty of shimmering metal or the financial aspect that it offers. Your East Indian science of Ayruveda understands properties of Silver and Gold in a valuable way. Silver provides cooling energy; Gold provides warming energy. Each of these may also be ingested for medicinal benefit. Yet the vibratory energy carries more information than this. When humans learn how to appropriately use the *true* value of Gold rather than attaching financial importance to the metal, much will be attained towards peace.

Is there anything else of importance for humans to understand about colors?

Colors help you see through the mist or fog of duality. Not only do colors help you define and understand reality, they help humans to recognize the vibrations you are using as you are co-creating the new reality of the future of humanity. If you understand the use of colors, you may more cohesively join with the universe in creating by invoking certain energies to support what you wish to create. For example, when you are asking for a clear communication, you may invoke the color of Blue, which we use when we communicate with humans, for Blue promotes Trust. Blue also enhances clarity. If you are looking for greater understanding of something, you may invoke the color of Yellow. If you are looking for Transformation or Transition out of a situation in which you are not comfortable, you may ask for the Violet color to aid in your creation of a new reality. Colors swirl around you, and you are able to call upon their energy to promote the creation of the changes that need to occur. It is important to understand the vibration of colors so that you understand the choices you make through these colors: what you choose to put out into the universe and what you choose to call from the universe towards you. Does this sufficiently answer the question?

Yes, I believe this is quite complete. As we evolve as humans, will we learn to communicate with colors and lights?

Yes. Human awareness becomes more able to perceive in non-dimensional understanding through the understanding of colors and their vibrations. Human perceptions of color open you more to beauty and Truth. When you look in the sky and see apparitions in the clouds, the colorful patterns, you see more in the way we wish you to see colors, and you may call them into your awareness through your focus and intent. Your understanding and relationship to the Truth of reality grows every day. The two of you have been experiencing the expansion of color for some time now, a number of years, as you look in the sky. Work on being able to sense varying vibratory levels when you see colors to enhance your understanding. Humans are beautiful, each of you, whether you accept that or not. We all are beautiful, each of us. When humans assess themselves without judgment and evaluation, looking for the light you carry, you may see your beauty. Colors help you raise your vibration to understand your own beauty. Each of you needs to look for and remember the light, for that is where both beauty and Truth live, in the light. And the light is Love. Remember these things, for there is no need to suffer.

The man who embodied the Christ energy in human form was a wonderful example of using the vibrations of color. He utilized them well. The Pink light of Love radiated from his being. The Green Healing light flowed through his hands to support others Healing. The Blue light of Trust caused him to turn towards higher understandings. The White light of Truth led him to reject existing beliefs and dogmas of his time. He used the White light to speak about universal Truth, rejecting what was popularly considered true at that time. He used the Violet light to help people raise themselves from their lower vibrations to attain higher states of being. Yellow light around him showed the Illumination of his understanding. All humans may do this as the man Jesus tried to teach you. He is not the only human capable of using colors to access divinity.

We wish humans to understand that all of the colors are present within light and all of the colors that surround you are present within your environment all the time, and you may call upon them for your own growth and Healing anytime. We would like humans to become more aware of colors and to use your imagination to call colors up on your own. Imagining that you see them will bring their presence into your reality vibrationally, and you may explore their energy. Doing this will help humans experience and transcend challenging physical or emotional states. You may ask for Grace while imagining the Golden light; invoke the Pink light of Love to open your heart; ask the Blue light of Trust for greater clarity, and invite the Violet light of Transformation to help you transcend your challenges. When you are ready to give up your beliefs, ask the White light of Truth to pour down upon you.

Pay attention to how you feel when you look at colors. Surround yourself with colors physically and in your mind's eye. Bring more color into your life as you bring flowers into your home. You know you can receive the vibration of color along with many other gifts from the flowers you enjoy. Most humans believe they choose colors because they like their visual impact. It is more accurate that you choose colors because you resonate with their vibration. You may notice many people wearing the same color on a particular day. They didn't all just wake up and decide to wear Blue. On these occasions, the collective consciousness is resonating with a certain vibration, and those who are tuned into the collective vibration resonate with it. There is an actual resonance with the vibration of the color that matches their emotional/physical state. Color choices often come from the subconscious of humans. We find more women than men in the human species practicing the awareness of color vibration by making conscious color choices with their clothes; some are even perplexed when they wish to wear the same color vibration a second day, thinking they cannot do so because they wore it the day before. It is a mistake. If they are called to wear a color, they should wear it for as long as they are being led to do so and not be distracted by what they believe others will think for seeing them in the same color repetitively.

The colors humans wear put out an energy signature into the world. Your choice of Blue shirts daily, Cullen, has long been a beacon drawing others to Trust you. You emanate that you are trustworthy, not only through your personal vibration but also through the color Blue which you so often choose for your outer wear. Rebecca often wears Pink, emanating the vibration of Love, and many who are in her presence sense Love without judgment or conditions. All humans may choose colors to enhance their own vibratory condition and to call similar energy towards them. Thus color serves as both a signature and an invitation. The vibrations you send into the world affect all beings. You have the ability to use the vibrations you draw from the universe towards you to co-create your reality. When you learn to direct those energies while flowing with them, you may use colors for communication and eventually transportation, especially if you combine them with sound. What we teach humans about colors helps you to understand movement and omnipresence. Colors contain energy; they allow movement and direction. When humans understand how to direct those energies, how to navigate the system, you grow closer to melding etheric and physical forms and you move closer to your goal of zip zip zip (meaning what Cullen refers to as the ability to move timelessly from one place to another instantaneously or omnipresently.)

That adds another dimension to travel. It must be Love and the light of colors together that create the magic that allows zip, zip, zip, whether the movement

***is for a ship or whether it is for a singular being
without the need of a ship.***

Yes. Love and light used together guide the movement, so you do not even need the zip, zip, zip (instant movement); you are already there (omnipresence.) The two of you already know this, of course, for you have been saying, "In Light and Love" for a very long time. Understand that light and Love are the same thing. All colors emanate from Love and light; colors are varying aspects of Love and light. Since colors all come from light, using them invites more light into your vibration. Your science has taught that White is the absence of all color. We believe this is a misunderstood concept, for light contains the beauty of all colors, including White. Think of a candle flame and the way you can see Yellow, Blue, White variations within the flame. Light carries all colors. You may enjoy the light externally if you open your eyes or internally if you wish to keep them closed. It is all the same. If you look at a candle flame you will notice the varying layers of light and color in the flame. There is Blue in the Center (Trust); there is White (Truth), and there is Yellow (Illumination). Blue-Trust. White-Truth. Yellow-Illumination. There is good reason many choose to focus on a candle flame that contains these colors for meditative practices.

Doubt is the opposite of Trust and grows from fear. Doubt stems from fragmentation within the human system. Doubt is a cloud that confiscates light. Light obliterates doubt. Light also obliterates fear. It obliterates negative emotions, dispelling them, absorbing them, leaving only the light. Proper use of colors as varying aspects of light realigns humans with their own divinity. The light you experience as the breaking of day is symbolic of breaking through doubts and fears, penetrating the darkness, dispelling the darkness, and bringing you to Unity with Trust. This is one reason many humans enjoy sunrise and seeing the light arrive. The universe sends the many colors of light to invite you to remember your own divine light. Your own divinity already exists; no one places it in you. It is placed there universally as you spring from Source. When humans Connect deeply with their High Selves and their inner light, opening the channel which moves it back and forth from your physical body outward into the universe and from the universe and Source back to your physical body, you become light conductors. Some call these light carriers. Human beings are light carriers, not because they carry light within themselves as is commonly understood, but because they open the pathway from what exists within them to Source in a broader manner, allowing the light to move back and forth simultaneously.

As we close our conversation on colors, we suggest that you use your imagination and spend more time thinking about and visualizing the understandings we have shared about colors. Learn to enjoy and utilize colors in your daily life. The more you recognize their power, the more you may create your own reality!

15

CYCLES, PATTERNS, AND CHOICE

If humans are going to ascend with their physical bodies, dysfunctional patterns must be disbanded. The wheel of karma goes around because humans come back with an agenda and an intent to fix what they failed in the last go round, but they get distracted by their emotional states and fears; they forget why they are here and they seek safety and comfort instead. They also become too immersed in the pleasurable sensations of their physical bodies. Humans lose courage; they lose heart; they increase the fear vibration as they join their beliefs to those of the collective consciousness, which largely resides in fear, negativity, and hopelessness. Reactive patterns are set up, and humans begin to focus on how to soothe their emotions through pleasurable sensations or distractions, or they focus on how to uphold their beliefs with thoughts such as, "This is my belief, and I'm sticking to it." It is the very definition of the wheel of karma. Because humans live in duality, you experience cycles, cyclical patterns in everything. Yet those cycles do not have to be hard. Most of you assume when you are at the top of the cycle things are great, and when you are at the bottom of the cycle things are awful. This assumption, this belief is invalid. A better way to experience cycles is to recognize that some days you will be completely in flow, and on some days you need to rebalance yourself, to rest and regroup because you have shifted out of flow. Humans are trapped in cycles and patterns that are based in fear; staying in those cycles of comfort and denial only perpetuates your fear. Rest when you feel you are out of sync or out of balance. It is important to take the time when it is needed, not later. When humans begin the work of clearing out their shadows and the emotions to which they have attached meanings, using intention, you disengage from them in order to disintegrate the patterns that have kept you trapped in dysfunctional beliefs lifetime after lifetime. Emotional blowups may be *quite* beneficial in disbanding and dispelling beliefs that no longer serve, beliefs that have been kept alive in the subconscious from your past/parallel lives. When emotions arise, you may consider your subconscious is acting as a big vacuum cleaner, pulling out negative things that need to be examined in relationship to the incorrect beliefs you are holding. This approach breaks the patterns that keep humans stuck.

So you are telling us that uncomfortable emotional states are the very tools that we need to use to clear ourselves in order for us to live in a re-remembered state of our divinity and our Connection to Source.

Yes, but emotional states were never intended to rule your behavior. They are merely signposts pointing you to higher and more conscious thoughts in order to make better choices in your lives. It helps if you make fewer assumptions in your thinking, for it is your assumptions that often cause you pain. Assumptions and belief systems are the reasons you remain stuck in old patterns. Assumptions and belief continue the loop of collective consciousness that creates a reality that is not working very well for you and all of humanity.

Is assumption a polite way of saying judgment?

They are related but not the same. Assumptions are underlying belief systems that lead to judgment. Judgment is harsher and full of more emotion than assumptions are. While judgments are not the same as assumptions, they come _from_ assumptions. Look to your emotions, and you will understand whether you are making judgments or whether you are simply _discerning_ the world as it is. If there is great emotion involved, you can be very sure belief systems, assumptions, and judgments are present. Love has no assumptions. Fear is full of assumptions. Separation is judgmental. Unity is non-judgmental. Oneness, unity, peace, harmony, ease, Love, these are different ways of saying the same thing. You, Cullen, have coined a favorite phrase:

> _"If you are in a state of compassion, you cannot be in a state of reaction. If you are in a state of reaction, you cannot be in a state of compassion."_

This Truth that you have discovered is very close to what we mean when we say, "Assumptions, judgments, and separation are not the same state of Love, oneness, and Unity." You cannot be in both states at the same time.

We notice from our perspective that humans choose to suffer over and over again in cycles of making assumptions, judging, reacting with emotions, and feeding their belief systems. Humans refuse to watch the thoughts they think when they experience emotion. They continually refuse to make the choice to detach from their emotional places and choose thoughts of compassion and Love, after they have experienced the emotion. They prolong the emotions, feeding them through their thoughts and beliefs, rather than simply separating them and saying, "This is out of proportion. I will come back and examine this when I calm my emotions." Humans typically make very poor choices when they are engaged in that pattern, and so they perpetuate a destructive cycle of separation. We watch the lack of compassion as many humans in relationships move away from Love and into separation because of destructive emotional cycles, judgments, and beliefs. They turn away from Love, choosing instead to judge and react emotionally rather than engaging in compassionate thoughts. Most animals know not to foul their own backyard, yet humans continually spoil their environment by throwing their own emotional garbage on those in their very backyards, causing further and further separation. It is not necessary to suffer that much. It seems most humans consistently choose the familiar reactive emotional state rather than choosing compassionate thoughts and *refusing* to react. You may break the cycle by simply detaching from your emotions and recognizing emotions are present *only* to show you that something is out of balance and must change. Remember we have cautioned you to use emotions only as a pointer, not as an environment in which to wallow. Emotions are actually opportunities to choose better thoughts so that you can change your reality. Feeding them with thoughts based on incorrect, yet familiar patterns of belief only makes the cycle worse. Emotions are more wisely used as a gauge of imbalance, a signal that a belief or pattern needs to be broken, rather than as an excuse to react in harmful ways.

We humans live in a loop or a circle of patterns that create drama without understanding we can use simple choice to break the destructive pattern. We must make changes by using our skill of choice to stop living in that loop of drama.

Yes, we know. So when you stub your emotions instead of your toe, you suffer throughout your entire being. Your body suffers, your mental thoughts go rampant and wild, catching you and reinforcing the same old loop. So learning to be more careful where one walks emotionally would be a good idea. A simple guideline to watch for when situations begin to get out of hand and out of proportion is to remember that if you are feeling emotional, a belief system is presenting itself for clearing, and a pattern is asking to be broken. Can you be compassionate with yourself and with others in making a better choice? Are you wise enough to recognize the power of what you create through your own thoughts and how you fuel them with your emotions and your words? If you allow your emotions to control your thoughts, you are attaching to the very reality that causes you such emotional discomfort. It is your choice to break the pattern. It is your choice to train your thoughts to rise from compassion rather than reacting to everything that greets you. It is up to you, and the power of your choices will affect all of humanity, for you are co-creating the new reality. We suggest you choose well. You cannot move towards Love, oneness, and Unity while you perpetuate the cycle of separation through clinging to familiar assumptions, judgments, beliefs, and old patterns.

That is a very good understanding of what humans do; we humans miss the point that once we've done it, it's time to stop doing it, rather than clinging to pain, sorrow, negativity, and the lesser choices that we make. Even though you're not judgmental in your makeup, is there some mechanism that tires you of dealing with human mistakes and ignorance?

No, our Love is too great for that. We are never tired of you. We never tire of supporting, helping, Loving, and communicating with you. And don't forget we also have gone through the process of our own evolutionary growth. So how could we ever get tired? It would be an impossibility. We only have great compassion for human pain, joy at your abilities and your growth, and a sense of camaraderie when we work together. We are one, Cullen. We are guiding you towards Unity. Through darkness and fears, humans make the mistake of moving towards more separation. When humans move away from separation towards Unity, you find each other once again, and you find us always present. Unity. We are here because of our choice to be of service to those who wish to listen and evolve.

Can you address the role of mistakes in learning to break patterns and cycles?

Mistakes are actions, thoughts, and words that arise from fear. Actions, thoughts, and words that arise from Love are never mistakes. They may not take you where you expect to be; yet because they are generated through Love they are considered explorations, not mistakes in the universal cosmic understanding. Mistakes come only from fear. One of the most frequent mistakes humans make from fear-based choices is rejecting Love, either because they do not believe that they are worthy of Love or because they do not Trust that Love is real. These mistakes cause further separation and move you away from Connection. The condemnation of self, which arises from fear, is a related mistake. Thoughts that express feelings of being wrong, incorrect, invalid, judged, or unfulfilled, take you away from your divinity. Humans judge themselves for failures when they are not failing; they are learning, breaking patterns and moving forward. As one of your friends once told you, "Humans learn more from their mistakes than they do from their successes." We agree with this and feel much is learned from mistakes if the lessons are taken seriously to your heart. One thing you can learn from each mistake is how fear led you to make that choice. Notice how your own positive emotions lead you to make choices from Love rather than fear, so you make less and less mistakes and more and more Love directed choices.

Another frequent human mistake is falling into feelings of powerlessness, where you feel powerless to change your circumstances. You have great power to create a different reality through understanding that Love is all there is. Human fears and emotions cause humans to feel that they cannot be themselves and still be loved, and thus humans make fear-based mistakes from feeling powerless in their own lives. When you learn to regulate your power and Connect it to your heart, you will find you are more comfortable within yourselves, and when you are more comfortable within yourselves, you are more comfortable with others. The power of Love is Connected to Trust, and Trust is Connected to listening to your First Sense, directing your thoughts in a positive direction. Again we tell you, if you allow your emotions and your fears to direct your thoughts, you lose your power. Your power comes from Love and Trust, where you know that you are divinely Connected to and part of Source. Most humans do not understand their true power; few of the experiences where they feel powerful are connected to Love. Rather they experience power much like sunspots, in surges. Boom. Explosion. Volatility. Powerful statements. Powerful tone of voice. Words spoken with only power and not Love are driven by incorrect thoughts and beliefs. Learn to regulate your power by Connecting it to your heart. The only *real* power resides in the heart; it is the power of Love.

Humans fail to realize that your choices have power. You always have a choice in how you think and how you manage your emotions. If you make those choices from patterns of fear and separation, you will continue to experience power in your life in negative ways. If you make your choices through compassion and Love, you will experience the power of Love creating a reality that is supportive of who you really are. We have repeatedly told you that you create your own reality through the thoughts you think and how you fuel those thoughts with your emotions. Humans have the power to steer their minds out of accustomed ruts, to make better choices, and to reach for each other. It amazes us that with such power of choice and the power of Love supporting you, that you continue to choose the difficult path. You continue to choose familiar patterns and beliefs, thinking that they keep you safe from your fears. You continue to cling to your assumptions, your beliefs, and your judgments even when it is obvious that clinging to these ideas makes you unhappy. Familiarity has such magnetism for humans, even when it is harmful. Even when you see over and over again that the same patterns are not bringing relief, you still make the choice to react in your familiar patterns. We are here to help you break those patterns. There need be no assumptions and judgments. If you learn to recognize your emotions as *signals* rather than allowing them to power your thoughts, you will begin to recognize the patterns that keep you stuck. Drop your assumptions and judgments. Be clear and direct and Loving. This is exercising your power to create a better reality; this is a good choice. Cullen, you recently experienced the beginnings of what humans call "a bad mood," and we watched as you steered yourself away from it by making a different choice. Would you please share how you managed that so we may consider it for teaching other humans?

I realized that something was changing; something was different for me when I woke up. As soon as I started to feel a change, I looked at it and I simply thought to myself, "There's something moving here; there's something I don't understand, but I feel and know that it is not happy, not joyous, and certainly not supportive of myself." I simply looked at it and went, "Hmm, I'm not going to go somewhere I don't want to go; I am simply going to take control of how I feel and make myself be OK." It was a process of acknowledging that there was something there that needed to be addressed and consciously choosing to go through it without feeding the emotions negative thoughts. It sounds simple, but it was more difficult than that.

Yes, we understand the human difficulty. Yet the simplicity of your explanation may be offered to help others, for most humans, it seems, have occasional bad moods. We are interested in the Connection between noticing emotional states and the thought patterns that ensue once emotional states are noticed.

I was able to see it and feel it before I fed into it emotionally and physically as deeply as I could have. I used what you have helped us with in a realistic understanding of the possibility of changing our reality through changing our emotional environment through our thoughts.

That is excellent. You have taken the principles that we have supplied you and the tools that we have given you, and you have used them well on yourself. This is an exploratory journey for us in understanding the loops of human dynamics. How would you share with other humans how to move away from negative patterns of thought and emotion?

When a person notices the very beginning of change, that is the time to make a choice, to make an alternate choice. If we don't choose immediately, it's too late. If we don't choose right away, we move into a familiar, undesirable place of emotional reaction and negative thoughts before we realize that movement has occurred.

We think sharing this from a human viewpoint rather than our Pleiadian viewpoint will be most helpful. It will take practice for each human to learn a new pattern of *choosing quickly* to do something different. A way of making a new choice is to say to yourself, "This is an old pattern. I need to

make a different choice about what I am thinking about this."
Steps to help humans learn to do this might include:

1) Noticing something physiological is changing;
2) Noticing that the emotional state is changing;
3) Choosing your thoughts consciously with the intention to break old patterns and habits.

What we must do is help others to understand that they must act immediately once they have a negative feeling. The only way to break an old protective pattern is to make an instantaneous choice. It is a way to nip it in the bud, to prevent the escalation of a physical or an emotional problem. We must teach people that as soon as they get the very, very first understanding that they are to about to fall, about to crumple, about to move in a downward physiologic or emotional trap, they must attempt to correct it immediately.

So what you are saying is that we as team members need to teach human beings to *claim* their choice. Because of their fears and old patterns, they feel that they have no choice. Together we must teach them how to focus their intent so that they understand that they *do* have a choice and to act on it immediately.

It seems this is the only mechanism that will help, because we are so habitual and we cling to what we know. Once we start down that slippery slope, it is very difficult to break the pattern of our actions and reactions. So making that choice as quickly as possible, knowing that there is a choice is important because humans often believe, whether they are depressed or not, humans often believe that they are helpless and there is no choice. So I think in teaching the best thing is to always say, "Yes, there is a choice, and the quicker you make a choice, the more quickly you will prevent that downward spiral." It sounds really simplistic, but it doesn't seem any more difficult than that. It is intent plus choice.

In order for humans to be healthy and whole, cycles and patterns must be broken. You must move beyond your understanding of what is real and be curious about what might happen if you do things differently. Break all the patterns and cycles that keep you trapped. Break free. It is as easy as that. You allow new energy and new understandings in breaking the old patterns and exploring things differently. Be curious about what might happen if you break old habits or change the way you do things.

There is an old saying that the definition of mental illness is doing the same thing over and over and expecting a different outcome. We could say that if we engage in habitual behavior, whether it is fear based or socially based, if we do the same thing over and over expecting a different outcome, it simply will not happen. It is up to us to make a different choice and to do it differently.

It is each individual's choice how they will create his life, and the reality created depends on what each of you intends through your thoughts and belief systems. This is each person's opportunity, and while each of you experiences the effects of what is intended through the collective consciousness, you can't change someone else. You can't change the patterns and belief systems of someone else. Each person has the choice to do that himself, and as each person does make positive, Loving choices, each one then affects the entire collective consciousness in how it manifests new ways of being. So choose consciously. Choose Love.

16

HEALING

You have taught us how important our bodies have been to keep us anchored here on Earth, and our spirits and our souls in place to be able to do what we are here to do. We know we must honor that. We must make our bodies realize how important they are, and how we must work together. What can you tell us about Healing?

It is very wonderful to hear that you know to honor your bodies. Humans may support Healing and development of their bodies by listening to what their bodies need. Determine where and when is the best resting place and when and what are the best nourishments by Connecting to body awareness rather than by habits or thoughts of what you should do. Learn to listen to your body and give it what it needs. Extend Healing thoughts to bridge the gap between what is expressing as an imbalance and what is possible as you move towards your future healthy self. This type of listening and intentional thought will prove most helpful to you, for humans tend to worry about their health and about the health of those they care for. It is more helpful to redirect your concern by inviting in Healing energies, making necessary changes, and Trusting the body's ability to Heal itself, rather than focusing your thoughts on what can go wrong. We wish to teach humans these techniques for Healing yourselves. Healing will become easier and simpler if you practice what we are teaching *every* time you reach a place of imbalance. Focusing your thoughts with intent and keeping an attitude of Love and Trust are extremely instrumental in correcting imbalances and moving towards health. Humans may practice this on themselves individually and on each other. All humans have the ability to Heal themselves and to support the Healing of others. Healing is partnership. The person receiving Healing support must do her part by working with her emotions and beliefs so as not to block the energy provided by her partner in Healing. Partnership.

How do we learn to do this?

Through practice and listening. Begin by listening to your body, and then learn to listen to the bodies of others. Have conscious daily interactions with your body, opening up your communication abilities and apologizing for not listening sooner.

Is it part of being in the flow to surrender to sickness when it occurs?

Sickness is a human term. Imbalance is more accurate. You must stop thinking of yourselves as sick. Think instead of imbalance, and Trust that your body knows how to correct it, for bodies do know how to correct *all* imbalances and will do so if given the support and attention they need. In answer to your question, until humans learn to better listen to your bodies, break harmful patterns, and make *immediate* corrections as the body directs, it is part of what you have to endure. Taking care of your bodies is extremely important now. Humans often abuse their bodies, stuffing them with foods and drinks they think are comforting when the body is saying, "I can't handle this" or pushing themselves to work beyond their limits. Your bodies experience too much distress from being forced to process things you believe will bring emotional comfort or being pushed to work like slaves, rather than listening to their requests for rest, fresh air, exercise, nourishment, and of course, adequate clean, pure water. Eating and drinking only substances that are helpful is important. Lighter foods that are easier to digest and foods that have more nutrition for you such as fruits and vegetables are good to consume. Let go of the belief that certain foods will emotionally comfort you, and listen to what your body *truly* wants and needs instead, rather than what your habits lead you towards.

Humans must deal with what you have called into manifestation as reality from your past thought forms and the physical neglect and abuse of the body. Humans allow the mind to decide what is necessary and how far the body can be pushed, as if the body were a slave to the mind. Because humans have been accumulating thought forms such as," I'm too fat," or "I don't like my body," those selfish, disrespectful, harmful, and abusive thought forms stack up in time, for your body listens to all your thoughts and manifests what you think. You must be especially careful with your thoughts about the body now, for what you think manifests more quickly than ever. If you *think* that you don't want to be here because of emotional or physical challenges, the body will oblige you through one dis-ease or another. Your body's functionality is impacted by the messages you send through your thoughts. You must ache to be fully here in healthy form, thanking your body for providing a way for you to move through life. That is your job, to work in partnership with your wonderful body so that you can create the higher vibration of health that helps your body move closer to your etheric form and ascension. Contradictory negative messages cause physical discomfort, imbalance, and disharmony, which in turn, inevitably lead to the consensual reality of disease, and often ultimately death.

The level of ignorance in humans about communication with the body restricts some of your Healing possibilities. We are telling you that the more you communicate with the water of your own cells through kindness and Love, the more your body helps you gain wisdom and knowledge to Heal yourself from all imbalances. When you communicate good thoughts to your body in partnership, Healing and maintenance of health become easier, as does the possibility for regeneration, which reverses situations of imbalance. Even though "time" may have caught up with what you manifest from previous thoughts, you should know that you can simply wipe away imbalances and accumulated patterns once you fully understand and begin in every moment to use the power you carry within you. Remember that time does not exist. So you may remove patterns from the past by traveling backwards and correcting them. Healing *can* occur in an instant. That is *possible*, yet not many humans have achieved the level of understanding to do it. The man you call Jesus and the man called Sai Babba understand how to manifest health by moving old patterns through time, manifesting a different reality in the present. To be able to do this, you must be consistent in monitoring your thoughts so that you can access your own power to Heal through the power of Love, and you must be consistent in supplying what your body needs each moment. Constant dedicated appreciation, respect, Love, and harmony with your body will allow you to more quickly reach the place of instant Healing. Combine what we have taught you about intention, Trust, "time," and Love.

Stop believing in patterns that have been set in the past. These patterns and old paradigms hold humans back through outdated understandings. Current medical science continues to lead humans away from the knowledge that you can Heal yourselves with your body's wisdom, knowing that your body is in charge. Humans often Trust that someone else can make them feel better, rather than taking the initiative themselves. Humans must learn to Trust that they have the power within them to make themselves feel better. Medical schools teach potential doctors that they are in charge. They are not, and they never really were. Good doctors support the Healing process with tools they have available and then stand back and watch the body perform the miracle of Healing. You must understand, correct your "bad training," and take responsibility to Heal yourselves. It is up to you to break the patterns. It is not so difficult. It simply requires constant, consistent attention and intention. If you do not regain balance as quickly as you desire, you may employ *temporary* outside support from someone who understands how to support your system. Practice Trust in yourselves, but do not be stubborn if you need assistance. Learn to feel confident and competent that you have it within your power to co-create your own health. Talk to your body; call upon the power of Love and the power of Grace to affect the necessary changes. When you go to sleep, comfort and Love your body. Tell your body you are sorry for what it has experienced because you were unaware and that you intended no harm. Communicate through touch, thought, and verbalizations that you do not wish for your body to die. Apologize for the misunderstandings where you have given harmful directions through your incorrect thoughts or beliefs. Offer Love, friendship, comfort, and promise of dwelling together in health and harmony. Make a promise for a future relationship of better communication. Once you have done this, instruct your body to do its part to re-regulate the imbalances within your system. Address each cell's own intelligence, asking all cells to join together for united change. They know how to do this, but through their fear and desolation at having been ignored, dismissed, and abused, they have forgotten how to communicate with each other. With your firm and Loving direction from the power of your own water, you may once again achieve harmony more quickly for a very long-lasting and more thorough relationship.

Avoid being fearful about your health (or anything else), for when you are fearful, your vibration is lowered and your thought forms invite possibilities for more severe imbalances. Without fear, your immune systems are stronger. A higher vibration results from good emotional attitudes where fear is absent. A higher vibration stimulates your immune system, giving you natural prophylactic properties when you come in contact with others who are imbalanced. A higher vibration also helps you to rebalance more easily. When you do not allow fear to enter your thoughts, and you Trust in your bodies' Healing abilities, knowing that health is always possible, you may be able to overcome whatever health challenges come your way. If you feel slightly out of balance, you may consider that your body needs to cleanse or slow down rather than thinking thoughts of illness. Imbalances have permission and support to evaporate more quickly with this kind of Love and Trust for your body. Humans also need to let go of what they believe about their bodies' capabilities. Your bodies may move in ways that you think are impossible. Many of your bodies have been feeling quite restricted for a very long time; they *know* what is possible, even though they may have forgotten. This is one reason why being in water is good for humans. When you find ways of moving your own body's water as if you are floating upon the ocean, your body's Healing abilities are enhanced. Movement frees your physical body to engage more with the etheric, which we will explain in more detail later.

What about specific imbalances that get pathological labels such as Heart Disease, Cancer, Diabetes, or Chronic Fatigue Syndrome?

Let us start with speaking about stress. Cultures around this planet have finally understood the principle that all imbalances, which are called dis-ease comes from stress. This is an important concept, and while humans believe there are biological factors or genetic predispositions for certain dis-eases, they also understand that stress is what opens the possibilities for those biological markers or genetic predispositions to occur. You need a deeper understanding about dis-ease. Listening to what others tell you or what your frightened self tells you also contributes to imbalances that the collective consciousness calls disease. The Truth that listening to what has been thought or spoken causes the deterioration of the human body is an undiscovered medical concept. What you know as strokes and heart attacks come from places where the flow is blocked, not from the hardening of arteries as you have been taught (although this *is* a physiological manifestation); they come from a rigidity and a hardening of *belief systems*, when humans can take in no more of what has been spoken that does not resonate with who they are. Heart pains are often experienced as a direct result of listening to what people you Love say about you that does not resonate with the Truth of who you are as a divine being. Stomach pains often come from being "unable to stomach" what you heard spoken that is not Truth. Each human being moves into the possibility or the probability of imbalance until you gain the ability to dismiss what you have listened to about who you are from those who speak judgments about who you are. Those who have been diagnosed with cancer or tumors have developed congested places where the energy does not flow; there is no longer resonance with the divinity of who the person is and with what they have been spoken into through listening and hearing others define who they are. Blockages in the energetic system are often blockages to prevent hearing unkind or judgmental words. These blockages create the beginning of the breakdown of continuing flow towards Source. Energetic blockages then turn into physical blockages. What normally flows energetically is stopped by taking in and manifesting the energy of what is spoken through harmful emotions, harmful thought forms, judgments, fears, and unloving words, all of these things congeal in the system to form a tumor, a growth, a blockage, a congestion, an aberration of what is a normal human flow towards divinity. Does this make sense to you?

Yes it does.

Diabetes, reproductive disorders, lung and other organ imbalances all initially come from the same cause. All of these stressful imbalances begin through listening to and manifesting energies of something that does not resonate with the Truth of who a person is. Once the human being can no longer take in the energetic imprint and the impact of what is being spoken into his system, the imbalance begins. This can just as easily come from internal thoughts and actions; it does not have to come from outside the self. The individual breaks the flow from her own divinity to Source through fears that arise from listening to unkind words and judgments about who she is or repeating those judgments to herself. He begins to doubt who he is rather than knowing the Truth that he is divine. Dis-ease is disconnection from Source and disconnection from divinity. Chronic Fatigue is somewhat different. It begins in the same way through the stress of listening to others viewpoints about the self. However, it is also related to past/parallel life trauma. Persons who are susceptible to Chronic Fatigue Syndrome in this lifetime generally have become chronically fatigued from the trauma they have carried in their body consciousness in other lifetimes. They become caught in patterns of emotional paralysis; unable to make the changes they wish in their lives. It is the emotional paralysis that keeps this particular imbalance in place.

What can you tell us about emotional trauma?

Emotional trauma is a form of disconnection. It is separation and disconnection from Unity. We have explained to you that judgment causes separation. Emotional trauma occurs when one human moves from Loving thoughts and begins judging another, insisting that the other is "wrong." Emotional trauma occurs when realities do not match. Such trauma causes humans to contract within themselves in order to hold on to what they know is True. Emotional trauma causes humans to forget who they are and how they have been separated from Unity. Expansion occurs as a form of Healing when humans move back into Connection with all aspects of themselves. They remember that they are *not* who they have been defined by others. In reconnecting to the Truth of their divinity, they come to understand that they are not what happened to them or what someone said about them. Healing occurs as they expand their understanding of who they are by remembering their divinity. Extreme contraction from trauma can have an equal and opposite reaction of extreme expansion in Healing, opening greater channels for communication with other beings, including the devic kingdom, the angelic kingdom, and interplanetary beings, all of whom are divine and waiting to be of service to all who are willing to listen. Releases of anger and stored emotion, if done with the intent to clear one's shadow, may open avenues for better communication within the individual or between others, as the person moves away from contraction and towards expansion of the divine. All humans experience varying levels of emotional trauma as part of their separation from their own divinity and from each other. The intensity of contraction into trauma and the individual's willingness to move beyond the effects of trauma direct how and when possibilities for Healing expansion may occur. If traumas accumulate one on top of another, they usually unwind one on top of another. If there is an extreme, intense initial onset of trauma, the contraction of separation will usually also be extreme, and the possibility for re-opening to divinity may occur through sudden extreme expansion. These extremes may explain why so many who have experienced intense trauma also experience intense openings of knowing. You understand from physical conditions that when a human cuts his finger or stubs her toe, the body allows slow healing. When a human experiences a physical trauma that severs an organ or threatens life, there must be an immediate and opposite reaction in order to save the life. In the same way, Healing from trauma may occur slowly as humans slowly expand out of their separation, or Healing and understanding may come in a sudden expansion of knowing. Either way, expansion leads towards Connection to the divine, to Unity, and away from contraction and separation.

We have talked about bad training; we have talked about the power of words and emotion; we have talked about listening. We wish to put these concepts in a context of Healing for you. One of Rebecca's favorite sayings is that humans listen each other into being. Humans listen to what they are told. The little ones come in with knowledge and wisdom about who they are, and are reshaped by listening to those who tell them they are something else; their caretakers give them information that is not always accurate or appropriate, thereby reshaping them into who they are becoming. It is the listening that causes humans to rigidify beliefs and build structures around who they are. As humans try to fit in with society, these structures contribute to the building of consensual reality. When words and thoughts are coupled with extreme emotion, they have more impact. So when the young ones hear a parent say, "No!" with a loud tone, they understand that what they did was not acceptable. If the parent or caretaker says, "How can you..." or "You are so..." those words shape the little one's understanding of who she is. When judgments are coupled with harsh tones, rigidity in structure occurs, breaking down the flow of that human's way of being in the world according to her own divine guidance. Judgments build patterns of behavior around humans as structures for protection, molding them into whom they think they need to be. The young ones grow up and carry the structures and patterns that have formed through their experiences into other relationships as they become older, listening even more to what is spoken about who they are. *You do in fact listen each other into being.* When one being listens to another say, "You are ugly; you are incapable; you are wrong" or "You are beautiful, you are smart, you are kind," either more protective structures are put in place or more openness for Connection occurs. The human is indeed spoken into becoming who he is. This happens over and over again from generation to generation.

It seems to me that rather than listening into being, it sounds as if we are spoken into being. It makes more sense to say it the other way around, that we are spoken into being because the little ones listen to what is being said to them. It's possibly an equal-equal creative force. We are listened into being as we are spoken into being or the opposite; we are spoken into being as we are listened into being.

Ahh... well said. This is accurate. This is a good understanding. And one of your books of religious stories says, "God spoke. And the world was created. But first there was *the word*." The understanding is missing that it is not just the spoken word that causes the structures to be formed; thought precedes speech, and the emotion and tone used with words contribute to what is created. We are teaching humans that speaking and listening are creative forces, for humans take in more than what they hear through words; they take in the tonal quality, the emotional fuel behind the words that are spoken, and the thoughts from which the words arose. The words that are spoken, the tones used with the words, the emotions fueling the words, and the thoughts Connected to the emotions do speak you into being.

It is important to understand it from both points of view, because it is the speakers who are causing the change. It comes from the outside because the little ones are eager to absorb the information. The little ones do not ask to be formed in a negative framework. They do not ask to be formed in a rigid structure. So it is important to know or understand that the formation of the listening comes from and through the speaking.

Yes, that is correct. Speaking another into being, or being listened into being also occurs when humans begin relationships. In a new relationship, whether it is a new job, a new friendship, or a new Loving partnership, each human being moves into a place of newness, openness, hope, and Trust as they did coming into the world as infants. This is particularly true when humans enter into Love relationships. The openness and the Trust signify a searching to be "seen" as divine. Humans search for the mirroring effect of "I am another yourself. I see your divinity and your light." When humans "fall in Love," they often experience shared views of each other's divinity in brief glimpses before their expectations, fears, and judgments cause unkind words to speak your special other into forms that are less than what you first saw. The one you Love becomes what you see and what you say if they are listening to you. It is a new concept for humans to understand that you speak each other into form, for you do not yet understand the power of your thoughts, your words, and your emotions and how they work together. You speak each other into being through speaking your expectations, your judgments, your dreams, your visions, your hopes, your fears, your wants and desires. Each human does this, although those who are most fearful speak most judgmentally. And when what is heard is judgmental to the ones who are listening, they experience the same repetitive shock as when they arrived in this world full of Trust and hope and innocence. The effect is a shocking thought of "Uh-oh. I thought I was ok. I thought I was divine. I thought I was Loved and accepted, and I see and I hear that I am not." And then once again old patterns of structure move back into their familiar place, armoring the human even more. It is no wonder humans have such difficulty in relationships, for they find it very challenging to remain in acceptance and Love. They separate themselves from the Unity and Connection they want through their beliefs, their expectations, and primarily their judgments, causing the formation of shallow relationships where they hide who they really are. You must be careful with your words. They are powerful. Understand that you speak yourselves into form; you listen one another into being. If you truly understand this, then you know why it is so important to use only kind and compassionate words towards *any* other human, and especially to those who are vulnerable and open because they Trust you. The power you have for manifestation is not only held in your intentions and thoughts, but also in your words, tones, and emotions. Each of you truly has the power to harm or Heal, and it is time you take responsibility for what you do. Choose wisely. Once again, we want you to understand how these patterns happen over and over again from generation to generation. The pain created through judgment will occur repeatedly. Now as you begin to realize and gain new understanding of how you have been shaped and have participated in shaping others through your words, you may experience waves of grief. Accepting your responsibility to break this harmful pattern is one of the most important parts of your shadow work. Know that whether you are Healing emotional or physical imbalances, once a pattern of imbalance has begun and been reinforced, because of its persistence it is much more challenging to break it in order to move back into the flow of Health. Humans always gravitate towards what is familiar. Best not to start such negative patterns at all. It will be wonderful when humans learn to stay in the realm of the young ones and the innocents of Trust and Love and acceptance and joy, rather than being motivated by and reacting to fear. The challenge for health is to step away from the negative impact of emotions and understand that emotions are merely sign posts, signals to direct you to another thought form. Change is necessary to clear imbalances. Change is necessary to Heal, and Healing is necessary to life, especially if you wish to evolve into the new human.

Can you tell us specifically how Healing practitioners may take these concepts into their work?

Pay attention to the power of listening and speaking in your Healing work. Learn to deeply listen through your fingers, your touch, your heart, your ears, and your eyes, all of your senses, beginning, of course, with your First Sense. Listen to all of your senses, even your smell and your taste. When working with others, you may sense how a client tastes life. You may also learn to actually *see* into the body as Rebecca and other medical intuitives are beginning to do at this time. All of your senses may be employed in speaking another person out of an imbalance and into Healing. Your First Sense opens all the other senses and tells you how to interpret what you receive. So when you are speaking another into being, when you are helping them to co-create who they are, understand that the tone of your words, the emotion, the intention, the kindness, and the actual words that you choose to give to them while they are in an open space will affect their ability to co-create an alignment with their own divinity, so that they may be whole and healthy human beings. A few healers are practicing this understanding at this time with great success. It can and will revolutionize Healing for humanity.

Many of us are experiencing body pain, headaches, and sleeplessness that do not seem to be imbalances within our own systems. Are we experiencing adjustments to world and universal changes, and if so, how do we approach these imbalances for Healing?

Yes. When that occurs you must move through it with patience and Grace. The human energetic system responds to waves of change as the earth begins to make changes and as the collective consciousness of humanity begins to experience more fear around changes that they do not understand. There are also universal influences that are affecting you by adding additional amounts of light and energy into your systems. You are being opened and "re-wired" through these gifts of change. All humans at this time are experiencing energetic differences in their way of being on Earth, and it does affect their physical bodies. Specifically the energetic magnetics of your physical systems are affected by the realignment of Earth's ley lines of energy, and you feel pre-cursors in your bodies of changes that are either occurring now or are to come. The changes you feel are developmental. There is nothing wrong. It is simply a way of disassembling patterns that are no longer functional for humanity and allowing in more light and understanding. Those of you who are sensitive feel the imbalances more quickly; it feels disruptive to your normal way of being. It is extremely important that you allocate times for rest during this transitional period while you are integrating your own water with the higher vibrations provided by the universe.

Many of you who are sensitive feel as though you are ill or your sleep is disrupted because it is out of a familiar pattern. However, it is not a bad thing. As some of our colleagues say, it is not pathological; it is developmental. It is time that your bodies begin to wake up, but as you begin to pay attention and listen to what they say and what they need, they express many fears about the changes that are occurring. They feel different energies arriving that they do not understand. Additionally, humans who wish to grow and have asked to help promote these beneficial changes for humanity are receiving specific energies from the universe to adjust the way that you are in the world. Most humans are fragmented by the parts of their lives that have been compartmentalized. Fragmentation prevents Connecting to divinity and Healing into wholeness, holiness, and Unity. Fragmentation is a stopping point for human development. All the fragments of your shadow are surfacing now so that you may completely Heal yourselves. The universe is opening and offering different understandings to those who are listening and are willing and wishing to grow, who are tired of the pain and want to move towards something better; the universe is saying at this special time, "Yes, we are listening. We will help." And there are many, many helpers around to do this. So there is an influx of energy that you may sense in an intuitive way as resonant understanding, or in a physical sense as an unfamiliar pattern that feels uncomfortable. If you move into it with acceptance, even though it may not be comfortable, the pain or disorientation of it goes away. Listening is important. Listening involves listening to your own shadow. What needs to be cleared out? What needs to be cleaned up? Where are you afraid? What patterns need to be broken? Where do you need to fill the places of fear with Love? This is cleaning out your shadow, and it is necessary in order for your etheric and your physical to Connect with each other, as we will explain later, to create more health. We refer to physical health and healthy emotional states. The physical body does not know what to do with the unfamiliar energies it is receiving, so the body responds with pain receptors, for pain is the signal that something is different. Although it may be uncomfortable, do your best to adjust, recognizing that you are receiving energies that not only will open you and help you grow into being who you truly are, but will also help you resonate with the birth of the emerging new planet.

The headaches many of you feel like a band of pressure around the forehead are connected to the magnetic shifts of the planet. They are partial readjustments in what we have defined as the Five Pack of the brain, basically the system that regulates your emotions, your sleep patterns, and your hormonal systems; all of these things are deeply affected by both the energies that are coming into your brain and the energies of how you are aligned with planetary changes. And so you feel the magnetics in your own brain shifting. You are part of the earth, so yes, you are experiencing birth pains both within yourself and in resonance with the earth. The more sensitive you are, the more you feel these new and disorienting energies. Recognize that the body is accepting many new changes and adjusting to extra energetic surges. Be compassionate with your body. Allow deep listening to what your body needs. Think of what you are experiencing as developmental changes that require rest and integration as your body rebalances. Listen to your own water. Somewhere within the deep connective portions of all humans, there is an awareness that you have the ability to sense energy through your hands and to use it to help Heal yourselves and others. As you become more flexible through dropping away beliefs and old patterns, you *do* become more like water. The more you are waves and stop being particles stuck in rigid belief systems and patterns, the more others will look at you and see something different, and then you may teach through your energy, whether you open your mouth or not. You demonstrate that your highest desires are for Love, light, Trust, joy, communication, service, Connection, and good company. This is the path for Healing.

17

THE ETHERIC AND THE PHYSICAL

We wish to share more about your human form, which is comprised of a physical body, and an etheric body, with your mental thought forms making a bridge between the two. The etheric body is a body of light of higher vibration that moves omnipresently around the universe. The etheric body vibrates at a higher rate because it carries more light. The etheric body holds the blueprint of perfection for the physical body and directs the creation of the physical body. It is also sometimes called the light body because it is lighter in formation than the physical body. The etheric body has the ability to travel between veils instantly. Your etheric body does not experience the same constraints of space limitations that your physical body does or the constraints of your artificial time. The etheric body is light and free. At the same time, it can be affected by outside forces, which we will discuss in a few moments.

We will tell you how your physical bodies are created. The physical body is created from the blueprint of the etheric, yet the physical body does not maintain the perfection of the etheric form because it is constantly shaped and directed by the thoughts you think and the actions you take or do not take to care for your physical form. Thoughts travel to your etheric and then manifest into your physical. You may have a deeper understanding of this through letting it settle within your consciousness. We and other Pleiadians have been actively opening receptors of many humans to higher levels of understanding. Your job at this time is to concentrate on your thoughts, moving away from what you hold as solid belief. When you do this, you are in full partnership with us for your expansion. We help. You help. There are others, friends, who have also been in assistance of opening your brains to be able to receive communication in a more positive, beneficial way. These others have visited, and you have felt the effects afterwards yet puzzled over what it was. They are friends assisting in "rewiring" and what we call opening your circuits to remember. For now, understand that your thought forms, which are neither physical nor etheric but exist in the mental plane, travel between the two affecting their relationship.

While the etheric body maintains a blueprint of perfection for physical form, it *is* impacted by the thoughts you think, as is the body consciousness. We have repeatedly explained that humans do not understand the power of the thoughts they think. When you think a thought, you contact the mental field and send energy into the etheric. The etheric body is affected by those thought forms, and it reflects the way it is affected instantly into the physical body, thereby directing the physical body to respond according to how the etheric body has been affected. This is quite Connected to the understanding that your thought forms go into your body consciousness to affect the health of your body. Both the etheric and the body consciousness receive impact from the thoughts you think. The thoughts you think powerfully penetrate the etheric, and the etheric then manifests the reality of your physical form according to those thoughts. All humans need to better master awareness of what they think, for thoughts act as a bridge between the etheric and the physical. We expand on what we have explained about humans listening and speaking each other into being by saying that in effect, you design your physical body through the thoughts you send to your body consciousness and to your etheric body. The pathway for the thoughts that reach your body consciousness *is* your etheric. Thoughts travel into the etheric, where it is either supported or damaged by the impact, and then the healthy, supported etheric or the damaged etheric projects its reflection upon the physical. Our explanation becomes complex for human understanding here, but in reality it is simple. Because the etheric exists outside of time and human space, it can be affected by harmful thoughts and hold the perfect blueprint *at the same time*. You might say the etheric *remembers* perfection but projects in the present moment what it receives from the impact of your thoughts upon the physical body. The etheric is quite capable of simultaneously doing both. It may correct the impact of harmful thoughts upon its own etheric form returning it to its blueprint of perfection, yet it simultaneously takes the directions from the thoughts and projects them into physical form. The link between the two is the mental body, which we have previously defined as mental constructs or thought forms. Part of what we wish humans to understand at this time is how to more closely align and integrate their etheric and physical bodies through the thoughts they think. Fill your physical bodies with light, which you do by Loving yourselves and others, creating positive thoughts with everything you do, and changing negative thought forms that are constantly being emanated by the collective consciousness *through* your Love and positive thoughts. The etheric body and physical body in humans are not as well integrated as they are for us, partially because we do not participate in thought processes; we communicate through our hearts and our First Sense. Our understandings are shared, not individual, and therefore our Pleiadian forms reflect an integration between etheric and physical that is obviously lighter and of higher vibration. You might say, our physical manifestation *is* etheric. We are wave forms. We communicate through waves of heart energy and tones rather than "human" thoughts.

Humanity is engaged in a process of acceleration where the etheric bodies and the physical bodies are being more closely aligned. This is why the physical forms of so many of you so often feel sluggish, tired, or sick. You are not sick; you are changing. Humans are in a process where your etheric and physical energies are meeting, a form of melding. This energetic melding is quite similar to what occurs when we meld our energy to yours to communicate, only our communications bring the vibration and energy of joy. Humans are generally unaware of the etheric body or how thought forms affect the etheric before traveling to the physical. Because of the process of acceleration in which you are now engaged, it is more necessary than ever for you to understand how your etheric and physical are connected so that you may assist the process through the thoughts you think. Humans need to raise their physical vibration in order to meet more closely with their etheric forms. This is part of the process of ascension, which we will discuss later. Those humans who apply consciousness towards their bodies and fill them with light and Love are more closely aligning with their etheric and divine selves. This alignment is almost impossible for some, for they cannot comprehend the importance of what needs to be done. Use your creativity to imagine your etheric body. Your scientist Einstein said, "Imagination is more powerful even than knowledge." Humans would have an easier time with the coming changes and with the process of merging their etheric and physical bodies if they would learn to utilize their imaginations for things they cannot quite grasp in mental understanding. We do not understand why human adults crush the possibility of imagination in your young ones, dismissing it as fantasy or unreal. It is one of the most puzzling aspects of human behavior. Why would adults who often are unhappy or dissatisfied in their *own* lives, crush the imagination of a young one? Imagination creates beauty, harmony, health, and wholeness, bringing artificial separations closer to Unity. We know humans do not understand how thoughts affect their etheric bodies; perhaps these adults do not understand how thought impacts the physical brain either. Children learn, grow, understand, and gain wisdom through exploration, curiosity, and newness. They are constantly laying down new neural pathways within the physical brain system that link to pathways existing in the etheric brain system. This linking brings them knowledge of Truth from places beyond the current physical reality. If humans wish to continue to grow and understand your potential, you must utilize your imagination.

Workshops and trainings inspired by interdimensional friends are beginning to surface in alternative fields of deeper understandings that will broaden human belief systems as you expose yourself to those understandings. Some of the trainings actually have practices that enhance energy movement. As energy moves through the human system, the energy field may be manipulated positively in order to open you. As the energy opens, understanding comes. The more you work with *energy* and enhanced awareness of energy, moving away from *time*, the more you will open the pathways for your DNA wisdom to emerge. Play with it. Seek it out. Explore between yourselves and explore among others. Humans may attend workshops that interest them and play with what they discover about energy, or simply practice what you discover that enhances your awareness on your own. There is no preference for you to be individualistic in discovering your own method or in following a method one of your brothers or sisters has already discovered. The thing that is important is that you explore. Explore energy in ways you have not even thought of. Move beliefs out of the way. Move time out of the way. Focus on energy, intent, and intentional thinking, for these are keys for opening the wisdom contained within your DNA. As you explore new ideas and understandings about energy, remember that you do not have to direct the energy or follow specific sequences that may be presented through training for human understanding. Intelligence is always present in *all* energy. When applied with Healing intention, the energy *always* knows where to go. It *knows* where it is most needed and automatically travels there. As you explore and learn about your energy, focus on feeling etheric sensations, which are wondrous. You may notice pleasant physical sensations as well as learn to match and meld your physical body with your etheric body. The two of you already experience the touch and the embrace of our etheric energy on your physical forms. Other humans may learn to sense the presence of amazing energy as they meld their etheric and physical forms.

If the etheric is the perfect form which can help and Heal our physical form, what affects the etheric, or can it be affected?

Remember that the etheric form is the blueprint for perfection for the human body, yet the etheric carries an energy of its own. The etheric is the first to receive the impact of mental thought form (individual or from collective consciousness) and astral energy (either from the universe or from collective consciousness.) The etheric is quite able to adjust and rebalance itself and return to perfection quite quickly. However, what it receives is passed on to create the physical, and so may create an imperfect physical form before correcting itself. The physical form does not have the ability to return to perfection as quickly and easily; it does not have the knowledge; it is too dense and does not know how to do that without etheric Connection. The etheric helps the physical to remember what it is supposed to be. Yet because the etheric receives the mental thought forms, astral, and emotional waves, the etheric can get slightly warped or bent, and need an adjustment itself. It still remains the blueprint for perfection, yet in an instant of thought it passes on to the physical what it receives from that thought. If you wish to assist your etheric to maintain its perfect blueprint and pass that blueprint of perfection onto the physical, pay attention to your thoughts and the emotions that power your thoughts. What else do you wish to know about raising your vibrations?

How do we increase our vibrational frequency?

The first thing for increasing your vibrational frequency is to reach deeply into the recesses of the places you do not like yourselves and begin to Love them. Go into the places where you are fearful that you are not good enough, and forgive yourself for the mistakes where you have judged yourselves too harshly. Start there to raise your vibration. Start with Loving yourselves. You cannot truly Love yourself if you are not willing to reach deeply into the corners, pull out your shadow, and dance with it. Hold it in your arms and Love it until it no longer feels scary or frightening. Love it until the light fills the shadow so that you are unified and one, until you are whole with all those pieces of yourself that you do not like.

Once you have done that, the second step towards raising your vibration is learning not to judge others. Look at those who are not like you and if they hurt you or if they say something that is wrong, you may use your power to correct the situation, but you do not need to judge them. Instead you may simply say, "Wow, that person must really be scared, frightened, or unhappy to have such judgmental thoughts and words come out of them." Just send them Love. So you stop judging and blaming yourself; Love yourself and then you begin Loving everyone else. We like the understanding taught by Christ, by the Maya, and by the Buddha; it comes in many flavors and forms. Christ said, "Love your neighbor as yourself." The Maya said, "I am another yourself." All of the wise ones who understand Unity rather than separation and fear have promoted that you not judge one another, but offer your compassion instead. Remember, *"you cannot be in reaction and compassion at the same time."* So when someone is mean or hurtful to you, offer compassion rather than judgment. And so you raise your own vibration.

The third thing we would offer for raising your vibration is to laugh. Find joy in your life as much as you can. Find little things that delight you. Joy is one of the higher vibrations, and if you do not have joy in your life or do not have things that tickle you or make you smile, then your vibration could use a little amping up. So seek out those with whom you find yourself laughing, those who you feel joy when you are in their presence. If it is not another person, it may be a puppy, or it may be a walk in Nature, watching a butterfly or a hummingbird on a flower. Find something that makes you feel joy. This will help you raise your vibration. We hope these suggestions are helpful. Also anytime you move towards purity, whether it is in the food you take, the air you breathe, the water you drink, or the thoughts you think, you are helping your physical body to evolve. You are raising your vibration to meet that of your etheric body so that they may ascend together and help create the new humanity.

Many of you are experiencing greater and greater etheric sensitivities. You become more and more sensitive to the energies of collective human consciousness and to the energies of the planet Herself. Be aware that your increased sensitivity results from the shadow work you have accomplished, the improvement in your listening abilities, how you speak things into manifestation through the use of intent. You are intending to grow and to meld your physical and etheric bodies more closely to match the vibration of the earth as She changes. When you feel agitated, your sleep is disrupted, or your sense of well being is affected from the energetic changes that are occurring, focus on sending light wherever it is most needed; send calm energy and peace. You do not need to direct light to a specific place; just direct it to go where it is most needed. When you do this you will find you also benefit from calm and peace as well, and you will increase your own light. Humans make leaps and strides when you raise your vibration and when you use your intent to create a positive reality.

Apparently humans struggle somewhat with vibrational changes living in our three dimensional reality and because our vibration is not high enough, we cannot yet fully visit other dimensions. If I am correct, at humanity's normal dimensional vibratory rate, we are not yet able to meet or greet beings from other realms usually because we cannot yet sustain the higher vibrations. Would moving too quickly to a higher vibration for a sustained period harm humans?

This is a partial understanding. At this time humans differ in their levels of ability to Connect their physical and etheric bodies. Those who are more attached to their physical without understanding of the etheric, which is most, are more challenged with the concepts of melding the two in order to participate in other dimensional understandings. Moving back and forth in vibration stresses the physical body because the elements that comprise the physical body develop slowly. Remember, human etheric bodies form the blueprint for the physical body and show the physical body what is *possible*. Yet that does not mean that the physical body, which carries all of the impact of years of incorrect instructions for manifestation, *can* instantly match the perfect blueprint. While it is *possible* for the physical to instantly copy the etheric blueprint and manifest perfect health and abilities to visit other dimensions, it is challenging for most humans to maintain constant attention to all of the elements necessary for manifesting perfection in the present moment. Most of you must approach what we are teaching through your linear understanding, step by step, practice by practice. We restate the Truth that Healing and perfection can occur in an instant in the present moment, yet the challenge for humans remains in the belief systems and misunderstandings about your illusionary concepts of past, present, and future. We wish humans *not* to lose Trust in possibilities when they attempt what we teach, for it takes practice and constant attention to every thought in the present moment for what we teach to occur.

Human bodies view differences and changes as a preliminary for death, for this is what each body consciousness remembers. The concept of ascending *with* the body is new, and each human body must learn through repetition of receiving these new energies that death is not going to occur because different or unusual energies are present. Yes, it is taxing for the human body to continually sustain a higher vibration. Many humans feel the stress as their vibrations shift and do not understand why they experience feeling tired, seasick, or out of balance, or conversely, heightened experiences of joy and Love. Because of our melding with the two of you, we are more able to sense the ability and limitations of human physical bodies. It is continued resonance with these levels after a higher vibratory experience that is confusing for the human body. Yet the distress is educational; it is not harmful. You may feel temperature fluctuations that are related to the increased energy from the etheric waves that you are experiencing. The physical body must learn how to handle the excess energy and light. The integration period requires resting. Listen to your body's needs while recognizing compassionately that the body is accepting many new changes. Receiving excess etheric energy, light, and Connection is certainly an advantageous thing. You will accommodate the changes. In etheric-physical melding, the body adjusts to the extra energetic surges that cause temperature fluctuations. It is good for humans not to do mentally draining or physically exhausting types of activities after experiences of heightened vibration. It is also good to allow time to integrate the sensations you have experienced into your bodies as you prepare to rejoin conventional reality.

Humans need to understand that honoring their physical bodies and listening to their needs will help you gain the body's Trust. Remember that most human bodies have been abused and ignored lifetime after lifetime, including this one. Eat when you are hungry, and eat what your body needs. Rest when you are tired. Walk when you need movement. Swim when you are able. Laugh at every opportunity. Take deep breaths. Enjoy physical sensations of touch. All of these things let the body know that it is safe, Loved, cared for, and supported in the growth and the evolution of becoming something different. With that Trust, fears drop away. Death, as we have already said, is not necessary for ascension. Each human body must adjust to the understanding that death does not have to occur and search into the body's deep memory from long, long ago that Lemurian regeneration is indeed possible. The Lemurians have understood and taught this for a long time. Through listening to and caring for your body, you help it understand that melding of the physical and etheric for regeneration is possible. Rest and allow. Allow yourself awareness of your full expansive abilities when these changes occur. Allow the spaciousness, the disorientation, occasional headaches, temperature fluctuations, and seasickness that cause you to feel out of balance, to come into awareness with acceptance. They will eventually balance themselves as your physical and etheric grow closer and higher vibrations are sustained. As human bodies learn to adjust to higher vibrations, they may also experience sensations that you may perceive as tingly, fiery, or wavy. These sensations come from melding the etheric and the physical and can be puzzling because they are new to how the human body normally understands itself. Simply allow them. Three simple things are all that are required during a period of integration: rest, nourishment, and the most important, watching your thoughts and what you believe about what is occurring. If you focus on believing you are ill, your thoughts support the possibility for more serious imbalances. If you think of what you experience as needing rest and reintegration while developmental changes occur, you promote rebalancing and Healing. The physical body is slower than the etheric to respond to energetic changes; it will take its cue from the thoughts you generate about what is occurring. As humans meld their etheric and physical forms more and more together, more light emanates from you. These light dynamics have Healing benefits of regeneration. They can assist in erasing human disrepair and filling humans with wholeness through Connecting to the etheric body and the etheric world. Any time humans move closer to their etheric bodies, there is more light and there is more natural, automatic nurturance of the physical body; hard, rigid places of structure and resistance soften, and you move towards the plumpness of childhood. All the cells within the body become fuller because they are nourished.

Is there anything else we need to understand about how etheric or other dimensional energies penetrate and affect things in this dimension?

Humanity's idea of what is stable is beginning to change and shift as you understand more about density and levels of vibration, and most importantly, wave motion. Reality in the third dimension is only an outward projection of the etheric. Without the etheric blueprint, it would crumble and not exist. Thought forms and intent make reality; therefore, understand that etheric forms create your reality in physical form. The level of the third dimensional reality dissolves as the etheric becomes melded to the physical in large and small moments, and aware humans begin to have increased experiences that are out of their usual understanding. There is a Connection to etheric-physical melding and the collapse of time as duality ceases to exist, and you move towards Unity. You will see gaps in time, where something doesn't quite fit, gaps in day and night, and gaps in understanding about weather conditions and seasonal changes. There are all kinds of gaps that don't fit into the constructs of your former belief systems. Third dimensional reality *is* falling away, and those humans who are working to meld their etheric and physical selves will see that escalate more and more. Others will simply be puzzled. Some of this has to do with the ending of time and the ending of duality. Some of it has to do with elevating your vibration as you ask for and continually receive assistance from us and other beings somewhat like us who help you in raising your vibration and melding your etheric to your physical forms. As the etheric impresses its reality onto the physical reality, things merge in waves that are unpredictable, surprising, magical, and instructive. Focus on the wonder and the magic and just ride with it, flowing with the synchronicity and the wonder, as if you were riding on the back of a dragon from long ago, taking you between the veils and showing you what is possible and real.

Rebecca and I have both been looking at each other and saying we are feeling expectant that things will be happening to us, things that are unusual, magical, and unknown to us. I believe what you just said is that we are aware on some level that these changes are beginning, and we are now realizing them consciously, with an increasing awareness of how we are being affected, as well as how others and the entire planet are being affected.

Yes. You are. Isn't it wonderful? Full of wonder. Full of magic. When humans take the trouble and spend the time to work with their own water and allow and encourage the body to move spontaneously when it hurts or becomes rigid, you may approximate the experience of moving in the etheric. Be fluid. Flow in your thoughts and in your body. Wave motion of your own body's water is not so different from wave motion in the etheric. Understanding wave motion in your bodies helps humans know what it feels like to move between the realms; it is the etheric body that transfers the experience to the physical. This is why Rebecca teaches wave motion to her clients. Most humans have resistance to this form of freedom, for they are afraid of moving without the structure that they believe is solid reality. The more you let go of the resistance you have to what you believe your physical body is capable or not capable of, the closer and the quicker you approach finding your own key to being able to move in waves, which facilitates etheric-physical merging.

Some advanced humans who have extreme mental focus, intent, and non-emotionality are already able to merge their etheric and physical spontaneously to remove themselves from danger when circumstances suddenly change. This is a form of shape shifting. All humans may learn to do this. For instance, if death were impending and a human makes a conscious choice to avoid death, it is possible to facilitate that choice through asking for help to meld etheric and physical bodies together. As long as there is no *fear* present, it is possible. Fear prevents manifestation. We wish to instill in you the ability to navigate the creation of your reality through focused intent. Much as you steer your car with focused intent, you may steer into the reality you wish to create with focused intent, even leaving behind physical infirmities and difficulties by intending your physical to be more in sync with the blueprint of your etheric. We have spoken of this before. We think refreshers and presenting things from different angles with different examples enhances your ability to remember and know what is possible. We would like very much to see the two of you and all humans who are working to Connect to their own divinity use the Violet light of Transformation to Transcend, thereby letting go of uncomfortable and painful physical and emotional imbalances your physical body carries. Intend yourselves towards merged etheric and physical form in a different reality that does not include pain and discomfort. Transcend the mental state where human belief systems live and are firmly entrenched in habitual patterns of what you *think* is real. Belief systems keep you trapped in old patterns of rigidity. Transcend your beliefs and move towards etheric-physical merging.

The two of you have experienced travel in your etheric form when you have not been together physically and wish to Connect directly to each other. Your Unity and shared vibration respond when you need to contact each other. Rebecca has been able to leave her physical body and travel with her etheric body to where you are sleeping when you are absent from each other in another state or country. And you have been able to travel with your light body to her. Each of you does the same thing. She is more aware of the activity than you are, Cullen, although you have a long history of doing things outside of your body and not consciously knowing where you have gone or what you have done. You were preparing for what you do now. Many others have been preparing in the same way. Travel in this form is extremely tiring on the physical body until you learn to meld your etheric and physical more closely together. This why we wish for you to accelerate the vibration of your physical bodies to match more closely to your etheric so that you may travel at the same rate in physical and etheric form, for greater access to traveling between the realms and for better communication with each other and beings such as us. The more humans are elevated, the more beings come to assist. Humans sometimes experience the inability to speak when interdimensional beings approach them to help in the sleep state. This is because in etheric form, the physical vocal cords do not work. You cannot speak in the same way in your etheric body as you speak in physical form. The way to communicate in the etheric is through thought waves through your water. This is how you communicate with each other from a distance. It is not physical hearing; it is mental thought form from your water; you communicate through your water in telepathic thought forms.

Humans who are more aware of their etheric form, may receive symbolic messages from the chaotic order of the world. You pick up on astral and physical disruptions as humanity accelerates in their separation, their over-amped activities, and their sinking into self rather than Connecting with others. These activities and thought forms are represented in the astral plane in symbolic form and may be read in the dream state, where the etheric communicates with you. Rebecca experiences this through active, lucid dreaming. You, Cullen, receive similar messages through visions. You both are acting as "seers," prophets of what is occurring and what may come if humans do not alter what they co-create in collective consciousness. Such awareness is merely an extension of all human abilities when you begin to develop the knowledge of how to use your water to receive deeper and broader intuitive information.

I have noticed Rebecca seems taller lately. How does that relate to etheric-physical merging?

She is expanding the devic qualities within herself, creating more space along her spinal system according to her etheric blueprint. You and other aware humans may do that as well if you so choose. When a human makes a conscious step to move away from pain and discomfort towards Love and Trust, you create a space that did not exist before. You and others may do so as well. The more the etheric and the physical are blended, the more the physical takes on an increasingly holistic, rounded, and balanced shape. The physical can become actually quite a bit more beautiful when it more closely matches the etheric and they begin to meld together to create a whole. Broken pieces of the human body may be Healed. Compressed places where human emotions and physicality have been squished or compressed by life, can be infused with space, light, and Love, and the physical body may begin to reflect more accurately what the etheric body intends. Life is Connected to beauty. Life is beautiful. We are all beautiful.

The two of you are noticing waves everywhere. You begin to understand the significance of being a wave. You begin to understand more fully the impact you have on others and the world through your own wave motion. It is easier for humans to maintain harmonious states when surrounded by others who also carry harmonious states. We will give you an example of the opposite of spreading harmonious states. Sour clerks in stores who are unhappy and complain spread negative energy, and then everybody else around them begins to complain; it becomes the norm. Wouldn't it be much more pleasant if the norm were clerks who spread happier energy around as they work, rather than spreading their thoughts and words of being over tired, over stressed, and unhappy. Whether it is positive or negative, the wave motion influences, like a wave on a lake rippling out to its furthest shore. We have been trying to explain this to you for some time as we tell you the importance of keeping your own water in a positive state, rather than in an uproar. Humans struggle to maintain calm waters. They need the influence of positive waves, such as the two of you and others who are doing the work to evolve. When one or two consistently maintain calm waters, the calmness spontaneously affects others in positive ways. We believe your scientific terms call this the hundredth monkey effect. When one learns, suddenly all the others learn. This is what you and Rebecca will be doing as lead monkeys, so to speak, teaching through your joyousness and your Love and allowing others to pick up the vibration. Teach each person that it starts at home and travels outward. Consider your work now as moving more coherently into being waves. Change moment to moment. Listen to your bodies and learn what they need. Listen and continue to raise your vibrations when you reach places that are not comfortable, for it is through the energy of waves that necessary changes will open the doorway to the reality of etheric-physical merging. Everything else opens and changes from there.

You may practice experiencing waves by using your imagination. When you experience discomfort, anxiety, apprehension, or inexplicable feelings that are challenging to manage or understand and you are sure they do not belong to you, (this would be when you are picking up on chaotic or painful energetic waves of collective consciousness) remember that the mind is habitual and will *seek* an explanation of what you feel that fits within what you *believe*. The mind seeks the familiar. When humans have no filing system for what you experience, you may momentarily feel etchings of old emotional patterns because the mind does not know what to do with this energy. So your *thoughts* travel to old patterns. The mind will present something to give a framework for the emotional response. When you feel such energy, change your *thoughts*. *Wave* yourself away from old patterns. Remember that everything is Connected and both what you feel and what you express affect everyone around you, the collective consciousness, and the universe. So don't get stuck like an unhappy particle. Be a wave, and move, move, move towards the merging of your etheric and physical; move towards Love. Be waves. Be Love. Be yourselves.

18

LIFE PURPOSE AND ASCENSION

We wish to speak to you today about life purpose and ascension. Many humans struggle between finding their life purpose and staying in patterns that feel comfortable and familiar. We honor and recognize the importance of familiarity in making humans feel safe and comfortable. The changing conditions in which you live are not familiar to many of you, and yet you may find a sense of familiarity by gathering with others who share your experiences in one manner or another. We have spoken for some time about the power of your thoughts in creating reality. In Lemuria when human beings were less complicated and more developed, humans had a greater understanding of the importance of being careful with what was thought or spoken. Simplicity and directness of thought are invaluable. Convoluted, complicated thoughts create convoluted, complicated reality. What we are trying to teach you is the importance of understanding the concept of "simple and deep." The world around you holds much complexity because of so many complicated human thought forms. These world complexities tire humans physically, for they require you to think in many directions at once. There is no help for it but to do one thing at a time, continually allowing time for rest and regeneration, and not allowing all thoughts to impact you at once. The power of your thought is still unrecognized by most of humanity. Many of those who intellectually understand this concept are not adept at employing it because of rampant, constant thought activity and unmanaged emotions. If you wish to understand your life purpose, you must rid yourselves of complexities and move towards being simple and deep.

When many humans work together with focused thoughts for a simple intent, it is easier to generate the intentional reality you wish to create. Rebecca and Cullen's purpose at this time is not only to bring our communication forward and act as intermediaries for interdimensional communication, but also to focus your thought patterns for manifestation and to share with others how to manifest through intentional thought. It is of more value if there are many than few practicing intentional thought. By example, if you have a car engine with only one spark plug, the spark can try to manifest to make the engine move, but try as it might, the engine will not move. If you join the spark plug with other spark plugs, every one in its own place attached to the intent of movement, each plug jumps as it needs to, the engine begins, and movement occurs. You manifest the reality of moving through space. In the same way, if you join with other light beings who share the similar purpose of elevating humanity and understand the power of manifestation through intentional thought, you may move the things which challenge you, the things which tire you out, the things which throw you out of balance, and the things which keep you stressed. You may at this point actually manifest the world you know is possible. This is your life purpose. You will benefit through Connection with those who have similar interests at heart.

Know that there are negative energies present on Earth at this time that understand the power of thought for manifestation, and they seek to manipulate a future opposite from what you wish through spreading fear and confusion. They focus thought forms to generate more and more fear, causing further separation and complexity. You *must, must* realize the importance of banding together with others who are light beings to focus on learning how to manifest your reality through intentional thought. It is imperative for the ascension of the earth and Her humans for both to make the necessary changes to ascend together. Humanity has a unified life purpose: the evolution of humanity that returns you to your divine state of Love. There are three goals on which you and other humans who wish to assist in the evolution of humanity may focus:

Number 1- Learn how to manifest the reality that aligns with divinity. Increase your power by joining with like-minded light beings who have the same focused intent to help humanity align with divinity. *Become* what is possible.

Number 2- Foster communication between helpers such as us and others who wish to share in helping humanity align with divinity to evolve.

Number 3- Be a counterbalance to those who control through negative thought forms of fear and separation. Show how fear is counterproductive to what humanity wishes to create.

Each human may ask his own High Self angel to define additional specific life purpose goals. You and Rebecca have an additional life purpose that is specific to you: you are to act as ambassadors to our Pleiadian group, fostering communication between us and all humans who wish to hear how they may be part of the evolution of humanity.

This life purpose is excellent. In this work we are always filled with more light, and we always know we are doing the work intended for us here. It is good to invite other humans to share the life purpose of the evolution of humanity.

Excellent. Notice the beautiful song of the bird outside.

We have been listening. One of the benefits of living on earth as a human is to enjoy that kind of experience; it lifts us up.

That is a very joyous earth creature. That bird's complete life purpose is to bring joy into the world. Can you not hear it in its song? Each human must look into her own heart and find her own purpose. It is helpful if individual life purpose goals are combined with the goals we have given you for the evolution of humanity. Combining both individual and larger goals helps to create a sense of overall Unity among us all.

We understand that humans feel stressed physically as they experience shifts within the current consensual reality moving towards the universal reality. We understand the emotional discomfort that occurs as humans work to clear out their own shadow fears and beliefs, bringing subconscious awareness to consciousness. It will help you during these changes and challenges if you focus on being uplifted by work with purpose and Connection with others who share that purpose. Then issues such as disrupted sleep and imbalanced health become secondary, and by becoming secondary, they Heal themselves. Do not withdraw from life because you do not feel well or because you become frustrated. Do not focus on such thoughts. Instead focus your thoughts on your life purpose and find joy in unsuspected places. Each human knows within them how to do this. Thought forms lead the way. Familiarity is not your friend if it keeps you stuck in incorrect beliefs and reactions. Welcome the changes and make changes yourself. Move towards intentional thought and create humanity's future reality.

Humanity's future is of interest to many, many, many interdimensional beings who watch as humans awaken and struggle to recognize that they are divine and that they hold the power for creation within them. If you understand the implications of watching such powerful life forms reclaim their divinity, you understand why all of the others are interested in you. If you understand *that*, you understand why those who do not come from Love seek to stir the pot to further the separation and fear that have caused so much suffering for humanity for so long. Looking at those opposite polarities, it is clear to see the necessity and the importance of moving forward to join with others such as yourselves, learning together how to create the reality you are destined for as divine beings. While we speak of duality and those who promote separation, know that as time collapses duality will cease and you will move towards Unity in Love. Do your part. Live your life purpose.

We would like to speak now about the process of ascension. Ascension may take two forms, but with the exception of a few examples you call "masters", most humans hold the belief system that they will leave their bodies as their spirits ascend. There is another form of ascension, as we recently mentioned: that of merging the etheric and physical bodies together. Because most humans do not understand how to make this bridge between etheric and physical while in physical bodies, many souls on this planet will ascend through death, leaving the physical body and re-entering again the karmic wheel for another lifetime. Death is a form of ascension. However, death is neither necessary nor appropriate for those such as the two of you nor others who wish to ascend *with* your physical body. Yes, we hear your concerns and questions about taking the physical body with you, with its pain and its imbalances, and the tiredness that has accumulated through living on Earth. We hear that concern in the back of your mind. However, we tell you, your physical form is not necessarily as you think. When it is matched with the etheric body it can do things you would assume are miracles. You would see the physical body be able to do many things that are only now possible in etheric form. Yet humans do not understand this concept because their thoughts are based in duality. Most humans still separate the reality of the physical body from the reality of the etheric body; most of your species view death as necessary and a natural part of that cycle. That is no longer true. You may choose your way of ascension now according to your thoughts and your beliefs. If you believe you are going to die, you will. It is your *choice*, and most choices are made from misunderstandings about how to honor and care for the physical body and misunderstandings based on beliefs held in consensual reality. As humans learn to listen to and honor their bodies' requests, merge their etheric and physical together, and use intentional thoughts, the process of ascension may include taking both the etheric and physical bodies together to the next stage of your evolution.

Each human *will* ascend. Whether you choose to do it as the masses through death, realigning with the karmic wheel, or whether you choose to do as we have suggested by merging your etheric and physical bodies together is your choice. To choose the second path, you must nurture your body and feed it much light. This does not mean you should not allow darkness to surface when necessary, for this is part of the process. However, do not get stuck in the darkness. Instead focus on allowing the darkness to be Illuminated by the light that you carry. If you cannot find the light within yourself, find it outside for the moment and be grateful for something of beauty in Nature. The more you shine lightness into your physical body, the more you attain a chance of taking your physical body with you, which *is* the desired procedure for those who wish to participate in the evolution of humanity. Do not believe diagnoses of illness. Do not believe diagnoses that define you pathologically. Each human can and probably will have periods of being out of balance, needing attention. When this occurs, do not focus on fear-based thoughts of illness and death, for if you do, those thoughts attach you to the physical cycle to which you are accustomed and you manifest death as the choice. If you choose such thoughts, you choose death. Is this clear? Again and again we caution you to watch your thoughts. Thoughts come from the mental body, which is a sort of bridge between the etheric and the physical.

Understand that your physical vibration must be raised to match your etheric vibration for the merging that allows ascension with the physical body to occur. We have already explained that when your own physical body receives vibrations to which you are unaccustomed, humans sometimes experience disorientation and discomfort or distress. You may also experience the opposite sensations of joy and Unity. How quickly you accept and acclimate to these higher vibrations determines how quickly you may raise your physical vibration. Please remember we have agreed to communicate and help each other, and we are deeply engaged with you as you proceed with raising your vibration. When you understand what you experience, you can move through adjustment periods with greater ease and more quickly align yourself with the light beings that you are. Bring more joy into your vibration. It is the joy vibration that enhances your ability to lighten your physical form, which helps your physical form raise its vibration to match your etheric form. The higher vibration of joy also helps you to communicate without words, and to do many, many other things. We have attempted to explain how emotions power the thoughts that create your reality. Joy is one of the most benevolent and highest energy vibrations to propel you towards places of Love and Trust which were familiar to you before you re-entered human form. We wish for you to be able to dwell in joy and Trust while *in* human form, elevating yourselves, others, and the planet for the highest good of all. This will additionally assist the process of merging your etheric and physical together for ascension.

Does a vegetarian diet help prepare humans for an easier time at ascension?

Delightful. Yes. But because humans are accustomed to a denser diet based on meat, if you choose to begin a vegetarian diet, you must make changes slowly, easing yourself into the lighter vibration of vegetarianism. Vegetarianism is a lighter form of eating that prevents the body from overworking to clear out toxins, which helps the physical body become lighter and lighter.

Is there a vibratory difference in the vegetarian diet versus a meat eaten diet?

Oh, yes, quite obviously to us, and we know quite obviously to you two as well. You, Cullen, are one of the humans who understood early on the energetic impact of eating flesh, not from a mental conceptual understanding but from the vibratory understanding. Although you do have compassion for the animals and wish not to eat them, your higher consciousness actually understood the vibratory components and steered you in this direction at a very young age. Most humans come to vegetarianism through an intellectual understanding or from the heart place of compassion for the animals, not from the vibratory understanding, which although not better, is certainly a more developed understanding. As the human body gets lighter because it does not have to process toxic and dense material that it cannot handle through letting go of wastes on a regular basis, the body works better and the body consciousness is happier with less of the work load. With less work load, the body consciousness can communicate more easily with humans who are willing to listen. The listening is important. The body can tell you what it needs; yet those needs can change as you elevate your physical vibration. As you get lighter and lighter in your body and as you communicate more with your body, you quite naturally are more open to listening to the body's needs and honoring the body's requests. The open communication helps your body understand the vibratory changes that raise it to match the etheric body without so much distress. Vegetarianism does help in the ascension process.

Do elderly people in deteriorated bodies have an equal chance of taking their physical bodies with them in the ascension process if they are spiritually evolved enough to understand that process?

Most do not make this choice because their physical bodies are already oriented towards returning to the earth. The physical body will follow the directions given to it, and if it has been ignored or given poor directions ("we are getting sick," "we will die,") it will continue following those directions and may not change course fast enough to ascend without death. Some could, of course, make the choice, and our Lemurian friends and we would assist in regeneration of the form, but it would take great intent and freedom from fear. Regeneration does not occur when fear is in the way. It is deeply ingrained in the collective consciousness of humanity to be afraid of death. So it would depend on the individual elder's ability to move beyond fear, ask for help, and intend regeneration. Many humans wish to leave the physical form because they experience frustration, challenge, and pain. If you wish to evolve and live into the new reality, you must stay in physical form. We wish you to know or re-remember something inside of you. You volunteered to be in human form at this time of great opening in order to accomplish your life purpose of helping the collective consciousness of humanity evolve. This is another reason we encourage you to honor, respect, and care greatly for your physical form. We encourage the melding of your physical and etheric bodies to promote the most desirable ascension possible when it is time for that. There is no longer a need to die away from the body in order to ascend.

How do we learn to regenerate the physical form?

Lemurian consciousness knows how to regenerate physical form. Rebecca has long had the concept that she may age backwards as the mythical character Merlin did. She is right. It is done through accessing memory of vitality retained within one's consciousness. This method of regeneration is part of the secrets encoded within your DNA. It is also related to understanding how to step out of time. When one understands parallel existence, it is easy to sidestep physical manifestations in one reality and bring more fully functional physical manifestations into your present *from what you might call a prior time.* Humanity's biggest impediment to accessing and acting on this knowledge of regeneration is the mental constructs of both individual and collective consciousness. Collective consciousness bears down heavily on your individual consciousness with the word "impossible." We tell you it is *not* impossible, and yet it takes great strength of mind to break old mental constructs, beliefs, and fears when one is suffering physically. Additional impediments occur when thoughts are fueled by emotions of despair, hopelessness, frustration, and general lack of belief in abilities. So at this time, most humans keep themselves from even beginning the process of ascending. Human elders have lived for a longer time under the weight of the collective consciousness of impossibility, and they have lived within time frames where rules were important and needed to be adhered to for social conformity. Therefore it is more difficult for elders to put aside accumulated experience, accumulated belief, and accumulated emotional energy that has affected the form they carry in their elder years. Of course it is possible for an elder to simply make the leap, understand, and decide to take her body with her, but it is harder for them to do this because of those things that we have just explained. Additionally, life purpose must be considered. Most elders alive at this time were here for their own specific purposes in the wheel of life, which may not match the life purpose of those who are younger. Yet many humans who are exposed to our conversations now may make the leap, regardless of their age.

There is a reason the two of you and others like you were born in this time, and associated with that reason, is the need for you to ascend *with* your physical bodies. You are rewarded for understanding that your physical body is more than you perceive. Your higher vibratory bodies are necessary vehicles for the work that you will do as time drops away and the new Earth begins life differently. You will need your physical bodies, *if* you can manage to take them with you. It is still a work you must focus on *every day*. You must on a daily basis apologize to your bodies and thank them for what they are and how they support you. You must tell them that you did not understand the importance of respecting and taking care of them and begin to listen to their requests no matter what you *think* you need to do. Put the body first for once in your life. If humans wish to ascend with their bodies, it is imperative that they focus on this to combat what they might have begun to manifest through previous erroneous thought patterns and attached emotional clearings that occur through shadow work. The two of you and the others like you who are able to do this work are making an evolutionary leap for humanity. It is your opening and your leap of consciousness and understanding that makes the difference. You are in a position to drop away karmic patterns, to drop away habitual beliefs, to drop away physical and emotional traumas you have carried lifetime after lifetime, and to create new possibilities with your thoughts.

The only way to ascend with our bodies is to do ample shadow work.

Yes, or course, and direct your thoughts in every moment.

Do humans become taller in the ascension process?

That is correct. We have given you the example of Rebecca's creating more space as she more closely matches her etheric and physical bodies.

How else do our bodies change? Will they change in form or vibratory density as we ascend?

Oh, yes! You do not currently have this understanding. Many humans still believe their bodies will remain as they are, broken and painful. It is not the Truth.

Oh, no, I don't mean that. I mean will our bodies be of a lighter fabric? Will our bodies actually become more filled with light and have a higher vibratory sense upon ascension?

Yes, they will. The first thing you will notice is that you will feel taller, and more expanded, for as you stretch into the Truth of who you are, places in your physical, mental, and emotional bodies will become more spacious. You will feel larger, taller, and fuller. You will also feel lighter, for much of the density will drop away, and you will feel as if gravity has lessened. It will be an introductory step to zip-zip-zip. It will be like leaping, or running in ways that are seemingly impossible in human form today. By example, it will seem as it did to the astronauts who first walked on the surface of the moon; they were able to move about as lighter beings without the constraints of normal gravity. It will be a very joyous stage. Additionally you will have less hair coverings, for you will not need those. Hair will become a matter of personal choice for personal appearance, not a biological necessity to retain warmth on the head or provide protection as the hair on your bodies does now. Yes, you will feel much more filled with light, but that is a feeling sense only, for you carry all of that light within you now. You are just not aware of the brilliance or how it shines or how it feels because while living in duality you have equal amount of awareness of the dark. So it is not that you will *be* more light-filled, it is that your sensation will *feel* more light filled. We wish to stress this so that you may visualize or imagine the actual amount of light you carry within you now. As you move towards merging your etheric and physical bodies, the light will be seen through the eyes more. The light out of your eyes is an indicator of change in physical form. The light will be seen from form to form, whether it is human to human or Pleiadian to human. Humans who do not ascend with their physical forms may not be able to see the changes that are occurring within you as you adjust and shift while they sink into old patterns, yet many will note something different about you and not understand what it is they see. To some advanced humans your physical form or existence may flicker as though you are here and then you are not. It might appear as though you are blinking on and off, rather than appearing completely in dense physical form. What they are viewing is the beginning of the ascension process.

It sounds as though we will shuck or leave the limitation of gravity, and it also sounds that we may look more like you, with more light, no hair, and a different understanding of light and zip zip zip.

Yes. Although it is a personal choice for humans. We ask you again to please focus on apologizing to your bodies and making a conscious daily practice of asking them what they now need, and how you can elevate their vibration as your own conscious vibration is being elevated. You do not want to leave them behind or treat them as most humans view and treat animals. Most humans feel they have to control their animals without understanding that they are equal life forms. In the same way most humans have a similar view of their bodies. It is time that advanced humans wake up and set the trend for raising the vibration of your bodies as equal partners to the totalality of who you are. This is the biggest work for humans once they have surpassed, mastered, and understood the cyclical patterns of emotional outbreaks and emotional clearing and cleansing. Once you have learned to use your emotions to direct necessary change and to practice intentional thought, focus on elevating the consciousness of your physical body. Teach it to talk to you. Teach it to listen to you. Teach it to take directions lovingly as a joint effort. We do not say this will be easy, but we do say it will be rewarding.

Do we drop our emotions when we ascend?

When you ascend, the emotions are not emotions. Emotions are replaced by a state of bliss, peace, calm, and Love, which are not truly emotions. Emotions are human. States of Love, joy, and peace are universal. So yes, you will be able to discern without emotional attachment, and you will drop emotional extremes when you ascend. Remember. Remember. Remember how you felt at times you have experienced peace and joy. Focus on that. Let emotions drop away once they have served their purpose of pointing you in the needed direction of change.

The earth is also expressing changes during Her ascension process. Earth's transition is not just from changes you see in physical flora and fauna that are occurring, and in some cases, becoming extinct. You may see it in many environmental differences. You must begin to accept the beauty of what you may see as starkness from human eyes. Learn to see the etheric form as Earth Transforms: the geometric patterns, the colors, the shapes, and the beauty that they hold from a new perspective, rather than being frightened by the differences you will begin to see. If you were out of human form, as we are and as you were prior to this birth, you would simply be aware of light and color, movement and form. But as your physical and etheric forms begin to merge, you will need to be as easily at home and feel resonance with all types of landscapes that are strange to your human eyes and your other senses. The ascension process offers much possibility for what humans would consider magic when you merge your physical and etheric together. Think of bending space and time, moving the molecular structure in order to intend physical form into something other than the way it is currently perceived. This has always been possible. The Lemurians knew this and used this in their Healing practice. It is what we have explained to you called Regeneration. It is possible for humans to do this regenerative practice, yet most humans allow their belief systems to prevent them from doing what is possible and previously misunderstood. Through understanding possibilities of regeneration and constant Connection to divinity even at the microscopic cell level of physical form, humans may learn to merge their etheric and physical for ascension. These understandings cause density to fall away, allowing the physical body to truly become a light body while still in physical form. Those who are unable to grasp this very challenging concept, which is most, follow the consensual reality of dropping away from physical form, allowing the body to return to the earth and stepping into etheric form for the next step of the journey at death before they enter the wheel again. Yet many human ascended masters knew how to do what we are teaching you, melding the etheric and the physical together to ascend with the full body. The man you call Jesus was one of these. There are those from the countries of India and China also who have been able to do this. They have made up a very small group in what you call your past. Sri Auribindo's companion, known as "Mother" approached doing this through her understanding of cellular communication. We support all humans who wish to learn to do this in order to ascend with the planet as the planet makes Her changes for existing in a new reality.

Ascension is not an overnight occurrence. *It occurs as an ongoing wave.* You ascend moment by moment as you are moving through and releasing things that have held you in certain patterns. You move beyond the dense physicality of human form, to a merged form of the etheric and the physical together. As you pay attention to and flow with the changes you make, you spontaneously evolve. All life is spontaneous when you are in the flow. This will continue to unfold, as duality and time cease to exist and the earth makes Her many changes. It is now time for humans to *really* understand this opportunity in order to become the future of humanity. Remember you agreed to come here at this time to help birth this process. You will be parents to the new humanity.

19

KNOWING AND UNDERSTANDING

Humans have great difficulty discerning between "belief" and "knowing." Knowing comes from a place of Love and Trust. Knowing is heart-based wisdom, while beliefs are mind-based ideas, usually arising from fear. Beliefs are based on human hopes that they will be safe from what they fear. Humans form habitual patterns from their belief systems to keep them safe and comfortable. Do you wish to co-create your reality from fear or from Love? Humans need to understand the power of their own mental constructs in creating their reality every moment of the day. When your mental thoughts are in places that cause pain or suffering from unrealistic belief systems, you manifest that reality in your physical body. Your etheric takes the mental instructions more or less and the reality is created and set into a pattern that joins consensual reality. This is why humans have difficulty in Healing, for they do not understand the power of their own water, their own thoughts in creating the reality in which they dwell. They often hold on to an old reality that no longer exists nor helps them form a positive energetic environment. This is why *knowing* is so much more powerful than *believing*. Humans must learn to open their own doors and windows to fresh knowing while leaving stale beliefs behind. Reality is formed through your own thought creations more than you are aware. The weight and the burden of consensual reality is dense, heavy to bear, and difficult to penetrate, yet humans do not realize that they are helping to create such reality every day by their thoughts about that reality. When you choose better thoughts and disregard beliefs as illusions, better realities become more and more prevalent, building one upon the other to create a higher consensual reality for all to move forward towards a new creation, one thought at a time; it is that direct and simple.

We have explained that human physical bodies are created from your etheric bodies through the thought forms you project. All of your reality is created this way, so know that it can all be beautiful and safe; intend that in your thoughts and actions, and move towards it with Trust. We do not suggest that you subscribe to the illusion of New-Age affirmations of simply *believing* something into being a certain way, expecting it will magically happen; there is more to it than that. Belief alone will not do the trick. What we are teaching you is beyond belief. It is knowing. Knowing allows you to de-create, as if you have an eraser, erasing incorrect patterns that lock you into a reality that doesn't work. Be a conscious co-creator erasing misunderstandings and incorrect belief systems through accepting pain and challenges where they are, while releasing any ideas that such challenges must continue. Instead focus your intent with

Love on *positive* possibilities, erasing *negative* possibilities bit by bit. Make small steps towards awareness of possibility; small is how it starts. Small is really all that matters, for it is in microscopic smallness and slowness that the kernel of Truth begins. Part of the human dilemma is not being able to stretch beyond what you know through your senses to the knowingness of universal Truth. Many understand this concept on a spiritual and mental level, yet they still struggle with the belief that what their five biological senses tell them is the only Truth. Others ignore what their biological senses and First Sense tell them, relying only upon mental ideas for Truth. It is an interesting dynamic in which humans have trapped themselves. Humans continually trap themselves in what feels comfortable and familiar by using *only* their minds or *only* their biological senses, when they could open their awareness to divine knowing through using *all* that is available to them. You may choose alternatives to your habitual patterning by dropping your beliefs, Trusting, and being open to what you may *know* is Truth.

We must get out of our own way.

Yes. This would be a very good guideline in leaving behind all of the old habits and patterns that keep you stuck. Do not be afraid to go back and correct things that you feel you have chosen incorrectly. Many humans have a tendency to feel that once a choice is made, it cannot be changed. This is not true. Be kind to yourselves, and be open to possibilities. *"Life is movement,"* as Rebecca is fond of saying. Stillness is necessary for rest, yet life requires movement. Movement does not mean "fast." The most beneficial movements occur in slowness. Life requires both physical movement and movement in changing habits, patterns, and cycles.

We are learning that being the same, staying the same virtually gets us nowhere. We may stay the same in Love, in our compassion, in our divinity, and in our commitment to Source only. For all other places of non-movement do not help us.

Yes. And as you contemplate movement, do not forget that in these times there are possibilities and necessities for stepping between realities. You move more and more towards being able to look at a reality that is not beneficial and step aside, saying, "This does not apply to me.'" This is one thing you may do with epidemics so that you are always in another reality when you are exposed to those who believe that imbalances are contagious. You do your human part by being cautious and then move into a higher awareness of possibility by shapeshifting your attitudes and moving into a dimension where you *know* illness does not exist; co-create another reality to prevent contamination. You may also ask for your light to cleanse the negative energy all around you so that not only are you protected, you are clearing the path for others as well.

We are most interested in promoting Unity in human teamwork to help you move towards Source. You need to know and fully understand that the intent of a group, or even two, does more to shift your current reality than the intent of a single individual. Humans must take responsibility for the control of their own thoughts and join with others who wish to raise their combined thought vibrations. We are neither allowed nor capable of making changes for you, for humans control their own attitudes. That is your power, the power of your water, and we cannot affect that. We can help to open the pathways, educate, and show you other possibilities, yet nothing can be done without your controlling your own water, your own thought forms, and ultimately making your own choices. Always remember that it is your choice to make these changes in attitudes and possibilities. Know and understand that human thought forms have been holding you back for generations and millennia. Humans have always had the power to live in a higher vibration; yet most of you simply refuse to relinquish your patterns and beliefs in order to do so, preferring instead to perpetuate the illusion that everything is OK as it is, or you attempt to change the world using tired old patterns that do not work (actions such as protests, petitions, and debates.) Often humans are so much more familiar with discomfort, pain, and misery than joy and ease that you fall into familiar old patterns rather than making new, joyful patterns. You are the only ones who can control your thoughts and your attitudes. Joining with others who live in the higher vibrations of Love and Trust supports making better choices in your own thoughts, and together you make a greater impact on the collective consciousness.

Let us explain our view of the percentage of responsibility you have individually for co-creating reality. You must know and understand how it works. Humans have responsibility for 50% of what is created and what happens to them. Humans are self-responsible *only* for 50% of what is created, for you have outside influences and outside help that create the other 50% of your reality. So humans can never control the entire 100% of what happens to you and what is inevitably created.

However humans must always use 100% of the knowledge and tools you have available to take advantage of your 50% of creative power. Take self-responsibility; make wise choices; govern your thoughts and actions, redirecting both thought and action when necessary. Forget the percentages, and do it every single moment. If you do it every single moment, you are contributing 100%; then you are doing *all* that you can do, and your 100% of effort becomes a full 50% of co-creating reality for yourselves, other humans, and the earth. The other 50% comes from the help that is provided when you ask. All you ever have to do is ask and focus your own thoughts. In these times of great change more help is now available for humanity. The help is always, we repeat, *always* there available to you whenever you ask. This is the nature of co-creating your reality.

It is a tedious, touchy business to get humans to understand the difference between self-responsibility, fully doing their 50%, and asking for help for the other 50% to convert outside circumstances that are not within their control into something they can work with. As you consistently do your 50%, know that amazing possibilities are made available to you (things that you may have imagined as miraculous.) We will list some of the abilities that you may call upon when you fully do your 50%, knowing what is possible. Shape shifting is a form of working with something out of your control. Seeing other realities, hearing things from other dimensions, traveling between worlds, are all ways that humans who are raising their awareness and their vibration may utilize outside influences and change them. Humans have been arguing about whether fate controls their lives for as long as they have had the ability to think. The simple Truth is that humans are co-creators with great power. Use your power and ask for assistance from the divine co-creators of the universe. They are always *willing* and ready to combine their 50% with the human 50% to form a greater whole together. It is important to remember that we always work towards the highest good for all.

Thought forms from consensual reality also contribute to what you experience; you are not completely in control of that, although every thought you think affects it. All kinds of things can come into your environment that are outside of your direct control. Consensual reality is built upon thought forms of all humans projecting their beliefs and their emotions into the creation of reality. Aware humans must begin to choose your thoughts with intention, and as you do this together, you raise the power of your 50% of co-creative abilities, positively affecting your individual reality and consensual reality at the same time. It is important that you know and understand this. Your focus and attitude immediately make a difference in what you create. It is your awareness that allows you to make a shift. When you make quick mental shifts, you are doing a human form of zip zip zip, moving somewhere else quickly, being flexible, shape shifting out of something that could harm you into another reality. Understanding how to do this is very, very much the same as understanding shape shifting abilities. The more you enhance your ability to shift realms through shifting your thoughts, the more you gain control over your 50%. You do not have complete control over the impact of consensual reality, but you do have some control over it as you raise the vibration of your thoughts, which in turn helps to lift the vibration of the collective consciousness. You have control over shapeshifting away from a reality that is harmful and contributing to the creation of another reality. Once humans figure out how to do this through Love and Unity, you will have more control over the reality in which you live. We are seeing this more and more with the choices humans are making. It is uplifting and heartening to see this shift in human consciousness. It takes great connection with divinity, through Trust and surrender when things don't go your way to make these positive attitudinal changes, and it takes great focused intent of the power of your own water to discover what you are capable of and to know how powerful you are.

Human beings dream themselves into reality through the power of your thoughts and what you speak. You are not aware of the order of creation. You are aware of what you sense in the physical about your world. From your physical sensations you move towards emotional reactions. From your emotional reactions and expressions you assign meaning to the thoughts that arise, and these thoughts go out into the world to create and sew the reality that you experience. Most of your thoughts are based on assumptions and belief rather than knowing Truth. Humans are caught in a loop of 1, 2, 3 physical, emotional, and mental, without understanding how to move out of the loop and create something different from your thoughts. *The reality you live is the reality you create.* When we speak of dreaming yourself into reality, we speak of knowing your own power and knowing that you are connected to other worlds. Knowing is universal. When you connect to your divinity through your water to universal knowing, you dream a better reality through the thoughts you project into the world and into the universe. Traditional Australian aborigines knew how to do this before Western consensual reality affected them. They moved into the universal rhythm and vibration so that they were constantly in the present moment, creating what needed to come next. They dreamed their reality into being.

We are trying to help humans understand that you can go beyond your beliefs by focusing your intent on creating your reality. Listen to the wisdom of your body and your First Sense, and direct your thoughts so that the etheric may help you create what you want and need. We say again and again, humans do not understand the power their beliefs hold over them. Neither do they understand the power of their thoughts, so when they focus their thoughts on erroneous beliefs or assumptions rather than focusing their thoughts on positive knowing, they keep themselves stuck in a loop of their own making. A whole new reality awaits the future of humanity once you know and understand your own power. It is all about the knowing. Know the Truth. Meaning and language are built upon repetitive patterns that cause looping in human behavior. Through assumptions and patterns that are not always correct, each human builds a structure of belief based upon his own meanings from his own experiences. The use of language and building patterns upon misconceptions and misunderstandings without listening to your water causes miscommunication, arguments, and wars. We do not care for history, for it keeps you in the loop of the past. Relying on history is the basis of making assumptions, which then lead to incorrect meanings and poor communication.

Notice the separation that occurs when language causes miscommunication or when communication is based on old patterns of assumption and belief. After you notice the sense of separation that occurs through poor communication, listen to your own body's water through your First Sense. Then reconnect through Love and Trust. Look past the words to the intentions that are present. Your water leads you past belief into knowing. This is communicating through the heart. *Teach* others that language is based on meanings and that these meanings have been built upon assumptions since childhood. Break the pattern of meaning held within beliefs. Move beyond to communicate through you water with Love and intent as the future humans. The wisdom of your entire being needs to be incorporated in communicating. Language serves to continue separation. This is why we do not communicate between ourselves with language. We use our First Sense and communicate through heart-knowing, which is what we are teaching you. As humans you now need to move beyond language for communication, moving more and more towards universal forms of communication through your water. The only way we know to teach you to do this is to suggest you practice moving away from fear into Trust, from Trust into Love, and into *knowing* rather than *believing* what is possible. We are here at this time to help guide you towards this understanding of heart language rather than mind language. While we have told you to use your thoughts, eventually we guide you to move past thinking into communicating entirely through your heart. We are available to help transform the way in which humanity can use Trust, Love, and knowing to move vibrationally towards Unity and back to Source, within which is the true understanding of Love. This is the future of humanity, if you choose it. Truth lives in your heart, not in your head. The heart of each of you *knows* Truth. Rely on that.

20

TECHNOLOGY AND WORLD AFFAIRS

As more and more interdimensional beings offer communication with humans, it will become increasingly important for leaders to be willing and able to receive and consider what we have to say. We need ambassadors to bridge the communication, which is one reason we have approached the two of you. Those who lead during the approaching end of time must deal with breaking the karma of old patterns and beliefs held by the collective consciousness. Additionally, they are challenged with a great deal of negative energy and negative intent aimed at them from outside influences of those who do not want the old ways to change. Even those leaders who carry great Love experience much struggle against the forces that come from fear. We ask humans to continually send light and requests for protection to those who lead from the heart, so that they may fulfill the possibilities of what they have to offer in leading the planet towards the new reality. As the collective consciousness of humanity changes, more leaders who make their decisions from Love rather than fear will appear.

Send them Love so that they may choose wisely. Leaders are arising who have the potential to show other leaders how to move humanity towards the energy of eight, the number of abundance, if they can rise above negative influences and listen to their own hearts. Of course, we cannot predict how this will unfold, for it depends upon human choice. As you watch for the possibility of abundance, do not look for it in terms of money, for that is an old pattern. Abundance is not necessarily financial. Look for abundance of heart; look for abundance of communication; look for abundance in community; look for abundance of people moving towards sameness and Unity instead of difference and separation. These new leaders hold the potential to move humanity towards Unity and away from separating concepts of duality and fear that have caused humanity to suffer for so long, yet in order to do this, they must rise above the collective human karma that they did not create and the pressures of negative intent. If they succeed, they may bring an abundance of needed harmony and peace through the challenges that they have inherited. Those who lead their countries making choices from Love, have the potential to help all of Earth, and all kingdoms on Earth, as well. Humans may participate by holding the intention that their leaders will move towards choices of Love and Unity for the greatest good for all. Many beings like us who are curious and supportive watch with hope that humanity will make the right choices

You may be surprised to know that we hold wishes and dreams as you do. When we speak of being co-creators with humans, we are truly hoping for a grand partnership of Unity, and we would like to speak with human leaders who are able to Trust rather than react with fear about what we have to offer.

Our wishes and our dreams can only come true if humans learn how to create a better reality through using their emotional energy and intent. Because humans have so much power through choice, we do not hold all the answers. Of course our obvious wish is for peace, harmony, and communication through Love; however, humans determine 50% of creating that possibility through the choices you make and the energy you choose to use. The importance of human choice is the primary reason we wish to meet with human leaders; we wish to let leaders know we are here to help and offer our service for the good of humanity. You are aware that we left your good company abruptly during one of our conversations. We explained to you that we needed to avert an attempt to cause harm for the planet. *(Laarkmaa inferred in their explanation that they averted a nuclear war or an attempt at "pushing the button" through pouring in Love to rebalance emotional energies.)* We and others who help guide your planet would *not* have allowed such a thing to happen. We are capable of stopping *extreme* events through our actions of Love, for there are things that could totally destroy the planet if they were allowed. That is the *only* way we are allowed to intervene with humans, for humans are responsible for co-creating their reality through choice. When human ignorance or negative influences interfere with the evolutionary divine path for this planet and the human species, we can help. We do our part to prevent, promote, and work for the good of all, *according to the choice of the collective consciousness.* We send Love to combat darkness. We fix things, make things apparent, or stop things, as we did on three of your recent airplane flights, making the pilots and mechanics aware that something concerning passenger safety needed their attention. We can help change these things for your personal and global safety. Sometimes we must rush away to join others for a big project or crisis, as we did when we recently stopped a nuclear potentiality. There are things afloat in the astral world that impact advanced humans because of your sensitivities; even some others who have never been sensitive are beginning to wake up to feeling things they cannot explain or understand. Humans may be sensitive to astral and emotional reactions of fear permeating the atmosphere, yet be unaware of what the fear is related to. When we successfully intervene and prevent catastrophic happenings, sensitive ones such as the two of you may notice. The planet *must not* be destroyed, and our assistance has prevented that on *more* than *one* occasion.

Do you mean that the planet will never be destroyed?

We mean that the planet is very close to ascension status at this time, and it is unpredictable how or when that will occur. Yet from our limited abilities to intervene, we have been able to intercede when governments choose grand scale harm that could cause the alteration or dissolution of the molecular space-time structure through their inappropriate and misunderstood actions. When those types of attempts occur, we are able to step in and stop them, *as long as we are acting in accordance with the intentions of the collective consciousness of humanity.* That does not mean that collective consciousness of humanity could not decide to ignite a nuclear bomb. Such things are still possible. Yet most of those intentions come from a minority of humans, and even those possibilities grow dimmer as more and more humans move towards frontier states of understanding as future humans and carriers of light. As humans grow in understanding and continue your intentions, your listening, your opening, your receptivity, shining of your own light and teaching others, negative possibilities diminish. Do not allow artificial fears to create your reality. Trust instead that Love can and will prevail. Then the amount of danger that is possible lessens, for many of you are learning to step outside of fear and into Trust and Love; that energy alone changes the possibility for peace more than you can imagine. When you make positive intentions from a place of Trust and Love, you act in accordance with the planet's own divine intentions.

We are curious about how Earth will look in the future reality.

Ah. So are we! Humans are co-creators. What it will look like will depend on your 50%. Earth has 50% say-so in how She will be different, and you have 50% in how you say She will be different. So it will depend on the emotional and the thought energy that you intend for what you wish to create. One thing we can be quite sure of is that as you move towards Unity and more into your heart space, there will be less separation and preferences for familiarity. You will find beauty wherever you go. You will learn to see the earth through a vibrational stance rather than through your eyes; this is one of the changes you will make. How it will be different and how it will look will largely be dependent on you.

What can you tell us about detriments or benefits of the computer age? Are we following in the footsteps of Atlantis and moving towards self-destruction because of technological choices?

Computer use does have detriments, and you are correct in remembering the harmful effects of misused technology in Atlantis. As always, it is human choice that determines what will occur. Humans need to be aware that computer technology speeds up the human nervous system beyond its natural capacity, moving humans further and further away from their Connection with Nature. It is not the computer that is harmful; it is the imbalance that occurs as humans demand quicker and quicker access to "information" without also listening to the information provided by Nature through their bodies and their First Sense. Humans incorrectly believe that they can speed up and speed up and speed up, getting more and more thought information without incorporating it into your water. Many humans know within the cells of their being that it does not feel right, and that they feel out of balance when they engage with computer use and Internet activities too often or too long. The imbalance of thoughts without connection to First Sense or body knowing leads to many lower vibrational activities, such as addictive behaviors and irresponsible actions, that separate humans and cause further disconnection from Nature. Computer information often promotes building upon beliefs from old paradigms that no longer apply in the new reality that is evolving. Yet nothing is ever black and white. You must find the balance. We see continual use of computers as harming the physical body through the constant speeding up of the nervous system, but more importantly, we see that humans are prevented from moving forward spiritually if they do not allow time for listening to their own First Sense, listening to their bodies, Connecting with Nature, and connecting with other humans who share intentions for moving towards light,

Love, and Unity. You may express your concerns to others by sharing that it saddens you that computers have replaced *real* communication.

Is our technology leading us towards simplicity?

No. Human technology is a long way from Pleiadian and other technologies, and you have much to learn. Your collective consciousness operates under the belief system that technology improves your lives. The key word there is *belief.* Those who promote computer technology have added incorrect information into the collective consciousness that technology will make your lives simpler. It is propaganda. It is not Truth. Many of the gadgets that fill your households now do not make your lives simpler; they cause more complications. Technology has many gifts, but technology is complex, not simple. Your technology currently moves more and more towards complexity rather than simplicity. Computer information builds a structure of instant gratification into humans, rather than promoting the deepening of understanding within them. Humans "go on-line," punch in a word, and instantly have a multitude of information on that subject. But we ask you, do you get anything other than what your thoughts can think about that subject? Do you have any direct Connection with what it means? If you look up the word butterfly and read all about it, does it mean the same to you as if you walk in the forest and one lands on your face? No. There are costs for using computers to instantly gratify yourselves with more and more information. Your young ones are being trained while they are still growing and developing to "go on-line" and look for information. Many parents put their three year olds in front of computers thinking it will help them be brighter, smarter, and excel more in school or in life. But gathering information from computers disconnects them from the insight and information they can get from Nature, and as they grow and develop they miss gaps in their understanding, so they disconnect themselves from life. They do not learn to listen to their body wisdom. They do not learn to listen to their hearts. They do not learn to listen to the whisper of the wind in the trees or the sound of the rain. They learn to see Nature's actions as interfering with what they want, and they will go inside and "go online," entraining themselves more and more in an artificial reality that is disconnected from their hearts. The neurons in their brains and in their systems, their total neuronal makeup, cannot accept this speed, so they are growing and leaving out portions of what helps make them human. They become automatons that are desensitized to life. This is a major concern for humanity. Humans are causing major harm to their young ones by pushing them towards artificial intelligence rather than encouraging them to Connect with the native intelligence that lives within them as divinity. You will note there is an increase in autistic types of behaviors in your young ones, for they cannot take so much stimuli into their nervous systems. You will notice there is an increase in hyperactivity, for it is against human design to sit still and learn; Nature teaches through movement. You will notice there is an increase in young ones being diagnosed with bi-polar disorder, for they are bifurcated from their natural divinity and the consensual reality to which they are being directed. All of these things are signposts to tell caregivers, "Stop this. You are pushing your young ones too far, too fast, away from Nature towards something artificial." You are creating a group of mechanized, very bright human beings who are disconnected from other people, Nature, and life. The more you teach disconnection, the more you will continue your experience of reality through fear. It is through Connection that humans learn harmony. It is through Connection that you learn how to listen to each other's hearts and how to communicate through your water without words. These abilities are being detrained out of humans. As you say, Cullen, "It is bad training."

There are addictive qualities within your current computer use as well. Once humans have found what they are looking for on the computer, many of you cannot stop looking. You continue to search for varying aspects of information before you are satiated or overwhelmed with information. Or something else captures your attention and you begin another search. What you are doing, humans, is feeding yourselves more and more and more information without allowing the still point, the time and the space to integrate what you learn. Further, you have no real life recognition of what it is you have been studying, for you do not touch it with your hands, or smell it with your nose, or taste it with your mouth, or hear it with your ears like a beautiful bird song. You do not connect with it through your First Sense; you only see written language that defines it; you do not see or experience the real thing. Technology used addictively further speeds human neurological systems, and we notice that many of you try to adjust to this by taking in stimulants to keep you at that speed. We watch much of humanity take in varying stimulants; they cannot move fast enough to keep up with the lives they are creating. One cup of coffee or soda begins before the last one was finished, as humans stimulate their systems to match the speed of the information they are receiving from their computers. You are in effect short-circuiting your neurological systems when you do this. The human system is designed to do everything in balance.

However, humans do have some technology that holds promise, particularly in the Healing fields, but that technological understanding is only a bridge to understanding what you can do in the future by yourselves as humans. There are many who are working to promote Healing with technology through understanding the liquid, crystalline of the energy of the human body and the crystalline formation of electric magnetic energetic combinations. This form of technology may be helpful, but it certainly is anything other than simple. It becomes more complex by the day. Nature is simple. Universal concepts of Love, Healing, Trust, Grace, Truth, Transformation, Illumination, and Connection are simple. The simplicity of Healing lies within the human, *not* within technology. Technology is only a bridge. Rebecca had a technical machine she used for Healing. It was a pad with energies that she could program on a computer and lie on to give her DNA certain Healing patterns. For a time it worked quite well, and her body accepted it. After a while, her body did not accept the energy from the machine. So she traded with a friend who gave her another technical Healing device. As she prepared to plug it into the electrical outlet, the machine turned itself on through her energetic touch before she could plug it into wall. She understood, "I have this electrical energy within me." Each human has this electrical energy within them. The future of Healing is within facilitating and channeling your *own* electrical energy, not plugging into a machine. You are in a learning period. Of course you may choose to experiment with Healing with the assistance of technology, but please understand that it is only a bridge. In the new reality you will power the technology you use with your own intent and your own electrical energy. And eventually, you will not *need* technology at all.

Humanity's collective consciousness believes that you must progress and continually move forward linearly. That belief, like most beliefs, is erroneous; it is not Truth. Life does not progress along a linear line. Life cycles. Life spirals. Life has still points, periods of rest, winters where everything sleeps. Humans do not often respect or honor cycles of rest, especially humans who are engaged with computers everyday for long stretches of time. While computers *can* provide useful information, if you rely on them only rather than listening to Nature and your own innate divine wisdom, you move away from the natural progression of your own evolution. It is extremely important for you to break your patterns of belief about linear progress and your incorrect assumptions about the importance of all the information that is available through technology. Technology is not the answer. We do not wish to be perceived as technology bashers, for we have our own technology, and we find it quite helpful when we *choose* to use it. It is powered with Love and intent. We see the future of humanity moving towards helpful technology. You just need to break some beliefs and patterns to prevent repeating what humanity has experienced on more than one occasion of technological disasters. Learn to use your heart with your technology, for the technology of the new reality will not be powered by plugging it into electrical outlets; it will be powered by your *intent*. It will be powered by the light you have within you. The future of technology is heart based. Those of you who are aware of and seeking to understand these concepts are the future leaders. Honor yourselves as such. Do not get caught in belief systems where scientists tell you what technology can or cannot do. Listen to your hearts and teach those with whom you work how to listen to their own hearts. Communicate through your water, human to human.

Can you tell us, will the current computer age come to a crashing halt in order to stop the human addiction to instant information?

The answer is dependent upon the consciousness of humanity and the choices that you make. So much of your reality is dependent upon the consciousness of humanity and your choices. The doom and gloom predictions for your planet were turned around by the conscious intent of a small group of humans during the 1987 consciousness-raising event we have spoken of, the first Harmonic Convergence. Likewise, as more humans elevate their consciousness now, clean up their own shadows, refuse to be ruled by those who seek to control them through fear, spend more time in Nature, and encourage their children to play rather than doing computer games, the possibility increases for the computer and other technological devices to be more useful components in your lives like your stoves and your refrigerators. Yet at this time the probability for that is not strong, for most humans have become addicted to a speed that hurts them. There is a great likelihood that computers will jumble their information, break their circuits, cross their wires, be affected by the changing magnetic grid, and solar flares, and humans will suffer the loss of their instant information gratification. There may also be periods of times when no computer communication is possible. This is why it is so important for you to learn to rely on your First Sense for communication. Relying on machines locks you into a reality of separation rather than supporting your natural flow towards Unity. Natural ways of communicating are *always* better than artificial ones. Computers can *never* replace or duplicate the intended design of person-to-person communication through the First Sense of your water and your hearts.

What can you share with us about extreme weather conditions that we are experiencing at this time?

We have already told you about how you affect storms and storms affect you through human emotions. As time and duality fall away, cycles of weather that humans have come to rely on as "normal" will no longer be predictable. We see the changing patterns of the earth's environment Connecting to and promoting changes within humanity. Just as you experience unexpected emotional storms arising within you, external storms of the earth arise unpredictably. The movement is necessary to break apart patterns that no longer work both for Earth and for humans. It appears to us that the unpredictability is manifesting from the shifts within the crystalline structure beneath the earth's crust, the shifting magnetic polarities of your planet, and the increased winds caused by solar flares as they interact in your environment. Humans have similar unpredictable shifts as your own vibrations are elevated. You and Earth move together. Humans have the opportunity to change your liquid crystalline form and the form of Earth by directing your thoughts and intentions when Earth's storms and your inner emotional storms arise. We will support you as Earth goes through Her necessary changes causing uncertainty in your environment and as you go through your own human changes.

Can we be warned in advance if there will be adverse weather conditions in order to stay safe?

Your bodies already have an advanced warning system much like animals you have noted who know when storms approach. We can assist in enhancing that function by opening it for better receptivity; this we can do. Yet you must do your part by listening to your First Sense and Connecting your inner water to Earth's water. Be aware of your own emotional terrain. Changes are occurring very rapidly, requiring your flexibility in making plans. Listen to the land; hold your hands out palms down, enhancing your abilities and helping you to find resonance with the earth. The two of you and many others are growing in your abilities to perceive. The feeling sensors in your hands and feet are more important than humans are aware. Humans may feel others' energy and the energy of the earth through these sensors. This ability will grow when humans shed restrictions and allow themselves to *feel*. Walking on the ground barefoot is an excellent example. Holding out your hands to assess someone's energy will become a sort of greeting in the future, where you allow your energy to extend through your eyes and heart, and you reach out, extending your palms outward to Connect with the energy of another. The more work, willingness, listening, and surrender you employ, the more you integrate your changes and develop potentials such as these. You may use these abilities to keep yourselves safe.

When the earth escalates Her cleansing process and magnetic-electrical changes occur as Earth approaches Her own ascension, there will be some places on the planet more heavily affected than others. What occurs at each location is Connected to the human consciousness at that location.

However, human safety is not necessarily dependent upon where you are physically. Your safety depends on your communication with your body and your ability to listen for the changes in the earth. Humans are also kept safe through your continued work to meld together your physical and your etheric bodies so that you may shape shift to other spaces when necessary. As you learn to raise your vibration, move your molecular structure, and manifest what you need through your intentions, you will be able to do your own human form of zip zip zip in times of danger.

Rebecca and I, and others we have spoken to, are feeling that something is going on here on Earth (or it might be outside our world) that does indeed affect us. Can you help us understand what it is we are sensing or feeling when we know that it does not come from within us?

It has to do with energies that are adjusting on the planet. For a very long time humans have been controlled by negative energies. Most humans have been quite successfully trained by listening to the nightly news and other media to focus on this fear-mongering energy, which adds to their own fears and their own negative thoughts. Those of you who are using emotions as directional signals for positive change and working to redirect your thoughts make a difference in altering the direction and the force of these negative energies. You are in effect helping to change the outcome for Earth. Additionally, the human energetic-magnetic templates and the earth's energetic-magnetic templates are becoming more aligned. Those of you who are more sensitive and aware feel the movement of these templates away from the great separation of fear and darkness towards Love and Unity. The willingness to sit in darkness with your light and the work you do to focus your thoughts on Love and Trust make an overall energetic difference for yourselves and for Earth. You have been told, and it is true, it does not take many to change the direction of what will happen. A small number of humans have been directing the creation of reality for the many by spreading fear. Since the first Harmonic Convergence, more of you are reclaiming your power to create your own reality. The number of humans is growing who understand how the process for co-creation works, and you are using your power to direct the creation of a new reality through spreading Love. It is not the number of you who do this that matters (although the more of you who intend Love, the stronger the impact); it is the intensity, integrity, the intent, the Love, the compassion, and the joy that you energetically put into what you do and how you think that makes the difference. One person *can* make a difference. Many of you together make a bigger difference. Remember, part of your journey is connecting with like-minded people. It does not matter if it is only a few. It matters how much the few focus their intention and their thoughts. Advanced humans help change others who don't yet know *how* to co-create through better thoughts. It is a great service you provide. And remember, the second Harmonic Convergence creates another opening for the light of Truth to flood humanity.

Last night as Rebecca was gazing at the stars, she noticed a bright light. She began communicating with it, and it moved very, very rapidly twice in the night sky towards her and then stopped. Was that some sort of communication, and can you tell

***us if we are going to begin having more interstellar
communication?***

The quick star movement that flashed across the sky two
times was an interdimenstional response to her request for
communication. We are present. We are so very often present.
Rebecca may consider that what she saw last night was an
acknowledgment of her desire to Connect. We took her impulse
and intent for Connection and planted a dream within her. In
the dream, there was a circle of humans on the land communing
and Connecting. The dream is a symbol for all humans: seek
Connection through like-minded beings of many kinds who
can bring the harmony you wish. In the dream she asked about
Connection to land, and we explained: it's *all* Connection; it's
all communication. Find other like-minded beings with whom
you can communicate, for through your shared positive intent
you may assist in the birth of the new reality. Send your Love
and Trust like laser beams into the collective consciousness to
shatter and break apart rigid belief systems and old patterns
that hold humanity captive. It is a time of calling together
those of you who have waited all this time to do your work.
Remember, you came here for a purpose.

This is a special time for opening communications between
species and interstellar beings. Situations and understandings
will be changing rapidly as time and duality collapse. As you
change your belief systems, your abilities to communicate will
also change and expand. You will be able to initiate conversations
and dialogues with interdimensional beings as never before. It
is more important now than at any other time on Earth, for
"time" as you know it is coming to an end. This end is not
finality: it is the potential for a new Earth, a new humanity, and

a new reality to be born. This birth has challenges and great changes, yet it is ultimately worth all the shifts that you will experience. Use the power of Love and move towards Unity. The birth of the new reality has begun.

21

THE POWER OF LOVE:
UNITY AND CONNECTION

We've been leading you towards the understanding that in Unity, Love is all there is. Love is the most powerful force in the universe. It is the answer and the way to all you've wanted. Love everything, even the challenging times, but first of all Love yourselves. We have told you, until humans face their fears and do their shadow work, they cannot consistently contact the Truth that light and Love are always present. Until humans do their shadow work and learn to Love themselves, they simply have fleeting glimpses of light and moments of human Love (which is often misperceived) and moments of divine Love. The human perception of Love is not as encompassing as the divine, universal understanding of Love. Love is powerful. Love has the ability to change everything. Many humans have perceived Love and power as opposites. While power can exist without Love, Love always contains power, for Love is everything. Power has much more force when paired with Love. When humans express power from a place of Love, you make an actual difference in the fabric of the world and the universe. In understanding the essence of Love, you may imagine a triangle with power as the base. Make the sides Unity and draw them to a point at the top, representing Trust, for Trust points you forward. Then fill in the triangle with Love, for Love is what fills the entire universe.

When humans experience Love, you experience a higher vibration. This is the vibration we are guiding you towards as future humans. It can be reached and held virtually all of the time by monitoring your thoughts and emotions and using your intent; the higher vibration helps you move away from fear and separation and achieve Unity, Trust, and Love. When you are in a higher vibration, there is a wave effect on others, and they perceive it. There is an energetic magnetism of wave motion that emanates from you. People will want to be around you, for you make them feel better. There is no judgment present in the vibration of Love, and others can feel that lack of resistance. Therefore they are more able to flow towards you in their own wave motion, and you may approach Unity together. That is the way human Connection is intended. That is the way of peaceful harmony among humans that was intended from the beginning. Love is an actual vibratory change emanating a different wave frequency that changes the reality within you and around you. Suddenly the world is no longer hard; the world becomes easier because you are living in a different vibration, being a different vibration, and inviting others to join you in that vibration, so you are creating a better reality.

It seems so simple. Why don't humans get it?

Because humans are fractured by fears that reside in the subconscious of their present and past/parallel lives. And because living in duality complicates everything. Humans have these internal battles going on within them because of their unresolved fears. The fears feed insecurities and emotions that keep fractured belief systems alive. The more humans step out of fear and into Trust, and the more they clean up and clear out their own shadows using the power of Love, the more they raise their vibrations and the complications fall away. Complications cannot exist in the simple flow of Unity. *Belief cannot compete with Truth. Fear cannot exist in Love.* This is a simple answer for a very complicated form of living. There is more light pouring in right now to help humans break free from the complications caused by living in fear, and there are more angelic and other interplanetary beings who approach to help at this special time in which you are so privileged to live. We, Pleiadians, are simple beings who live in Truth, Trust, Love, and Unity. And we bring you ways to move towards living that way yourselves as the new humans. This is the path that you must reclaim. We are one. As we work together, we can bring this new understanding and the new humanity into being. Working together through sharing wisdom and knowing can only help this wonderful process.

I have the image of the number 8, the infinity number as we discuss this. Can you tell me why that's coming up and what that means?

You are sensing the meaning of the symbol of Infinity: connection of all; you are coming into fuller understanding of the principle of "the highest good for all." The Infinity symbol is represented by the number 8 turned sideways; it is a loop. That loop shows the connection from one to all and from all to one; it moves in flow in both directions at once. It is a continuous loop of understanding that we are all one, and that we are moving towards Source, divinity, and Unity in a continuous loop. When all is Connected in Unity, you have abundance of everything you need. The number 8 carries the energetic vibration of abundance. The Infinity loop and the number 8 are the same. Understanding the symbolism of the Infinity loop can provide a major breakthrough for humans in understanding the concept of Unity. And the more you understand Unity, the more you understand the power of Love. The more you understand the power of Love, the more you Trust the highest good for all, you let go of your fears, and you more readily meld your etheric and physical bodies together, moving towards ascension.

When humans arrive at the point of ascending with our physical bodies, will we be finished with our time on Earth, or will we be moving from another dimension back to Earth with our physical bodies?

When your vibration is elevated to the point of completely melding your etheric and your physical, you may choose to travel back and forth between dimensions at will. When you have reached that understanding, you will see so much beauty around you that it won't matter to you whether you are here on Earth or whether you are with us. The veil is thinning all the time. You will understand that it's all the same place! So you will be able to choose where you wish to go, and you will no longer make duality-based choices of being either "here" or "there." Movement back and forth between the veils is a form of shape shifting. Humans who develop the capacity to do this through their higher vibration will seem to simply disappear and then reappear in a recognizable form to the eyes of others. Humans who cannot imagine themselves operating at that vibration with complete ease and Trust find it difficult to imagine what is coming. There is no experiential base, and thus far, humans base most of their understanding on experience, although many of you also employ imagination, which is a very good tool for moving towards the new reality. Expand your perceptions of speed and movement. Now is an excellent opportunity for you to expand your perceptions while in physical form. Practice moving beyond the constrictions of duality and time in your awareness. This will assist you in making the coming changes. Time and duality are only illusions of consensual reality. When those of you who understand begin to move beyond this stage of development through practicing what we are teaching you, the process of changing reality will be accelerated for all.

We will simply be in a greater reality. We will not be traveling backwards, nor will be we traveling forwards. We will not be crossing a veil; we will be eliminating the veil.

Very well said. You will be living in Love and Trust, Unity, and Connection with abundance through the power of Love.

Understanding a new reality.

Yes. You are beginning to get a view of what *will be* for humans who choose to help manifest the new reality. You know, all things done from Love have a simple nature, for they come from the heart, and they direct you to what is necessary. Everything else can be taken care of later. Humans complicate things; it is a human trait. Moving towards simplicity is moving towards Love and Trust. Simplicity is much like Unity. Complication is born of separation, and as we now all know, separation is attached to fear. So when you make complications in your lives, stop and ask yourself, "What part does fear play in my making so many complications in this project or decision?"

You once described yourselves as simple beings.

We are indeed. We are not fragmented by complications, beliefs, and private thoughts. Fragmentation promotes complication. Many humans believe it is a complement to be complicated, as if that makes them smarter; it does not. You may hear someone say, "that person is so complicated," or "I'm a very complicated person," or "It's complicated." Humans believe being complicated means being brighter or more intelligent; they do not understand complications are based upon separation and fear. Love is simple. Unity is simple. Trust is simple. Truth is simple. It is much better to practice, "I am a simple being."

We could probably equalize the words complication and drama because drama always brings complication.

Indeed. And humans who crave attention because they cannot feel their own self-Love complicate their lives, in attempts to receive the Love that is actually right there within them. If they clear the complications from their thoughts and their lives, returning to the simplicity of self, all the Love they need is right there in their own divinity. Stepping away from complications into simplicity allows humans to become simple like us and to find the Love they seek. The simplicity of Love is the most powerful creator. Loving oneself first opens the floodgates to Loving all others. We Love ourselves first, then we Love others; this is the Loving of life, and in Unity it is the same. The two of you experienced an example of Unity expressed through your water. In a restaurant Rebecca silently wished for extra cilantro but said nothing. The server brought more cilantro, telling her he knew she wanted it. Incidents such as this prove to humans how you may create what you wish for through the power of your water, with simple intention.

Was the young man who brought us the cilantro an unwitting participant or did he understand Rebecca's water message?

Unwitting? Is the universe ever unwitting in drawing humans towards Unity? As humans approach more understanding of and participation with Unity, other humans become more susceptible to the power of Love in your water and wish to join you. So in this example, his water was magnetically drawn to Rebecca's water, and he understood. This is communicating through Love and your First Sense. He will begin paying attention to his own First Sense because of Connecting with another; he was changed forever by the incident. We hope you and other humans will begin to teach such communication, not through words, but through your being. It makes a difference for humanity, and although it may seem like it is occurring one person at a time, there *is* a hundredth monkey effect. We have told you that Love is all that is present in Unity. In moving towards the new reality, you move towards Unity. We are pleased when humans notice reality is not what you normally perceive. Such perceptions mark a beginning of human movement away from fear based consensual reality and towards a greater understanding of the new reality of Unity and Love. When you move your fears, you Connect with everyone and everything who shares your vibration, for you understand that all is one. It really doesn't matter whether you see a human in front of you or a star sister or brother. We are all one, sharing the same reality, wishing for the same thing.

In the new reality interactions will be determined in the present moment by the vibrational blending of all present and each one's capability to receive and comprehend through their First Sense. You will affect each other, and you will affect the entire environment. This is true *now*, and it is becoming more true as duality falls away and you move closer to Unity. This is evident when you notice storms in your environment; through Unity and Connection you notice the earth shifting under your feet. Elevated sunspot activity and changes in energetic frequency support changes of your perceptions of the new reality. Electromagnetic frequencies that occur during storms allow much interaction with alternate realities. Storms have somewhat of a magical quality. Many humans are frightened of them, for things they cannot explain occur during storms. We see the electromagnetic frequency changes as opportunities to experience reality from another perspective. Storms can actually fuel the needed changes that are appropriate in changing Earth at this time. The electrical energies present in storms are capable of allowing humans to experience the same vibratory changes that are happening within Earth Herself, a kind of matching of energies.

I have always felt that I would gain something unknown to me by standing directly in storms.

And you do. We would not recommend standing on the top of a mountain in intense lightening, for that would not be taking care of your physical form, but standing safely in storms when lightening and thunder occur is not at all dangerous and can be done with the intention of learning. It can help you transcend mental states where belief systems live and are firmly entrenched in habitual patterns of what you think is real. Some humans must transcend their beliefs about what *is* or *is not* possible. Others must transcend their expectations of *how* the new possibilities will occur. If humans believe changes or magic should fit within certain parameters, it limits other opportunities of which you may be unaware. Humans are part of the earth and the divine. Storms affect you, and you affect storms. You may co-create reality with storms through your thoughts. It is significant that storms are occurring more often as humans experience more emotional storms within themselves. As you become more and more aware, you may notice the impact and interactions from environmental situations related to your emotional states. Sometimes humans stir up their own storms. You two have noticed in the past that the wind is often stirred up when you become upset. When human emotions disintegrate unnecessarily over a tiny thing, emotional energy is magnified in the air and can reflect on the environmental devas, who may create storms in response to the energy you are creating;

it forces you to look at your own thoughts and actions and take responsibility for what you are co-creating for others. As you become aware of the power of your own water, you may see that your own emotional storms create storms in the environment or that your thoughts and emotions can calm Earth's storms. You work together through Connection. You have read stories of the man you call Jesus calming the storms of the sea; this is an example. He cast his thoughts outward on the water from his water with the intention of calm and Love. The sea responded. This is a perfect example that what is inside is reflected outside. It demonstrates your divine Connection to Earth. It shows you how powerful your thoughts are and what you can do when you understand the power of Love.

Humans have much to learn about the amount of power you have. You fail to realize the impact you have on your personal environment, your social environment, all the way to Earth's environment, from inside to outside, small effects to large ones. You have the power to change them all. You are powerful beings with a veil over your eyes, unable to recognize and see your own power. *Wake up!* Claim your power; it is yours for the taking. If you wish a peaceable kingdom, you must *be* peaceful inside yourselves. Remember the higher the vibration you attain and regularly maintain, the higher the incidence of Connecting with helping beings from other realms. We are here to help you create the new reality for your new humanity, and this new humanity will have an untold affect on the rest of the universe. The more Earth and humanity change, the more we *all* will feel the change. The power of Love leads to Connection and Unity.

We repeat, Love is the answer and the way to all you've ever wanted. Your power lies in the choices you make about *what* you think and *how* you direct your thoughts and emotions. Humans are being watched from all over the universe to see what choices they will make. You have no idea how important you are for the future of humanity and the new reality. Will you choose Unity and Love with us?

22

THE DIVINE COUPLE

In many of our personal conversations with Laarkmaa, they referred to us as "The Divine Couple." We silently accepted their loving choice of words and determined to leave that out of the book. We really did not intend to include Laarkmaa's personal reference to us as the Divine Couple in this book, but Laarkmaa disagreed and strongly suggested that we include this part of our dialogue. To us, it sounded a bit too lofty and, well, embarrassing. We have no ego around who we are or what we are doing. We are just grateful for the opportunity. As the book was coming together, Laarkmaa insisted over and over again that we make the choice to include the name they lovingly called us and explain it. Reluctantly, we include this portion with Trust that our readers will use it as a guideline for understanding their own divinity and for making their own relationships

divine. After all, if we can do it, so can the rest of humanity.

Yes, we have suggested quite strongly that you explain our reference to you, as well as more information about how and why you were chosen. We acknowledge that you did not wish to include this for the public, and as it is always your choice, we appreciate your honoring our request. We call you the Divine Couple not because you are more special than others, nor because you are the only humans who are Connected to your own divinity or who have struggled with their shadow making steps towards growth. Of course there are many who do this, even many who do it as couples wishing to grow together through their Love. Many couples may correctly consider themselves divine couples through acknowledging their own divinity and through acknowledging the divinity of their union. This is appropriate and as it should be. We wish more humans to be bonded in Unity with their divinity. All humans are divine, and they need to wake up and realize it. The more we speak of human divinity, the more you may listen yourselves into being who you truly are.

We refer to you as the Divine Couple because you are the example that best represents our work and our teachings at this time. We call you the Divine Couple because through your example you show others that they are divine. We call you the Divine Couple because of the energy you carry together. *It does not mean that you are more divine than any other humans.* It means that you carry a greater responsibility because you know what must be accomplished. Your task is to be an example: to teach, to Heal, and to bring this energy to the world through your own light and your shared Unity and Love. You are the couple who has been chosen by Laarkmaa, a Pleiadian group from the star system Pleiades. While Pleiadians have worked with many other humans in the past, our relationships have always been through *individuals* chosen by Pleiadians because of their individual sparks of light. There has never been a couple chosen for the unique dynamics that they carry. This is another reason that we call you the Divine Couple, and we wish for you to share it. We wish those who read this work to understand that it is not about your being better than others or having an ego about who you are. *You are no more special than anyone else;* the two of you are simply ready at this time. Most other couples have not yet created opportunities for being able to reach through the veil to receive this type of communication as you and Rebecca are. When they do, they often color what they hear with their own beliefs and concepts, which filter and change the information. Through the dynamics of your oppositeness, the two of you are actually able to listen without adding or subtracting anything on your own.

This is the first time a human pair has been chosen to join a Pleiadian team for an interdimensional, interplanetary, group collaboration for aiding the evolution of humanity towards its own divinity. *You are Laarkmaa's choice. You are a Pleiadian choice.* There is no other couple like you. All couples have similarities and differences within them. And although you may find similarities with others such as the way you come together in Unity and Love, the way you argue or resolve your differences, the way that you communicate, your shared interests in world work, or similar Healing abilities, your coupledom is different from all other couples on Earth. You carry unique energy. It is how you work with this energy together that makes you who you are and our choice of team members. We say "the" Divine Couple because through your polar opposite differences, you are illustrating for others how separation moves towards Unity to become divine. While there are many things that you share, the two of you are about as polar opposite as any two human beings can be. It is not simply a matter of maleness and femaleness. It is a matter of the different elements that you bring into this unique formation of the totality of yourselves. One of you reacts with distress to heat; one of you reacts with distress to cold. You most often see things from completely different vantage points; one of you sees from the inside out, and one of you sees the whole and takes it from the outside in. While you are both human with devic qualities, one of you carries Pleiadian qualities and one of you carries angelic qualities that show you different ways of seeing and moving towards Unity. Together, you are a perfect example that shows others how polar opposites can move towards Unity. We spoke earlier about the cross as a symbol of two energies coming from two different directions and meeting at the center, where the spark of Illumination occurs. So you and Rebecca bring your differences together to light your way towards Unity. You move away from the polar opposites that have made you individuals and into the Unity of your one shared heart. We call you the Divine Couple because your movements are in alignment with Earth's movements. Just as Earth quakes and moves away from duality and separation caused by time, moving towards the birth of Her new reality, you experience birth pains as you drop away from your individual beliefs and patterns, continuing to flow towards each other and Unity. It is in the center of your one shared heart that you create the divine spark that Illuminates who you are. It is *together* that you *remember,* and this is what you are here to teach others.

If we were not so different, would we not understand as fully the necessity of not judging each other's differences? Has our oppositeness supported our movement towards divine Unity?

The 180-degree difference you share as a couple is a tool to help you see, understand, and move towards Unity through your differences. The discernment of your differences helps you to see how the differences complete the whole. And as you merge your differences into divine Unity, you show others how *they too may become Divine Couples.* The two of you have persisted with courage in consistently making friends with your shadows, no matter how painful or frightening. You have insisted on using your intentions with the power of Love to shape your lives. You may now live the integration you have achieved, showing others how to move towards the future of humanity. Each individual has the right and the inherent knowingness of his or her own divinity to develop and evolve into who she or he truly is: a divine one. Each couple has the opportunity to bring their oppositeness together in Unity. Yet until the shadows are cleared and the light is shining with a higher vibration, the divinity does not show through with regularity. Through the spark of your extreme differences, you light the way.

Through this process your brains have been "re-wired" and expanded to match your already expanded hearts and are in alignment for using the power of your water with focused intent to move into full integration and Unity. We care not what this is called: evolving into something new, or devolving away from something old, as long as you are aware that you are opening channels that Connect you to the light of your own divinity and ultimate recognition of who you are. Divine. *We wish all humans to open to their own divinity.* Your intent to grow past limitations, to explore new methods and new dimensions, and to expand your capabilities makes you perfect candidates for our explorations together. We know that this process has been challenging at times. A portion of the public may deem you crazy, and some may be somewhat curious about you when our teamwork brings our information to the public arena, for dropping old patterns and belief systems in order to accept new and little understood ones is challenging for most humans.

There are other universal aspects that reflect in who you are that further explain why we call you the Divine Couple. Your karmic patterns are closely aligned. In human terms, you may call yourselves twin souls or twin spirits, with one heart, which is unusual among human incarnated beings. You have carried your Love lifetime-to-lifetime, working out your lessons, sometimes together and sometimes separately. You must know that you have been granted the gift of being together now because of the work you have already accomplished. Each of you was born under certain energies that help enable you to be who you are in this lifetime. These energies may be seen through your Western, Vedic, or Mayan Calendar astrology. You were guided to meet on May 27th so that as a couple you would be in alignment with the energy of what is about to arrive for humanity and the planet. The two of you were brought together during a point of light in the midst of darkness; that light was beaming down to promote changes for humanity. The day you met, May 27th, was an auspicious day. You met and were opened and changed on that very auspicious point of light. As a couple, you became a seed that has grown into a plant reaching upwards to the heavens as you bloom and grow.

May 27, 2010 marks a point of return of that same light energy to open humans and the planet even more for evolution into your divinity. May 27th, 2010 is a cosmological point of energetic light beaming into the earth to open humans to greater possibilities for more Unity. It is the second Harmonic Convergence, and the changes in consciousness that are possible are even greater than the changes in consciousness that occurred during the first Harmonic Convergence roughly thirty years ago in Gregorian time. The light will shine for humanity to have the opportunity to see who they are as divine beings and to step into position if they so choose. As you celebrate your own anniversary, we invite you, by calling you the Divine Couple, to continue your evolution and show the way with the light you carry. How you represent your togetherness through your one shared heart makes a difference, for it is up to you to let your shared light of your United heart be the beckon for all to see that there is something different here. And that light may be reflected back for all to see what is possible for humanity as you reflect the understanding of "I am another yourself," *supporting others in becoming divine couples or individually divine.*

You two must fully sense into what you are feeling and beginning to do. Each of you has strengths and gifts that *will* be utilized for speaking the Truth we share in the future. We would call you Ambassadors to the Pleiadians, for you join energies and understandings from one world to another. Your future is calling you to do what you've always known you could do. It will be different from the other work you did as Healers in the past, yet you may offer Healing support to humans to raise their vibrational levels far beyond what most are doing currently. When humans feel the difference within themselves through the Love and support of Healing you offer, you will begin to be known for who you are. We watch you with great Love and Trust that you are incorporating all the things we speak of on a daily basis, for each concept we teach has a special purpose in elevating human awareness. Many will eventually come to you because they are awakening to Truth. Some may try to follow you rather than doing on their own what you teach them. You must take their hands and tell them the power for change is within *them*, not only within you.

Humans have known for some time that the Christ energy is returning. It will return as a light that shines through many humans, not through only one. *As humans reclaim their divinity, the Christ light returns within them. The two of you and many others, are pieces of the Christ.* You all have the potential to manifest the Christ light within you. Those who are doing their work, are now accomplishing this. Stop being embarrassed and know that you are divine. Share with others that *each human is divine.* Stop being resistant and remember that you agreed long ago to accept this task. You have waited a very long time for the opportunity to assist this birth. Use your Christ Light to move humanity into the new reality.

Laarkmaa, you approached us. We had told the universe that we wanted to communicate with other dimensional beings and with other species. When

you nudged us with the radio signal, did you know that we would accept?

Since you were small children we have known it was a great potential. And while we say we chose you, you also chose yourselves through the choices you made with your intention. Certainly you have worked for this with complete dedication to moving all of humanity as well as yourselves towards the divinity that was always meant for humankind. No humans get to the place where you are without doing their 50% to be able to perceive and live within the level of light that pours into you for our communication. There are rewards for being so persistent in doing what is necessary to communicate and yearning to share with others in our vast universe.

So was there a knowing that went beyond a potentiality?

We were certain of the potentiality, for you have communicated your desire to us through many lifetimes. There was a possibility that when we approached you, you would react in fear, and for a while, you were somewhat confused about what was happening around and to you. You could have stayed at that level; we could not predict that, for it was your choice. Yet Rebecca's steadfast Trust and openness and your intent to connect with Truth turned the potentiality for our Connection now at this special time into reality.

You heard our requests to communicate and said that you worked with us before our births. Can you say more about that? Oh, yes. We worked with the two of you, and you worked with us. We were partners on the other side of the veil and in some of your lifetimes on Earth. Certainly we have been present; however with the exception of our communications in Mu, Lemuria, and Atlantis, you were rarely aware of our presence or our help. We supplied one-way assistance to you as you experienced certain dense human existences during parallel lifetimes. Communication such as we have now is not possible during human incarnations where the vibration is very low. When humans are disconnected from their heart wisdom and their First Sense, they do not understand other modes of communication very well. Yet when you use touch or energy, communication also occurs. We have communicated with humans in this way for a very long time. So we say to you, you two are unique. We do work with others, but not in the way that we work with you. We do hope for their growth also, for all humans are capable of this, yet the percentage who are able to do this is small, for most humans do not carry the combination of courage, heart, integrity, and brilliance of mind that you and other humans on the spiritual path bring to this endeavor. We are aware of a small but growing group of humans who are truly striving to do their work with courage and intention. That number grows. We are hopeful that the percentage of these humans will grow to reach the level of divinity and Unity that is required for Healing and teaching what we are sharing. The two of you have endeavored to reach towards your divinity with more dedication and willingness to face your shadow, offering your service with more heart, than most humans. This is why we have come to you and asked you to be Ambassadors for our work. It is your responsibility, if you choose to participate, to help reawaken the divinity that *all* humans carry by demonstrating and living this Truth. Divinity is possible for *all*. The two of you, other individuals, and other divine couples must teach others how to recreate themselves *every* day through managing their thoughts, their emotions, and their intent.

I think that our desire to communicate and yearning for the zip zip zip of being anywhere we want or being in multiple places at once by simply thinking about it, is what you are asking us to teach; we never lost that memory of those abilities. Am I close?

Yes, you are exactly, correctly, on point. And it is because of your special re-remembering, always remembering, never forgetting these abilities that the two of you are leaders now; it contributes to our choice of *you two* to be members of *our* Team. You have lived all your life waiting for what is occurring now. It is also connected to the empathy that is present because of your high vibrations. Empathy leads towards Unity, for with empathy you understand more fully the concept of "I am another yourself." Empathic beings such as the two of you often have difficulty with pain when you feel others drowning in it; you feel as if you are drowning also. That empathy comes from having a higher vibration, which makes you highly sensitive. You often see it as challenging, yet it is a gift, for it brings you closer to Unity. You do not have to experience empathy only as pain; you may also experience the joy of empathy that helps you feel Connected to the divinity of others. Anything that brings you closer to oneness and Unity is a gift. The two of you are closer to oneness and Unity than most other human beings at this time.

We see you as advanced humans. We see you as a united heart that has much to share in our work together to raise the vibrations of humanity. You must know that this is Truth.

Separation and Unity are opposites. As duality ceases to exist, each of you together moves towards Unity. Your and Rebecca's job is to help humans understand how to get away from separation and move towards Unity. There is no distinction between teaching and Healing, Healing and teaching. You and Rebecca teach through Love and through the simple presence of your raised vibration. And understand please, that the more you open to Trust, Love, light, and Truth and the more you accept your role as the Divine Couple, the more other beings rush to support you. Yes. You and Rebecca can be electric and magnetic, for the magnetism of which we speak draws those to you who need to be in your presence. And the electrical portion of which we speak is the light that you shine out to them. Those who are able to receive it will be drawn to you. The time approaches when many will need help. There are others who are more like you in their development who are magnetically drawn to you to accomplish your shared intent of helping birth of the new humanity. Link together with these and broaden your numbers to help all. Those of the higher vibration will be drawn to you first. Those who are more in need may then be helped as you and others link your intent together with group focus to reflect the light outwards and manifest the new reality. What you and Rebecca are teaching is that there is no running only towards the light. Humans must turn around and face the dark of their shadows, for in facing the shadow you dissolve fear through Love. As The Divine Couple you help others Heal from the belief that they are separate; you teach them through your presence that they are divine and others join you in becoming divine Healers and teachers.

You have given us the concept of shattering duality. We cannot move towards the light nor live in the light without embracing the darkness or the shadow. So it is possible that those of us who embrace that understanding will actually help change the loop of duality as time comes to an end. We humans must participate in this process through our ability to co-create, and Rebecca and I yearn for others to join us in our divinity.

Ah, now you are dreaming your reality. Your divinity is coming through to Connect you fully to universal consciousness. We are here to help you with that. You understand the enormity of the project you undertake, and you understand more clearly your position as the Divine Couple. Remember, *all humans are divine.* The more each human speaks of his or her divinity, the more you speak yourselves into being who you truly are.

Breinigsville, PA USA
24 October 2010

247942BV00006B/17/P